TURNING POINT

A Hennessey and Yellich Mystery

Hennessey and Yellich are investigating two parallel murders committed twenty or so years apart. First, Ebenezer Moulton goes from his father's funeral straight to the police to confess he witnessed his late father committing a murder. But things are not as straightforward as they seem, and the trail leads to the murder of a man in his twenties whose father is not exactly a pillar of the community...

*Peter Turnbull titles available from
Severn House Large Print*

No Stone Unturned
Once a Biker
Chelsea Smile
Fire Burn
False Knight
Sweet Humphrey
Chill Factor
The Dance Master
Treasure Trove

TURNING POINT

Peter Turnbull

Severn House Large Print
London & New York

This first large print edition published 2010
in Great Britain and the USA by
SEVERN HOUSE PUBLISHERS LTD of
9-15 High Street, Sutton, Surrey, SM1 1DF.
First world regular print edition published 2008 by
Severn House Publishers Ltd., London and New York.

British Library Cataloguing in Publication Data

Turnbull, Peter, 1950-
   Turning point.
   1. Hennessey, George (Fictitious character)--Fiction.
   2. Yellich, Somerled (Fictitious character)--Fiction.
   3. Police--England--Yorkshire--Fiction. 4. Detective and
   mystery stories. 5. Large type books.
   I. Title
   823.9'14-dc22

ISBN-13: 978-0-7278-7891-5

Severn House Publishers support The Forest Stewardship Council
[FSC], the leading international forest certification organisation. All
our titles that are printed on Greenpeace-approved FSC-certified paper
carry the FSC logo.

 Mixed Sources
Product group from well-managed
forests and other controlled sources
FSC www.fsc.org Cert no. SA-COC-1565
© 1996 Forest Stewardship Council

Printed and bound in Great Britain by the
MPG Books Group, Bodmin, Cornwall.

One

Monday, 27th June,
12.32 hours – 14.40 hours

*In which a man walks from a funeral to the
police station.*

An observer would see this, the following:
he, or she, would see a low grey sky with
cloud cover at nine-tenths, as the Royal Air
Force might say, and it would, for June, be
seen as unseasonably dull. Beneath the
cloud cover, the observer would see a housing estate of squat houses built of fawn-
coloured brick with the roof tiles being of a
slightly, but only slightly, darker hue than the
houses. At the further end of the housing
estate would be seen a green area of lush
foliage from which tall stones, carefully
carved, protruded. Beyond the area of green
and stone were open fields of cultivated
land. This was summer, as June edged into
July, and it had, thus far, been a particularly
wet summer in which rain had fallen in
biblical proportions, swelling the River Ouse

5

and causing widespread flooding to the surrounding area. The road surfaces glistened with damp. It was only the occasional sliver of blue sky glimpsed behind the heavy rain-swelled grey clouds and the close, humid, shirt-sleeves-rolled-up temperature which served to remind one of the season. Against this backdrop, the observer would see a man walking, and walking as best a man could walk with an aluminium crutch which encased his right elbow and which he clutched with whitening knuckles. The man, the observer might feel, was young to be so disabled, appearing perhaps to be only in his early to mid twenties. The disabled man would be seen as thin, to the point of being emaciated. He was drawn of face, gaunt, sunken eyes and he propelled himself along the pavement with a lowered, head-down attitude, as if searching for coins upon the ground, rather than looking upwards and around him at nature's bounty. In respect of his clothing, the man would be seen to be wearing old sports shoes, faded denim jeans, a blue waterproof coat, fully unzipped and open at the front and a dark-coloured shirt underneath the waterproof coat. The man walked making a rhythmic, metallic clicking sound as he did so, as the crutch supported his right side and his right leg would indeed be seen to be dragged behind and not at all supporting his body weight. Yet the observer might, were he or she sufficiently keen-eyed, notice something else about the man, particularly about the way he walked. The keen-eyed viewer of this scene might, perhaps, detect a determination about the man conveyed by the way he walked, perhaps an anger even in the scrape-click, scrape-click, scrape-click as he moved along the shiny wet pavement. It might also seem that the young man's eyes were downcast because, unlike any other foot passenger on the pavement at that time, or indeed unlike any other person in the vicinity, the reason why he was not looking ahead or upwards was that he was unconcerned about the possibility of another downpour of rain. It might seem that such was his determination and possible anger that the next massing of a cloud of darker grey had no significance for him. He was perhaps unconcerned with such a development. He was a young man committed to another issue. He would project that impression. Here, the observer might think, was a man with a purpose. A man who had sustained a serious injury earlier in his life, a man who now knew poverty, but above all, here was a man with a mission, a man with a task, an urgent task to fulfil.

The young man, who would be seen to display no sign of weakening, either in his hampered walk, or in his resolve, would be observed to have walked from the area of foliage and stone, through the housing estate to the main road. At the main road he would be observed to turn towards York and continue to have a strong air of determination about him. There was, it might seem to be, a hunger about the youth, more than the hunger of the empty stomach that his dress seemed to indicate. There was a hunger in his walk.

The youth walked into the centre of the city of York. It was a walk which had taken him fully forty-five minutes, perhaps longer, and would not have been, could not have been, easy for him. But he was a man driven, evidently so. There was not the slightest hesitation in his direction, in his route, and he would be observed to be a person who knew exactly where he was and exactly where he wanted to go and by exactly which route. Indeed said route would appear to be the most direct; he would be seen to cut corners when he could and to cross the road obliquely rather than at ninety degrees, and even though such practices would save him but a few seconds on his overall journey time, it was a policy he chose to pursue. Once in the city he walked up Micklegate with its shops and public houses, with an occasional small business premises also, but shops and bars in the main, and heavy with pedestrians, it being the summer when tourists visit in large numbers and whose presence hampered the progress of the disabled youth. At the summit of the hill he moved on, down to Micklegate Bar, being one of the gates of the ancient city, over which gate were the walls and elevated pedestrian way along the walls, behind the battlements. At the Bar he paused. For the first time in his traverse across York he would be seen to pause, and to pant, and to catch his breath, but he paused only to wait until the traffic lights changed to permit foot passengers to cross the road. The pause and the catching of breath was not at all a faltering of his resolve. When the traffic lights changed and the green man shone, the youth unhesitatingly put himself at the road, crossing it with perhaps but a dozen dogged steps, and entered the public entrance of Micklegate Bar Police Station. It was, as records would later show, 12.32 hours on the Monday of that week. DC Carmen Pharoah was the duty CID officer.

'Thank you, I'll be there directly.' Carmen Pharoah gently replaced the telephone and glanced up good-humouredly at Thompson Ventnor who sat opposite her. 'I knew it was too quiet. Calm before the storm.' She stood and smoothed down her skirt. 'You don't really get that in England.'

'What?' Thompson Ventnor carried on writing.

'Calm before the storm.'

'Oh, we do...' He stopped writing and returned her smile.

'Not like in the tropics. On St Kitts you know, the calm would last for days and days and then a tropical storm would come in from the Atlantic and that would also last for days and days. I think I prefer it here. You English, you complain about the weather but I tell you, you don't know what bad weather is. Anyway, let's see what this member of the public wants, the constable at the enquiry desk says he seems very agitated.'

'Well, that's the way of it, that's the nature of police work.' Thompson Ventnor reclined back in his chair and clasped his hands together behind his head. 'I mean, what's so special about New York being the city that never sleeps? Even quaint Olde York is 24/7. Not quite the humming metropolis that is the Big Apple, but it's still 24/7.' He stretched his arms like a man waking from a deep and nourishing sleep. 'It's probably nothing, despite the agitation, a bit like the woman who dialled three nines because her pizza was delivered with the wrong topping.'

'But she was insane – and she was on medication to prove it. Somehow, I don't think this particular member of the public will prove to be insane. Woman's intuition.' She waved her hand in a mock gesture of farewell. 'It's more finely tuned than yours.'

10

'So they say,' Ventnor growled and then returned his attention to the paperwork on his desk which, knowing its value, he addressed with a certain pride and care, despite a sense of weakness in his body and an emptiness in his stomach.

Carmen Pharoah walked slowly, yet confidently and purposefully, out of the office she shared with Thompson Ventnor and into the narrow, yet high-roofed CID corridor of brown parquet floor and sombre green-painted walls and from thence to the enquiry desk where she stood beside the constable who indicated the youth who sat on the wooden bench in the public area in front of the desk. She had learned that initial impressions are always useful and her initial impression was of a haunted-looking man, too haunted-looking for his years. His eyes were too drawn, his body too wasted for one still short, very short, of his thirtieth year. The man, she saw, was looking at her with an expression which Carmen Pharoah thought could only be described as pleading.

'Mr Moulton?' She asked softly, yet authoritatively.

'Yes, that's me.' The man slowly stood, with a practised struggle, extending the crutch out in front of him, leaning into it and then levering himself up. 'That's me, miss.' He spoke with a local accent and a voice which somehow conveyed a paucity of education.

11

'I'll come round.' Carmen Pharoah walked from the rear of the enquiry desk and emerged a few moments later on the public side of the desk by which time Moulton was standing quite steadily, leaning the greater part of his weight upon the crutch. 'We'll go in here,' she announced and she led the way to a door at the far end of the public waiting area. She opened it, slid the sign on the door from 'vacant' to 'occupied' and held it wide open as Moulton hobbled into the room. Once inside the room, Moulton sat unbidden on a metal-framed chair and Carmen Pharoah, having shut the door with a solid sound, sat in a similar chair. Between them was a metal table. The room was dark, oppressively so, more cell-like Carmen Pharoah had always believed, and not at all conducive to making members of the public relax and feel at ease as they brought their concerns and complaints to the police. It was though, she realized, hardly anyone's fault, no blame can be placed at anybody's door, at no living person's door anyway. It was just the way they designed police stations when Queen Victoria was on the throne and the Zulu wars were being fought. People entered this room of their own free will and often left equally freely, but it was, she believed, still too cell-like for the purpose it was designed to serve. 'So,' she said, opening her notebook.

'It's about my father.'

Carmen Pharoah held up her hand. 'Just one thing at a time please ... it really is quicker.'

Moulton nodded apologetically. He had a certain 'hum' about his person which suggested to Carmen Pharoah that he had not washed for a day or two.

'So you are Mr Moulton?'

'Yes, miss. I am Ebenezer Moulton.'

Carmen Pharoah could not prevent herself from glancing at him with widening eyes. 'Ebenezer...?'

Moulton shrugged. 'It's no joke – had it all my life. I'm used to it now. My parents liked weird names, they both had weird Christian names, they said it made them stronger. Character building they said and Ebenezer is a real name, not just invented by Dickens for Scrooge. There was a poet in the nineteenth century—'

'Ah ... Ebenezer Elliot?' Carmen Pharoah nodded. 'Yes, I remember reading about him ... the Corn Law Rhymer and the only writer of any note to have come out of Rotherham.'

'So it is a real name.' Ebenezer Moulton spoke defensively as though he had been insistent that his was a 'real name' from his earliest years.

'Yes, I know.' Carmen Pharoah spoke calmly and reassuringly. 'It is unusual, but yes, it is real. So how can we help you, Mr

13

Moulton?'

'Well, it's about my father ... like I said.' Ebenezer Moulton shuffled on his chair and hunched forward. He held eye contact with Carmen Pharoah with a look which she found unsettlingly, worryingly collusive. She felt it to be a 'just between you and me' look, which surprised her coming from one who seemed to be running scared, a character who seemed to be constantly looking over his shoulder. 'Don't know where to start.' He pointed to his head, moving his index finger in a circular motion. 'It's all going round in here ... these past few days ... spinning around.'

'Just plunge in,' Carmen Pharoah suggested, 'it's often the best way.'

'Plunge,' Ebenezer Moulton repeated and looked up at the ceiling of the room, smiling a knowing smile as he did so. 'Plunge. You know, miss, it's funny you should say that ... really funny ... weird.'

'Oh? How so?' She tapped her pen on her notepad and repeated. 'How so?'

'It's like this, miss, it's like this – see, I am twenty-five years old and–' Moulton looked down at the surface of the table and swept his palm across the surface, as if brushing away an unseen and imaginary fly – 'people tell me I look older ... much older. And I feel it – I already feel I am ready for the box.'

Carmen Pharoah breathed deeply. She let

the sound be heard. It had been her experience that people walk into a police station when they should walk into the office of the Samaritans. Dealing with such people was a matter which Carmen Pharoah always found difficult. It was always hard for her not to be cutting and dismissive, no matter how much she felt for them, but she also knew that she had to cling to the fact that the police are overstretched with a difficult and specific job to do, and the lending of a sympathetic ear really is not part of said job. 'I've never done anything that I am proud of.'

'Plenty of time yet,' Carmen Pharoah said, after a second audible intake of breath. 'You're still a young man no matter how you feel, no matter what people say to you, and it's good that you want to do good.'

'What I was going to be–' Moulton swallowed hard – 'when I was nineteen, I was going to be a professional footballer – I mean premier league ... international level. They all said that I had got what it takes.' He grabbed his aluminium crutch and shook it angrily. 'Now look ... now look at me.'

'What happened?'

'I got rolled. I thought it would only happen once, but it happened again.'

'Again?'

'Yes, again and again ... and again. I am ... what is that term ... a serial victim? That's another thing I was going to be – a great parent, a really good daddy ... an international soccer player with a family. But neither happened. I was lifted up and rammed against a metal post a few times ... you know, with my legs either side of the post.'

'Oh...' Carmen Pharoah's jaw dropped slightly.

'Yeah, oh...' Ebenezer Moulton's voice was angry, embittered. 'They were supposed to be my mates and that was my stag night. Some mates, some stag night. When I was supposed to be on my honeymoon I was in hospital. I was in the York District Hospital all bandaged up.'

'I am sorry to hear that but I really don't see what the police can do now.'

'I'm coming to that, miss.' Again, another collusive-seeming eye contact.

'Alright.'

'Well, the wedding wasn't delayed, it was cancelled. Off. I couldn't walk for weeks and can't ever run and so my career as a top-notch soccer player was over before it had begun, and she wanted to be a WAG ... you know, wives and girlfriends ... those models who marry soccer stars and go on million-pound shopping sprees. So out she walked. I was alone.'

'Well, again, you have my sympathy but where is this going?'

Ebenezer Moulton continued talking as if he had not heard Carmen Pharoah's ques-

16

ion. 'Then a few years later I got rolled again and they smashed my leg with a massive iron bar really making sure that when it came to football, I'd only ever be a spectator.'

'Random attack or were you a specific target?'

'Definitely not random – not a random attack – it wasn't just a gang of thugs looking for an easy victim, any victim would do, not that, they definitely wanted me and no one else and they got me and no one else and well, didn't they just get me ... didn't they just?'

'Why? Had you offended them?'

'Well, miss, that's what I am here for, to do good, to do some good for once because one of them said, just before I blacked out, one of them said, "You say nothing. Nothing. Nothing. You saw nothing."'

'You saw nothing,' Carmen Pharoah repeated softly. 'What did they mean by that? Sounds like you posed a threat to them.'

'Yes, that's what they said, word for word. I am telling no lie, miss, word for word,' and again, Moulton eyed Carmen Pharoah with a 'just between the two of us' sort of glance, '"You didn't see nothing", then they laid into me until ... well, I woke up in hospital again. The doctor said the rest of you is going to mend, it's all going to heal up like new but your right leg, well, that's so smashed up that it's like soup with bits of bone

17

floating in it.' Ebenezer Moulton paused and again he brushed an imaginary fly from the surface of the table. 'Later, weeks later, that same doctor told me that putting my leg back together was like doing a jigsaw puzzle, finding out which bits of bone fitted where and I said why didn't they just chop it off and have done with it? And he said that they had seriously considered doing just that. He said if I had been a war zone casualty where medical resources were limited with my leg smashed up like that, then it would have been sawn off at the hip without a second thought. It would have been "prag" something ... don't know the word but prag—'

'Pragmatic?'

'Yes, that's it.' Ebenezer Moulton nodded as a distant look entered his eyes. 'That's what he said, I remember now ... pragmatic. What does it mean, pragmatic?'

'In the case that you describe–' Carmen Pharoah inclined her head to one side – 'well, practical ... sensible ... that sort of thing, that sort of meaning. I think the word has a wider usage though, but in this case what the doctor meant was that if you had been a battlefield casualty the leg would have come off, not having the time or resources for the surgical skill that would be required to save it.'

'I see, well, I wish I had been a battlefield casualty but they said they recognized the challenge and they rose to it. They were pleased with themselves and the doctor who talked to me said that my operation was written up and published in a medical journal. Well, good for them, they might be pleased with themselves but they have left me with a yard of dead meat to drag around. If I could stand on it for a little while, that at least might be something, just some compensation, but I can't do that, can't weight-bear at all on it. One good leg, one aluminium crutch and in between them there's a dead weight.'

'Again, I'm sorry–' Carmen Pharoah spoke as softly as she could, the young man's bitterness and anger were clear and very evident – 'but where are you going with this? Where are you taking me?'

'I'm getting there,' he said with restraint, 'just let me explain ... I'm getting there.'

'Well, frankly, Mr Moulton, if you do not hurry up and get where you are going, wherever that is, I am going to have to ask you to leave the police station.'

'I saw a man killed. Murdered. Done in. That's where I am going.'

Carmen Pharoah sat back in her chair. She held eye contact with Ebenezer Moulton, he of unwashed body and clothing, a threadbare man of marginal existence. 'Now,' she said, 'now you interest me.'

'I've just come from my father's funeral.'

Moulton retained eye contact with Carmen Pharoah. 'I came straight here. I walked ... well, as only I can walk. I want to do good for once. I want to do something good, I want to be able to lie on my deathbed and have something to think about that I can be proud of, something I can think about and say, "I did alright there" ... feel good about myself for that, and I can relive it while I'm lying there waiting for the reaper to gather me.'

'Fair enough, we all need memories like that for that time ... but do go on.'

'It was a bad time.'

'What was?'

'The funeral. There were four people at the funeral in the chapel: me, the priest, and two guys in suits from the undertakers – and it was all over in five minutes ... and not a word about my father, just reading from a script for anybody's funeral and putting my father's name in a blank space. "We give thanks for the life of our brother Walpole", and that was it and I was ushered out of the chapel, out to the grave and that was that.'

'Walpole?'

'My father's name. He was Walpole Moulton, my mother was Liberty Moulton, née Ferrie, so at school she was called "Liberty Ship", but they said you grow into unusual names so they called me Ebenezer and said I'd hate it but I'd grow into it and I'd be stronger. I can't tell you how I wished they'd called me John or David. Mind you, I met a bloke called John once and he said he'd love to have been given an unusual name. You can't please...'

'You're wandering, Mr Moulton, let's keep this focused.' Carmen Pharoah held up her right index finger between her eyes. 'Focus ... focus ... focus.'

'Sorry, miss.' Ebenezer Moulton glanced round the room. 'It's a dark room, this. I bet it hears dark stories ... a lot of dark stories.'

'Yes, I dare say it has over the years, an awful lot of tragic tales, but Mr Moulton, focus ... focus...'

'Yes, sorry, miss. Well, I saw my father kill someone ... in the floods.'

'These floods?' Carmen Pharoah pointed to the wall, indicating the world beyond, because the land outside York was inundated; homes were under two feet of water, the army rescued householders in inflatable dinghies and took them to resource shelters, other householders remained as close as they could to their homes to guard against looters. 'These floods? So one of the four people known to be missing was murdered by your father, yet you have just come from his funeral? The river burst its banks just forty-eight hours ago ... how could it be?'

'No–' Ebenezer Moulton smiled briefly and again brushed away an imaginary fly

21

from the surface of the table – 'not these floods. I am talking about floods twenty years ago.'

'There were floods twenty years ago?'

'Yes. You weren't here then?'

'No, I was at school in the West Indies.'

'We must be about the same age, you and me, miss.'

'I am a few years older ... but carry on.'

'Yes, well ... I forgot about it for a long time.'

'Yes–' Carmen Pharoah nodded slightly – 'it's a common reaction to trauma to bury the memory and then in time, when you are distant enough and old enough to deal with it, then the memory is recovered. It doesn't do to dig up memories before they emerge of their own accord.'

'Is that how it works?'

'So I believe. It explains why some women delay for years before reporting serious sexual assault, but carry on...'

'What about those life and limb emergencies you mentioned?'

'My colleague can deal with those.' Carmen Pharoah remained stone-faced. 'You are reporting a murder.'

'It was twenty years ago.'

'It's still a murder. Was he an elderly person? The murder victim, I mean.'

'I don't remember him as being old, but I was just a boy, only about five or six.'

'And the perpetrator...?'

'Perpetrators, there was a gang of them.'

'Alright, just carry on, in your own words, in your own time.'

Ebenezer Moulton shuffled in his chair and leaned a little further forward. 'In my own words ... so I was young, really new, the world was still new but I remember this like yesterday. I was in the rear seat of a car and my dad and another man were in front. The other guy was driving, I remember that, and we followed a van, a green van ... now I know it was a fifteen hundredweight.'

'OK.'

'Anyway, we followed it out in the country somewhere, there were no houses about, just fields and trees – definitely out in the sticks. The van stopped and we pulled up behind it. It was raining heavily; water everywhere, like now ... flooded fields ... lots of bits of road underwater.' Ebenezer Moulton paused as if he found talking about the incident difficult. 'Well, I remember my father turning round and looking beyond me, out of the rear window of the car and saying, "It's clear." Then he looked at me and said, "Get down behind the seat," so I did. Then my dad and the driver of the car got out.'

'I assume you didn't do as you were told–' Carmen Pharoah smiled – 'otherwise you wouldn't be here?'

'Yes, that's right.'

23

'So, what did you see?'

'I looked up over the top of the front seat and saw my dad and the other guy open the back door of the van and two other guys got out of the van and the four of them dragged another guy. The guy they pulled out had his hands tied behind his back but he was struggling, kicking out. I remember the look on his face; his eyes full of terror and one bloke punched him in the stomach and the guy doubled up, and then his hands were untied and they pitched him over a bridge. Assume it was a bridge; it was a stone wall and he went over it backwards. I can't see them pushing him over a wall into a field.'

'Nor can I.'

'It was only later, a lot later, when I remembered it, that I realized he must have drowned, he wouldn't have been able to swim after being punched like that ... that punch must have winded him. Then one of the guys turned and saw me looking at them so I ducked back down behind the seat and I heard the man shouting. Then my dad and those other men they were clever, very clever alright. I mean were they clever.'

'Clever? How so?'

'Treated me right royally.' Ebenezer Moulton inclined his head to one side. 'It was as if they had suddenly got degreed up in what makes children tick. You see, if they had told me to forget what I'd seen I would

24

have remembered it. If they had threatened me with this and that if I ever told anyone then I would have remembered it. They came back to the car, my dad and the other guy, and they didn't talk about it as they drove off, didn't even drive off in silence, doing either of those would also have made me likely to remember ... but they talked to me, included me in the conversation and they just talked about where to go for a cup of tea and a bun. We were following the green van still and the green van turned off and there was no sounding of the horn or waving, nothing. It was like the green van was just another car on the road, driven by strangers. So then I was just a little lad in the back seat of a car with his dad and his friend in the front seat and it was so soon after it. I began to wonder if I had really seen it happen. Suddenly we were just out for a car ride in the country, and we did stop for a cup of tea and a bun and I was bought a fizzy drink and ice cream and got lots of warmth and attention. Talking to me, giving me a treat, making me feel wanted, sort of warm inside, and we walked out of the cafe with my dad holding my hand and they knew what they were doing. What I had seen was already seeming to be like a dream I had had.'

'I see.' Carmen Pharoah opened her notebook and wrote that day's date at the top of the page. 'Clever, as you say.'

'Well, someone clearly knew what to do. It wouldn't have been my dad because one of the mistakes he made was to tell me to forget things if he didn't think I had seen them. Once when I was about the same age we were watching TV and one character put a "V"-sign up to another and my dad said, "I want you to forget that".'

'But that just made you remember it?'

'Yes, and I also remembered who was in the room at the time, and the name of the TV programme and the weather outside.' Moulton brushed yet another unseen fly from the table top. 'My dad, in saying that, he made it a clear memory.'

'It was recognized.'

'Yes.' Moulton smiled. 'That's what I'm trying to say, the "V"-sign on the TV screen was recognized and so I remembered it, never forgot it. Every time I see someone give a "V"-sign I remember that sunny day as we sat round watching television and I remembered it all the time I was growing up ... recognized ... but the other time they carried on as though nothing had happened. I remembered the attention, the fizzy drink and the ice cream but I forgot what had happened just a few minutes earlier, and I have read that the tendency is for people to bury bad memories.'

'Yes, it is, but they never stay buried, as I said.'

'No, they don't.' Moulton shook his head slowly from side to side. 'No they don't, they stay buried for a long time but eventually they surface and I was of an age when I was expected to remember things ... reciting the alphabet, learning the times tables, I was letting things into my head.'

'Receptive?'

'Yes,' Moulton smiled. 'You're good with words, miss, but yes, it happened when my mind, my brain, was receptive, taking things in, that's what an education does for you, you take things in and at first the memory came back like a dream when I was having a pint. You know, you don't drink to forget, you drink to remember. It's happened to me a few times, a pint or two has loosened a memory and up it has come, not when out of my skull on booze, but just one or two beers and ... wow, a memory.'

'So I believe.'

'Maybe you forget if you are seriously out of your skull and well drunk but, like I said, one or two beers and you remember long-buried memories. Anyway, this memory came back over a few days, a different bit at a time but in the wrong order, sort of jumbled up. It took a while to put the bits in the right order, then it was another while before I realized that it had happened, that I had seen a guy pitched to his death into a river and then the memory stayed. Once it surfaces it stays surfaced … it stays with you.'

'Did you ever talk to your father about it?'

'No.' Moulton shook his head vigorously. 'It was just one of those things, it was one of those families. Things were not talked about, not a good way to live.'

'No, not healthy–' Carmen Pharoah raised her eyebrows – 'not healthy at all.'

'It makes things very stressful. It was like that for me and Dad, just the two of us in a little council house sitting in silence when we should have been talking things over.'

'Just the two of you? Where was your mother?'

'She died when I was twenty.'

'I'm sorry.'

Moulton shrugged. 'Just another battering along the way. You know that saying, "If it doesn't kill it toughens you" … or something.'

'Nietzsche.'

'Who?'

'Friedrich Nietzsche. A German philosopher, thought by many to be fascist in his thinking but he said that, "The blow which does not kill me only serves to make me stronger." Not true, sufficient non-fatal blows can wear a person down completely, but that's the origin of the phrase.'

'You're well-educated, miss.'

'You pick things up along the way. I've just got one of those minds – it makes me good at Trivial Pursuit, but let's get back to this–' she tapped her notebook – 'remember ... focus.'

'Focus ... yes, but like you say it isn't true, each blow makes you weaker until eventually you don't get up again; loss of my mum, then being ruined down below on my stag night; loss of fiancée, then long-term dole money, never had a job; then attacked with a crow-bar which turned my right leg into a dead weight; living in a damp council house which I'll take over from my dad ... but damp. You know what me and my dad did one winter about three winters ago?'

'What? Tell me?'

'One winter there was a lot of snow and we couldn't stand the damp in the house, couldn't heat the house at all, so we went outside and dug a snow-hole, piled snow up all around us and lit a tilley lamp which gave out heat and we were warmer and drier in our snow-hole than in our house.'

Carmen Pharoah, aware of the quality of housing stock in York and the Vale said, 'I can believe that.'

'Well, that house, that's where I am going to be living on my own, on the dole, until I die early. That's what's ahead of me, watching the seasons change, growing old in the house I grew up in until I die early, like all long-term doleys but at least I've done this. I've done – I am doing – one good thing in my life.'

'So, when you were attacked–' Carmen Pharoah brought the interview back to the issue in hand – 'you think that that was to intimidate you into silence about what you saw twenty years ago?'

'Yes–' Moulton slowly nodded his head – 'like they knew that the memory would surface.' He paused. 'It was the nearest me and my dad ever got to talking about it. You see he came to see me in hospital with my leg in plaster and hoisted up and he said he was sorry to drag me into it, that all his life he regretted not leaving me with a neighbour.'

'Alright ... now tell me about the attack.'

'The attack–' Moulton studied the table top – 'one minute I could walk, couldn't run, not really, I was no longer an up and coming soccer star – the boy genius – but I could walk and run a little. I was employable and the next minute I was disabled, went from unemployment benefit to disability benefit in less time than it takes to smoke a coffin nail.'

'It can ... it often does happen like that ... a life can change, or end, in an instant.'

'Yes ... yes, how true.' Ebenzer Moulton nodded and raised his eyebrows. 'Yes, indeed.'

'So, the attack?' A mustiness about the man reached Carmen Pharoah, the legacy, she thought, of living in a damp council house and a preference for snow-holes in the winter time.

'It happened a couple of years ago. I did report it. I mean it was reported because when I woke up in the York District there was a policeman sitting there wanting details. I couldn't give much. I had to disappoint him, I couldn't give much information, a sudden noise behind me and a bang on the head which sent me reeling. A voice in my ear said, "You saw nothing, right?" Then they went to work on my right leg. I passed out and woke up in the hospital. It happened right outside my dad's house, so it wasn't a random attack or mistaken identity. It was me they were after and no one else and being on the estate meant no CCTV there to photograph it all.'

'You saw nothing?'

Once again Ebenezer Moulton brushed away an imaginary fly. It was a repetitive action which Carmen Pharoah thought suggested a state of shock on Ebenezer Moulton's part, or alternatively that he was in a permanent state of emotional detachment, unaware of his actions. It was, perhaps, she felt, some form of coping mechanism. 'No ... saw nothing, felt and heard, but saw nothing ... and it had to be about the guy I saw shoved off the bridge when I was a little lad, no matter what my dad and the other guy

31

did to make me forget, no matter how clever they were. The other guys knew that after a few years the memory would come back, as they do, and as it has. There was nothing else in my life that I was witness to that anybody would want me to keep quiet about. So it must be about the bridge incident.' And yet again that brushing of his hand palm down over the surface of the table. 'I had had the memory from when I was about twenty or twenty-one and I can remember where I was when I first recovered it, like those older people who can tell you exactly where they were ... I mean to the millimetre ... that day whenever it was that they heard the news about President Kennedy being shot.'

'Yes.' Carmen Pharoah smiled briefly, 'I have heard the same.'

'I was playing with the reserves, York Town, with one or two games with the first team, set up a few goals in the first team but never scored one, plenty with the reserves but none with the first team, but I was on my way. Then I went out after a match. I was drinking Bloody Mary's all night and woke up in my dad's house and my mates had painted my face black and yellow, you know, York Town's colours, and the hangover lasted till Monday morning, and it was the first drink after that that I remembered. My dad gave me a tenner and said, "There you go, lad, off to the pub for a hair of the dog."

So I went to the "Monk".'

'The Monk?'

'The Merry Monk, the pub.'

'Alright, carry on ... please.'

'Anyway, it was when I was on the second beer that the memory emerged, it just flooded into my head, it came like a punch and I stepped back a couple of paces and, like I said, it came in bits that were all jumbled up out of time order, and it was then I realised how giving me ice cream and a fizzy drink made all kinds of sense, helping me to forget what I had just seen.'

'How did that make you feel?'

'Used ... let down. They were not giving me a little treat at all, it was just for their benefit, to suit their ends ... for their purposes.'

'So that ... the recovery of the memory was about six or seven years ago?'

'About that, yes, miss–' Ebenezer Moulton glanced up at the window set high in the wall – 'summer ... it was summer ... must have been right at the end of the football season.'

'Why wait all this time to report it?'

Moulton smiled. 'I had to protect my dad ... I mean, hadn't I? I wasn't going to shop the old lad for murder, not my own dad. He went up the chimney this morning and I left the crematorium chapel and walked straight here. Like I said, time to do something good.'

'Alright–' Carmen Pharoah leaned forward and clicked her ballpoint pen – 'that's what we call the overview. Now we need the details.'

'Won't be able to help you much there, miss. I told you all I know.'

'We'll see.' Again Carmen Pharoah smiled but did so only briefly. 'You'll be surprised how far even the smallest detail can take an investigation. So let me ask you a few questions.'

'Of course, miss.'

'Was there any incident prior or subsequent to the murder that you remember and which you think might be relevant to the murder?'

Moulton paused and again glanced up at the opaque window. 'Well, my parents argued a lot after it happened ... or it might have been before. I'm sorry it's hard to tell whether it was before or after.'

'Alright, so there was a lot of arguing about the time of the murder, that is, between your parents?'

'Yes, miss, yes, I think so ... they argued in the car. I remember the car my dad had at the time.'

'That wasn't the car you were sitting in when you saw the murder?'

'No, miss, my dad was in the front passenger seat of that car and I had never been in that car before, but I remember the car we had at the time and my parents argued a lot in that car. That's why I remember it more than any other car my dad had. That's when he had money; these last few years he had nothing.'

'What happened?'

'He went all to little pieces when my mother died ... drink, gambling ... drink mostly, it's expensive stuff.'

'I know.'

'Actually it's dirt cheap is booze ... dirt cheap, but a lot of tax gets slapped on it. About three-quarters of what you pay for a beer goes to the Government in tax.'

'Focus ... Ebenezer ... focus.'

'Oh, sorry ... well, I never knew he was such a weak man. He could hold it together so long as everything was going his way but when his wife died he just sort of took his bat and ball home and took to the bottle.'

'Yes, I have known that reaction – hard shells hide soft centres. So your parents argued about the time of the murder?'

'Yes.'

'So your mother probably knew of it?'

'Yes.' Moulton shrugged. 'In fact I'd say it was likely. As I grew up I got to know that she was in charge, she bossed my dad about quite a lot. So if there was secrets it is more likely she kept them from him rather than him from her. She'd murder someone and keep it from my dad. He'd tell her he'd done it ... you know, done the deed. I can even see him asking her permission to murder someone. I'm very sorry, I really don't ... really honestly can't remember anything else, not right now anyway. Something might come to mind in the future but right now ... I'm sorry, that's it ... that's all.'

'Alright, as you say, something might come to you later but tell me about the men who attacked him – one being your father – what about the others?'

'That's all a blur ... just these figures sort of milling about. For a long time I thought that they were soldiers but I realized later that they were wearing camouflage jackets which they must have bought from the Army Stores. I realized that when I bought one for myself. They had hoods, so I didn't see any faces ... apart from my dad's friend, you know, the driver of the car I was in.'

'Can you describe him?'

'Ginger hair ... short ... the hair I mean, cut short ... no name, don't remember him as a family friend and if I saw him before or later, I don't remember.'

'Alright, I'll go and get a statement form but tell me, do you think you would have come forward if you hadn't been attacked?'

'Possibly–' Ebenezer Moulton leaned back in the chair – 'but not so soon. Eventually I probably would have, but right up to the time I was attacked I was going somewhere,

I mean to the top in professional football, an international. I was looking forward all the time, making plans, you know – the millionaire lifestyle – houses in Monaco, the whole tax exile bit. Then I went from that to watching daytime television, living with my dad in a little council house. So I started to look back earlier in life than I reckon I would have done if I had signed for Real Madrid ... but I do want to do some good ... something good has got to come out of this.'

'Well–' Carmen Pharoah stood, slowly, elegantly, with practised, perfectly controlled poise – 'you have already done good, you have provided sufficient information to merit the start of a murder inquiry ... whatever your motivation.'

'Motivation?'

'Reason. Do you want protection?'

Ebenezer Moulton shook his head. 'No thanks, not afraid of anything else they can do to me. Not now.'

Two

Monday, 27th June, 16.32 hours –
Tuesday, 28th June, 09.47 hours

In which a burglar thanks a corpse, a woman who is younger than her attitude would suggest is visited and Carmen Pharoah is at home to the gracious reader.

Carmen Pharoah tapped confidently yet reverently upon the door frame of the office of DCI Hennessey and entered his office.

'Quite a bundle of paper and files you have there, DC Pharoah.' Hennessey put his pen down on his desk beside the report that he was writing and looked up approvingly as Carmen Pharoah approached his desk. 'Do take a pew.'

'Glad I caught you, sir, very glad.' Carmen Pharoah slid gracefully into one of the upright chairs which stood in front of Hennessey's desk. She tapped the files she held on her lap. 'This is quite important but it could easily wait until tomorrow if need be ... or if you prefer.'

'I don't leave until about six p.m ... hate driving home in the rush hour. If I wait until six I use less fuel and don't get home much later than I would if I left on time and stop-started my way to Easingwold.' He leaned forward, resting his elbows on his desk top and clasping his two meaty and somewhat liver-spotted hands together. Pharoah noticed a modest watch which might, she thought, be best described as 'mid-range' and a wide wedding ring. 'And you have whetted my appetite, Ms Pharoah. So what have you got there?'

Carmen Pharoah calmly, with a clear logic and a minimum use of words, all of which impressed Hennessey, related the information given to her by Ebenezer Moulton.

'And I see you have done the checks.'

'Yes, sir.' Carmen Pharoah gave the collection of files that rested on her lap two further rapid taps with the palm of her right hand. 'It's quite a family, sir, and it seems to make sense of what Ebenezer Moulton said about wanting to do good for once.'

'Ebenezer ... is that really his name?' Hennessey smiled. 'Knew an Everard once ... Everard Allcock...'

Carmen Pharoah suppressed a chuckle. 'Really, sir?'

'Yes really. That's quite a name to labour through life with, I would have been inclined to change it if I had been him and which,

39

when I ponder what was his dreadful living conditions, I am so pleased I am not, I was not, or whatever. Anyway, tell me about the Moultons.' He leaned back in his chair and glanced to his left out of the small window of his office and saw the curious sight of the ancient walls (though reconstituted, dear reader, in Victorian times) of the city gleaming in sunlight, as they often did during the summer months, yet that day also dominated by a massively towering black cloud which edged menacingly ever closer. The cloud meant more rain, he realized, yet more rain, and more flooding. 'Tell me about them.'

'Well, sir, it transpired that Mr Moulton was not wholly truthful with me, although he might not have been lying so much for his own ends, more the case that he was trying to convince himself, or trying to show himself in a better light. The untruths were of no real consequence I felt, though I have only had time to scan-read the files.'

'Alright.'

'You see, sir, he told me that he was finished as a footballer when his so-called friends badly damaged his physique on his stag night. I should have been suspicious because a few moments later he was on the verge of international stardom until he was rolled in the street and his leg smashed with an iron bar. He has the element of the fantasist about him.'

'But—?'

'It transpires that he was finished as a footballer a little before the incident.'

'Ah...' Hennessey stroked his chin. 'This has a familiar ring to it.'

'Indeed, sir, not his fault at all ... that sort of ring. Footballers it seems are like rock stars and film stars, the life they lead can be overlooked when it results in criminal prosecution for rowdy behaviour or snorting cocaine. It almost seems to be expected of them.'

'So it seems,' Hennessey said drily.

'But,' Pharoah continued, 'young Mr Ebenezer was, it turns out, involved in organized crime. He has a prosecution for being involved in the distribution of cannabis and collected six months in prison, and he was also investigated but never charged with a part played in alleged match fixing, but mud was slung, and, as they say, mud sticks.'

'And they say truthfully, believe me.' Hennessey glanced to his right.

'Yes, sir.' Carmen Pharoah paused, recovering the thread of her delivery. 'Anyway, that was the real reason why he lost his glittering future as a top flight professional footballer, if indeed he was of that calibre, because to be frank, York Town Football Club is fourth division, barely above amateur league.'

41

'I know ... I know,' Hennessey said smiling, 'hasn't produced a lot of star players. Players sign for York Town because no one else will have them ... well, that's probably unfair of me to say that but it's hardly a hotbed of star players, but please continue.'

'So he may be blaming his loss of stardom on other people rather than placing the blame where it should be placed ... to wit ... upon himself.'

'Always somebody else's fault, we hear that often enough.'

'Indeed.'

'You know I think I recall that that incident – the first incident – the ruination of his stag night and subsequent wedding and loss of marriage, involved a pole in the city centre.'

'Yes, sir.'

'So-called friends, as you say, caused quite a lot of talk in this building that night.' Hennessey grimaced. He extended his open palm as if to say, 'Carry on.'

'Well, sir, after that incident, he pursued a career in petty crime. Eventually he was convicted for drug handling and received six months. The probation officer's report is in here. He laid great emphasis on the ruination of Ebenezer's life on his stag night and the magistrates were lenient; six months in the slammer for possession with intent to supply seems lenient to me.'

'It is.'

'There were other offences: theft, petty theft, fines, a period of probation, and then he got "rolled" as he put it and which incident destroyed his leg, which is now apparently a dead weight between his left leg and his crutch. I think he was right, that it would have been better if it had been amputated but the medics wouldn't consider it, apparently, according to him they wanted the challenge of saving it, even though it was saved only to be a dead weight ... but I digress, sorry.'

'No matter.'

'After the attack there have been no more convictions. Whether the attack altered his attitude or whether you need to be able-bodied to be a successful felon, I don't know, but either way, he's been clean for the last few years.'

'Good.'

'Now to his father, one Walpole Moulton.'

'Walpole!' Hennessey put his hand to his forehead. 'Where on earth do they find these names? Thank the Lord I called my son "Charles". Anyway, do go on, please.'

'Mr Moulton, Mr Ebenezer Moulton, said that his parents believed in unusual names ... they both had strange names.'

'Tell me. I despair, but tell me.'

'Liberty.'

Hennessey groaned. 'Carry on.'

'Ebenezer seems to be ... have been ... a

chip off the old block, as they say, because his father had quite a bit of track.'

'You know—' Hennessey tapped the surface of his desk with his fingertip – 'that name rings a bell, distant but distinct, which tolls in my mind like a distant bell on a still, frosty night, when sound will carry a long way. Walpole Moulton, it's a name you would remember. If it is who I am thinking of, wasn't he a housebreaker? Aggravated burglary, something of that sort? Unpleasant sort of individual.'

'Indeed, sir, that's the gentleman. He also had a conviction for armed robbery.'

'Really? So in fairness Ebenezer, his son, is quite mild, not really a chip off the old block?'

'Seems so, sir. Probably I was unfair, Ebenezer hasn't done violence.'

'Don't worry, within these walls anything can be said, but it's coming back quite clearly ... he collected ten years for that, didn't he?'

'Yes, sir, robbing a post office, came out after five years or so. He committed other assaults, other acts of violence which does fit with Ebenezer watching him push someone to their death.'

'Certainly does and especially since I can't see anyone waiting until their father was deceased before reporting his involvement, his commission of a murder, unless he was being fully truthful.'

'My feelings also, sir.'

'So who was Walpole Moulton's name linked with?'

'Quite a few, sir.' Carmen Pharoah once again patted the files on her lap. 'All now burned out it seems, none with convictions less than ten years old but quite a gang of felons and ne'er-do-wells in their day it appears; they were quite active in York and the Vale. Walpole has a few co-defendants mentioned here. I didn't dig out their files but they are easily accessible if needed.'

'Yes ... yes ... fair enough.' Hennessey again glanced out of the small window of his office. The large black cloud was by then much closer, the sun had dimmed and the battlements of the walls had been cleared, it seemed, of all persons, citizens and tourists alike. 'So, if we can identify the unfortunate man who was pushed to his death some twenty years ago, we can begin to focus this inquiry.'

Carmen Pharoah beamed. 'His name is, or rather was, Hill, sir.'

'Good for you, DC Pharoah–' Hennessey smiled warmly at her – 'I am impressed. Good for you. I do appreciate it when my officers bring me the full package. Well done.'

'Thank you, sir, but it wasn't difficult, hardly onerous at all. The deceased is likely to have been one Oliver Hill, aged forty-one when he was murdered. He was one of the people who was reported missing in the floods of twenty years ago. That was when the Bishop of York rowed a rowing boat up the aisle of York Minster.' Carmen Pharoah paused. 'There is a newspaper cutting of that event in the missing person's file, sir. The constable who took the report clearly thought it was a good illustration of the flood conditions in which Mr Hill vanished.'

'Clever.'

'Yes, sir, I thought it was a neat touch. To continue, Mr Hill's body was never found. Four others were deceased in those floods, their bodies were recovered, but not Mr Hill's. The details of Mr Hill do tie in with Ebenezer Moulton's memory of a tall gentleman, his height was given as six foot one inch and his photograph shows him to be neat and well groomed which fits with his occupation, given as that of "accountant/self-employed".'

'Accountant/self-employed? What does that mean? A self-employed accountant, or an accountant who has other sources of income over and above his professional fees?'

'Possibly either, sir, but this is ... this was the initial report, taken by a constable at the enquiry desk, in the middle of floods – a very busy time if it was anything like it is now...'

'Fair enough.' Hennessey felt himself impressed by Carmen Pharoah's sense of fair-mindedness. It can be, he had observed, very easy to be cynical about the shortcomings of others. 'And he disappeared.'

'Yes, sir. Of the five reported missing in the floods, missing presumed drowned, his was the only body not to have been recovered, so the file is still open. He was reported by his wife,' Carmen Pharoah read from the file. 'She would notify us if he had returned.'

'We hope so.' Hennessey spoke with a certain edge of anger in his voice. 'I mean, the number of misper files that are still open because the next of kin, who were quick to report their loved one as being missing, have not been so quick to inform us of said loved one's safe return.'

'Indeed, sir, but the description given by Ebenezer Moulton of a man being pushed off a bridge spanning a river in flood ... I walked across Lendal Bridge this morning, sir, and glanced over the parapet. The force of the water was terrifying, no one could survive in that ... the power of the flow ... just tremendous and if he had been disabled by a blow to the stomach he had no chance of survival at all. The rivers here drain into the Humber.'

'I know.'

'If the body caught the tide, he'd be washed out to sea. But what does surprise me, is that the body was not seen.'

'Not seen?'

'When the rivers are in a state of flood, they hold a fascination for people, who just stare at the water flowing so powerfully. At Lendal Bridge this morning I could only glance at the water from the parapet where there was a place for me to stand, folk were lining the bridge, all of them were just staring down at the water. It would have been like that twenty years ago and we know that Mr Hill, if it indeed was he, was pushed into the river during the hours of daylight.'

'Good point. Ebenezer Moulton could only have witnessed that in daylight.'

'So, I would have thought that someone would have seen a body floating by, unless his body was carried sub-surface ... but anyway ... if his body was seen, it didn't appear to have been reported and once it reached the Humber Estuary it would have been carried out to sea, never to be recovered.'

'We'll have to assume that was what happened. What was his address at the time?'

'It was in the Vale, sir, out by Malton way.'

'Money.' Hennessey raised his eyebrows. 'Lots of green Wellingtons out there ... Range Rovers and shooting sticks and top-of-the-range shotguns but also a lot of poverty which gets hidden away. So what do you think we should do? What would be considered the next step?'

'Interview the reporter, sir?' Carmen

Pharoah felt implicitly complimented by DCI Hennessey's question. Far, far better, she felt, than being imperiously told what to do. She had never experienced any such haughtiness from Hennessey, and coming to know him as she was, she doubted, pleasingly and gratefully, that she ever would. It just didn't seem to be his manner or method of team leadership. 'Visit her home if we still can. It was twenty years ago, she may have moved on. She'll probably be in her sixties now, if indeed she is still with us.'

'Sixty years is not old, DC Pharoah,' Hennessey replied with a clear and very noticeable 'there's life in the old dog yet', sort of gleam in his eye, which Carmen Pharoah found very appealing. 'Not old at all. In fact there's too many damned people over the age of sixty in the UK – one pensioner for every person in employment. Anyway, I think you are correct, quite correct, the next step will have to be to visit the reporter. Who is on duty with you?'

'Thompson Ventnor, sir.'

'Do you find that you two work together well?'

'I think so, sir. There isn't any friction anyway.'

'Good ... good. Then take Ventnor with you. Is he busy at the moment, do you know?'

'Catching up on paperwork, sir. At least he

was when I left him to interview Ebenezer Moulton.'

'Alright, paperwork is vital, but it can wait. Take him with you.'

'Yes, sir.' Carmen Pharoah stood.

'Leave the files with me, please, I'll read them while you are out. I'll wait for your return.'

'Thank you, sir.' Carmen Pharoah laid the files gently on DCI Hennessey's desk. 'We would appreciate that.'

The man walked along the line of cars. He did so as he was wont to say, 'For the good of my health'. Taking exercise when he could, and the break in the rain was an opportunity to be exploited. Five times out and five times back. Five times from his little wooden hut to the end of the line of cars and five times back. He did that exercising his legs, filling his lungs with rain-cleaned air, and then sat in the hut again and picked up the paperback book, and commenced chapter three of *Shoot Out at Comanche Creek*.

'Easy pickings, easy, easy, easy pickings,' Norman Budde whispered to himself as he moved silently and stealthily, catlike round the house, from vacant room to vacant room. He thought, suddenly, that it must have been like this for his grandfather in the war. The old boy had lived to be a good age

50

and as he had grown older he had begun to talk about, even boast and brag about, things which he had hitherto kept quiet about, knowing, like the good thief he was, the value of keeping his mouth shut. But as he grew older, he realized that the long arm of the law, while still able to reach him, had lost interest in doing so and consequently the old man began to entertain those who would listen, Norman Budde, 'young foreman' amongst them. The best job he ever had, the old man would say with a well-satisfied tone of voice, was being an air-raid warden in London during the blitz. 'Those old sirens would go of,' he would say, pronouncing off as 'orf' with his rich East End accent which he had never lost, 'and the old town was proper blacked out, the people was in the shelters or down the tube station and there was just us in the street, all those empty houses to go through ... watches, jewellery ... you'd have your old pockets full in no time flat. Had to be careful though, me and old Ken Chapel, God rest him, one looking for the Old Bill because they patrolled looking for looters. I mean bombs or no bombs the Bill was on the street looking for thieves, never thought it was a couple of air-raid wardens, they saw us as being on their side. "Lot of thieving going from the houses during the air raids, seen anything?" they'd say, and me and Ken would say, "No, we seen nothing", but didn't want to move in case all the jewellery in our pockets started to rattle. So the Bill would say, "Well, keep your eyes peeled and if you see anything, blow your whistles", and me and Ken said, "Yes, course we will, you can count on us", and once the Bill was safely away, we'd be back inside the houses. Well, one would, with the other keeping a lookout ... and did they suspect? Did they ever. Caught a few thieves who operated in the blackout, but never suspected a couple of air-raid wardens. We'd fence the stuff on the black market. I mean the trading that went on in the tap room of the Crown and Anchor and the King's Head and the Old Black Horse and a few other pubs ... nobody's business. I made a lot of good money in the war and at the end I got a letter from the King himself thanking me for my diligence and service as an ARW during the war. "No thanks needed," I would say whenever I got the old letter out and read it. So I slid in and out of prison for a few things but I never got near being suspected of burglary during the blitz. Good times they were, very good times, and if you were first there after a bomb fell and killed people, you'd get first crack at the rings and watches of the dead and badly injured. I mean, they were not needing them no more were they?' And that was Norman Budde's grandfather's war memories, how he ended the war with good money in the bank and a letter of thanks from the King himself, 'But,' he would say in a very serious tone, 'just don't do harm to no one, that's the trick – thieves' honour – there's honour amongst thieves, keep hold of it ... don't do violence, don't do damage inside people's houses, only steal from those who can stand the loss, and above all, don't ever, ever grass on your mates, no matter what the Old Bill offers you ... never give information on another thief ... do bird before giving information to the Bill.'

So his grandfather had been a thief, so had his father and uncles. Now, at seventeen, he was proudly following the family tradition and employing a few tricks his father and uncles and grandfather had taught him, and often fancied that his grandfather, the air-raid warden in London, who cleverly had used the cover of the blackout to go thieving, had himself been born into a family of villains. He wondered how far back was the lineage of thieving in the Budde family; it was after all a good way to make a living. He had found that seven or eight hundred pounds worth of stolen gear could be collected and removed from a house in less than fifteen minutes, and at a time when the minimum wage was £120 per week. He lost a lot of the value in fencing, he could never get more than a third of the actual value of any item, but it still paid, better, he thought, better by far than being a bus driver ... so Norman Budde told himself ... and so he'd been inside, well that's all part of the life and he recalled how proud his family had been of him when he collected his first prison sentence. Now treading softly, he thought fondly of his grandfather and how it must have been like this for him, poking about a whole street full of empty houses. He thought he was like a child let loose in a toy shop, for here he was, well over half a century later, doing what his grandfather Budde had done in the Hitler war. All the householders packed into emergency accommodation because there was two feet of mucky water in the downstairs rooms. All power had been cut off so no burglar alarms to worry about. Street after street of empty houses, all abandoned in a hurry, and if he heard a window smash somewhere close by, well, that was just another felon doing the same. Norman Budde smirked as he thought how lovely, how very lovely it was, the way that everybody pulls together in an emergency ... how it brings out the best in people.

Budde walked from the back bedroom of the house, moving slowly, cautiously, listening as well as looking, because his father and grandfather had both told him that the ones who get caught are the ones who dash about a house and leave their fingerprints everywhere or find out the house isn't empty after all. So he moved cautiously, knowing that the two feet of the River Ouse and raw sewage outside didn't mean the house was empty. 'Always think there is someone in the house until you know otherwise' was the good advice one of his uncles had once given him, to which his father, who was present, had said, 'That's good advice, Norman', and his mother who was also present had smiled and said, 'Can you pass the peas, please?' With that good advice and family support in mind, Norman Budde inched silently from the back bedroom, where he had seen much interesting stuff to return and search through. There was an equally interesting amount of goods on the landing; the family who lived in the house had evidently wasted little time in getting as much of their belongings upstairs as quickly as possible, and had, by his reckoning and comparison to other homes in the street, done better than their neighbours. The last house he had 'visited' had, by contrast, revealed no attempt by the occupants to have moved anything upstairs, they had just turned the door key and had gone to the emergency shelter, and that had made Norman Budde's 'mission' so much easier (for the erudite reader may be interested to learn that criminals of the ilk of Norman Budde attempt to induce the romance of a military exploit into their activities by referring to same as 'missions' and, if arrested, to their 'capture'). He did not, for example, have to clamber over armchairs and sofas which had been hastily deposited in bedrooms, nor did he have to remove the television and other electrical appliances from in front of the bedside cabinet to permit a search for valuables. In fact so absent was any noticeable reaction to the rising waters in the previous house, that Budde assumed that the householder(s) might be away on their annual holiday, it was, after all, the summer months. Nor had the householders taken any precaution at all in respect of their jewellery because there it had been in the drawer of the dressing table in the rear bedroom. It had probably been left there, Budde decided, because a good neighbour had agreed to turn the lights on and off and 'twitch' the curtains, and respond to the burglar alarm should it be activated. But, as his lovely grandfather also said, always expect the unexpected, like, for example, the stubborn old geezer what refused to go to the shelter and stayed in his house so grandfather had to 'tap him a couple of times' before the old geezer recognized the white helmet of the air raid warden; 'That was a close one, young Norman, about as close as you can get.' For the householders away on their long-looked-for holiday on Crete or some similar location, the unexpected flood that had caused the alarm system to be disabled and said good neighbour to be evacuated, then ... then ... the thieves move in. It seemed to Norman Budde to be exactly as 'Polly' Dobson had told them in those tedious science lessons, 'Nature abhors a vacuum.' The householders move out, but the thieves go on missions. Easy pickings.

This house, however, this present house, was clearly the house of a family who had the time and many hands and sufficient muscle that they had been able to remove much of the downstairs furniture and fittings, including carpets, and managed to place them quite neatly, Budde thought, in the back bedroom and on the landing. It was the household, he thought, of a man, his wife and their two sons aged eighteen and nineteen, that sort of household, and not a household likely to show much mercy to a burglar, likely in fact to break his arms and then call the police, if indeed they called the police at all. Budde was mindful, ever mindful, of the risks that mounting a mission, or in this case a series of missions, working along a whole street, could entail. He was ever aware of Johnny 'the Penguin' Lightfoot whose body had been found floating in the Ouse, with his arms and ribs broken in many places, his nose pulped, and his fingers also, and whose death was caused by drowning.

Johnny 'the Penguin' had announced his intention to go on a mission and his body was found two days later. One household clearly took the law into their own hands on that occasion, and they clearly showed no mercy for Johnny 'the Penguin's' tender fifteen years of life.

Fast money.

Easy pickings.

High risk.

That's burglary.

Norman Budde stepped on to the landing and found more items clearly rescued from below. He glanced down at the dank smelling waters that were menacingly still and into which the stairs disappeared. He glanced around him, a sound system, more carpets, the refrigerator, all stacked neatly. This household had clearly worked hard and had also clearly benefited from the forty-eight-hour warning of imminent flooding which the city had been able to provide.

Norman Budde found the body in the front bedroom.

He jolted as he saw the corpse, neat, fresh, an initial fear that the person was alive and would attack him in defence of the property. Then he relaxed as he realized that he was indeed looking at a corpse, and he began to stare at it with horrified fascination, it being the first dead body he had seen. Budde thought that the body had a strange aura about it. The body was of a strongly built male who seemed to Budde to have had the body of a weightlifter, powerful arms and strong shoulders and neck, for that was all that Budde could see because the remainder of the body was tucked up in the bed, neatly made up. The man was deceased, Budde decided, because of the deathly white pallor and also because of a small hole in the middle of the forehead from which a thin trickle of, by then, dried blood emanated and which had run down as far as the bridge of the nose. It was a small hole, but a hole nonetheless, sufficient, Budde thought, to terminate life. The man, in life, had a flattened 'boxer's nose' which had been pushed permanently to one side and which Budde found unusual to see on the body of such a powerfully built man, not, he thought, the sort of man who would be likely to take the second prize in any punch-up, and again Budde was reminded of more words of wisdom from his grandfather, 'You have to remember, young Norman, that you can't win 'em all. Win some, lose some, but win more than you lose, and learn that there's always someone better than you, no matter how good you are, and you'll meet him one day', and his father had said, 'That's good advice', and his mother had nodded and smiled and had said, 'Mashed potato, anybody?'

59

Budde glanced at his hands to ensure he had gloves on, though he felt them, he still needed to see them; it was an instinctive reaction to finding himself in the presence of an murder victim. It had to be a murder, he thought, no gun, definitely a gunshot to the head, but no gun, and the body left so neatly, and a guy with that physique is a guy who likes himself, not a suicidal type, so murder it has to be. Burglary is one thing, but murder, Budde did not want to become involved in a murder investigation. He looked at his gloved hands for a second time.

Then he relaxed. He smiled softly. This, he thought, this makes the mission very easy. No one, he thought, is going to disturb this house. The water below will keep the householders well away and they'll stay well away with the body there. They're probably on a plane somewhere, jetting off to where they can't be arrested, so thought Budde as he sought to turn the find to his advantage. The corpse, being a corpse, means that he is not going to rise up like in a cheap horror film and get him in a headlock. Now, Budde realized, now he can really take his time with this property. Then, only then, would he call the law. That was also part of the thieves' code of honour, so he had learned at the dining table over Sunday lunch, 'If you come across something that's well off-side, really well off-side, you call the law – like little kids unattended, animals being ill treated – you call the law, but only after you have turned over the drum, you have to take care of number one. So, thieve what you can, nick what can be nicked, then and only then, feed the kids or give the dog some water and something to eat, but don't leave the drum without stealing what you can ... stealing everything you can. That's the rule, young Norman. Self first all the time.'

'Thanks, mate.' Budde looked at the corpse. 'Thanks, you've done me a turn. Pity your kitchen's flooded, I could use a cup of tea but I suppose a good lad can't have everything.'

Budde began to search the room around the dead man. He casually, now feeling under no time pressure at all, began to open each of the drawers of the bedroom furniture and probed inside the wardrobe where he found a pearl necklace and a diamond ring and two gold rings hidden inside a thick and inviting-looking hiking sock. The household, he pondered, was clearly anticipating a burglary at some point but hadn't reckoned for a burglar of his skill and training. An old sock in the bottom corner of a wardrobe is a beacon for any housebreaker worth his salt, so Budde reasoned. It was always, he had also found, worth looking in the fridge, that margarine tub may contain margarine, it also may have been washed clean and contain valuables. In this case, the fridge, by then on the landing, had been emptied of all goods, whether edible or otherwise, and was by then slowly defrosting. In the loft of the house he had more, and probably better, luck, a wad of twenty-pound notes, about one thousand pounds he guessed, a neatly labelled collection of ancient coins, probably quite valuable, he thought, but too heavy to carry and so he was obliged, with a heavy heart, to leave them but he ensured he left them with the lid open to let the householder know that he had found them. The house had by then been 'harvested' to Budde's satisfaction and he returned to the first floor where he put the loot into an old canvas holdall which he carried to the back bedroom. Leaving the holdall on the floor by the window, he returned to the front bedroom and searched for something to use as a marker and came across a yellow scarf which he thought would do admirably. He opened a window, having first observed the road for any sign of human activity and tied the scarf to the window handle so that it dangled in front of the house. Budde then returned to the rear bedroom and, putting the holdall on his back like a rucksack, he clambered out of the window and shinned down the drainpipe into the chill, two-feet deep mire that covered the rear garden and lapped against the wall of the house.

'Buddy!'

The voice came from his right-hand side and a little behind him. Budde spun quickly in alarm to see, with no little relief, that he was looking at the drawn, pale, waif-like features of 'Nobby' Parsons, a fellow thief of good repute, and a one-time fellow inmate of Doncaster Young Offenders Institution. Budde smiled. 'How you doin', Nobby?' He spoke loudly and freely as had 'Nobby' Parsons, in the comforting knowledge that they were likely to be the only two people for many hundreds of yards.

'Wet,' Parsons replied from the other side of the fence which separated them. He too was utterly relaxed. 'Good mission?'

'Nothing much–' Budde patted the holdall – 'a bit of stuff ... had better luck. Don't bother with that house.' He indicated the neighbouring house that Parsons was clearly intending to burgle.

'No?'

'No. I done it ... nothing is in it. I just done this one, folk left a bit of trash. I done pretty well all this side of the street. Other side hasn't been done, no sign of it being done anyway, no open windows or forced gates in the rear garden ... but come back tomorrow.'

'Yes?'

'I'm calling the law, the filth will be all over this street in a while.'

'You're calling the law? Why?'

63

Budde told him. 'Just as soon as I am well away from this estate, just as soon as I am in the city centre.'

Parsons shook his head. 'Go to another estate. They got CCTV in the city centre, you'll be captured.'

Budde smiled and gave the thumbs up sign to Parsons as if to say, 'Yes, thanks, you're right. I should have thought of that.'

'He didn't leave us very much. He didn't leave us very much at all, and him an accountant. That's what he told me anyway.' Penny Hill seemed to both Pharoah and Ventnor to be a frail woman, both in terms of physique and personality. She seemed to the officers to be withdrawn, timid, seeming further to have retreated, rather than sunk, into the armchair in which she sat. Her home in Ripon was near the market place with its huge stone column where the horn blower blows his horn, as a horn blower has done so for centuries, once at each corner of the square, announcing the coming of the twenty-first hour, and doing so each day of the year, including Christmas Day and no matter what the weather conditions. The view from the cramped, to Ventnor's mind, but cosy in Pharoah's, pensioner's flat over-looked a road, then a small area of grass, opposite a fish and chip restaurant, down a narrow road on which stood a butcher's shop and the Post Office before affording a glimpse of the square itself. 'No ... not very much at all ... not at all. He didn't ... didn't give a lot in life. Left not a lot in ... well, death ... or disappearing ... whichever it was but it was one or the other ... had to be one or the other. How did you find me anyway, this is a long way from Hutton Cranswick, a very long way?'

'It was,' thought Ventnor, 'hardly any distance at all', but Penny Hill's claim to a great distance separating Hutton Cranswick from Ripon revealed the small world in which she lived. The 'long way' was probably, guessed Ventnor, about forty miles or two days' walk for an experienced walker in good health.

'I thought I had left Hutton Cranswick behind.' Penny Hill's voice was soft, almost a whisper, with a slight, almost pathetic whimpering quality about it, so observed the officers. She wore a long, brown woollen dress, a white blouse and a canary-yellow cardigan. She kept the windows of her flat closed and the temperature within was uncomfortable for the officers, both finding it to be of greenhouse-like stuffiness and unpleasantly warm, especially since they both stood, not having been invited to sit. The impression of both Pharoah and Ventnor was that if Mrs Hill sought warmth on a hot day by keeping the windows closed and wearing a woollen cardigan, feeling cold where none existed, then she was most likely to be of failing health, as if her life was, as an actuary might deem, not an insurable risk.

'We went to your last known address,' Pharoah explained. 'You know, the one in the missing person's report. It was the only thing we could do – all we could do. The present owner of the property gave us your address. They probably shouldn't have done, but they did.'

'But they were very good about it,' Ventnor added, 'insisted on seeing our identification ... our warrant cards; only upon their production did they give us your address.'

'No phone.' Penny Hill smiled. 'Yes, he's a good man, that would have been my son-in-law to whom you spoke. My daughter made a good marriage; she got herself a good husband there. I don't worry about her, I don't worry at all, he's a very good husband and she is happy to continue living in the house she grew up in. I would not want to do that but she seems happy. She is happy, not seems happy, and that's the main thing.'

'I'm surprised your son-in-law didn't phone you to let you know we were coming–' Ventnor glanced round the room, a calendar showing Scarborough, a china dog on the hearth next to the fire – 'a little warning of our arrival.'

'No phone.' Penny Hill raised an upturned palm in a 'see for yourself' gesture. 'When I moved here a few years ago I decided that I didn't want a phone. I decided I wanted peace. I have good neighbours in these flats – all pensioners – we keep each other's keys, front door keys I mean, and if I am not seen or heard for a day or two Mrs Tobin on the other side of the landing will check on me, as I would check on her. So I have that security, but I don't want to have to get up out of my chair each time the phone rings just to find out it's someone who wants to sell me double-glazing, or someone who doesn't reply when I answer but keeps me waiting because they're still trying to sell somebody else something. My daughter and son-in-law want me to get an answerphone, the type that the ringer can be kept switched off so I can listen to any message when I see the little light flashing and reply if I want to reply and also phone out when I want to, but I don't even want that ... just peace.'

'Seems that's a good idea, the answering machine, I mean, but if you prefer peace, well, that's up to you.' Carmen Pharoah sensed that Mrs Hill was beginning to relax in her and Ventnor's presence. To allow this rapport to develop would, she believed, make the interview easier, much better than jumping in with both feet, much more sensitive. They had called on her to talk about her deceased husband and they wanted, nay needed, her cooperation. 'I have just that arrangement in my flat in York. I never get bothered by telesales people, you should consider it.'

'I might consider it. So, please do sit down.'

Ventnor sat in the vacant chair and Pharoah sat on the sofa, and both did so thankfully.

'So, you drove from York to Hutton Cranswick to Ripon, that's an awful long drive.'

'An hour if that, and through beautiful countryside, so not unpleasant or difficult,' Ventnor offered, 'better than sitting in an office phoning total strangers, asking them to buy double-glazing.'

Penny Hill smiled. 'Yes, we are lucky. When I was young I so wanted to travel ... and I did, I really did travel, but then I got to an age where I didn't want to leave Britain, then I got to an age when I didn't want to leave England, then I didn't want to leave Yorkshire and now, I don't want to leave Ripon. Funny thing, your horizons shrink, but you're quite comfortable as they shrink. I am so content in my little box and once a month I go to Hutton Cranswick for Sunday lunch with my daughter's family ... I have three grandchildren. It's quite enough for me.'

Spoken, Carmen Pharoah thought, like an eighty-year-old, not like a woman in her mid-sixties. Women of Penny Hill's age are most often found on Saga holidays, looking for 'third life' partners, but then, she had also observed that people age at different rates. As when she was once standing in a bar and a couple entered whom she took as partners, only to overhear the woman introduce the man as her father. It seemed that the man had started his family very early in life and just had not aged as rapidly as other men of his generation. Penny Hill seemed to Carmen Pharoah to be on the other, less fortunate side of the spectrum, not only appearing older than her years, but ageing rapidly in terms of her attitude, being content in her pensioner's flat with the softly ticking clock on the mantelpiece, measuring her life away when other women of her age are taking their grandchildren out for the day, not visiting them once a month, or are walking strongly up Snowdon, enjoying life and good health and good company. Carmen Pharoah found Mrs Hill a somewhat pathetic figure and further found herself hoping that she herself would not succumb to such a fate. Adjacent to her she noticed Thompson Ventnor take his notebook out of his pocket and open it, signalling to her that it was time to commence the interview.

'Floods, though.' Penny Hill spoke softly.

'Sorry?' Carmen Pharoah raised her eyebrows.

'Floods. The countryside about here might be delightful, but floods now ... hard time for some folk and the land isn't pretty to look at when it's underwater.'

'No, but we saw little flooding on the way here, most of it is south of York, going towards the Humber. That area is very badly affected and parts of York also.'

'Ah ... I see.'

'So, could you tell us about your husband, please, Mrs Hill?'

'Oliver?' Penny Hill shook her head. 'Well, I had a lovely daughter by Oliver but that's all the good he gave me. It was a mistake ... the marriage ... another man was interested in me and he did well in life, but Oliver...'

'What did he do for a living, Mrs Hill? The missing person's report suggested he was an accountant but also said self-employed. We were puzzled by that, it covers a lot of bases.'

Carmen Pharoah looked at the wallpaper, loudly yellow to match Penny Hill's cardigan, but it was also a 'cold' colour and a colour which one recoils from, so psychologists have found, and much favoured by fast-food restaurants for that reason, so as to discourage patrons from lingering after their meal of burgers and tasteless chips. Carmen Pharoah could, she felt, never feel comfortable or relaxed in the room.

'Covers a lot of bases?' Penny Hill queried. 'Meaning?'

'Covers a multitude of sins, can mean a lot of things, that's what I meant. Could we have some clarification about his source of income, please?'

'Is that relevant? After all these years? He disappeared, probably in the floods that we had at the time. So why the sudden interest, has his body been found? Has he turned up alive and well and living under a new name with a new wife? That wouldn't surprise me; Oliver would do something like that.'

'No, neither has happened.' Carmen Pharoah spoke with a sombre, serious tone of voice. 'We have information that whatever happened to your husband was not an accident.'

A silence descended upon the room, a silence which was almost audible. Penny Hill's jaw dropped, she held intense eye contact with Carmen Pharoah. She turned to Thompson Ventnor and then turned again to Carmen Pharoah. When Penny Hill did speak, she did so with a note of fear and alarm in her voice. 'Not an accident? You mean someone did away with him? Someone murdered him?'

'It appears so.'

'Oh, all these years; days, weeks, months for twenty years ... minutes and seconds. I always thought that the silly soul had lost his footing and slipped into the flood water. Those floods were in the springtime and the water would have been cold, snow-melt rushing down from the Dales, not in the summer like these floods. Cold enough now

71

I would think, but in the spring they would be even colder. He wouldn't have lasted very long in those floods or–' she held up a finger in an admonishing style gesture – 'or, I thought the clever soul had used the floods as cover to make good his escape into a new life somewhere with a young floozy, leaving me and my daughter to cope as best we could, but now he seems to have been murdered ... well ... well.'

'Do you think he would do that?'

'Walk out on his family? Oh yes, he would have done that. You never really know someone unless you live with them. I mean, that is so, so true. I suspected that Oliver had a bit of a side to him, most people have, but I never knew just what a fly-by-night he was; always full of schemes to make money, some of them really far-fetched, the sort of thing that a lunatic would think of and some were downright criminal and those were the only ones he would share with me. I dread to think what other plans he was hatching. It was a terrible way to live, really terrible. I used to envy the women whose husbands had a steady job, and brought home steady money. Alright, they had to budget but at least they knew what was coming in each week, or each month. I'd see their husbands going to work and coming back at the same time each day ... how nice that was, how nice it must have been for them, regular money coming in and a car in the driveway, just a small car but they could run a car and a family holiday each year for the children; but we, the Hills, what did we live like? So he used to walk out of the house each morning wearing his suit and carrying his briefcase, but that was all show just to impress the neighbours. I never knew where he went. He had no job to go to but occasionally one of the neighbours said she had seen Oliver sitting in the bus station in Driffield or Beverley, like he was waiting for a bus; nothing wrong in that, nothing unusual in that.'

'But...' Carmen Pharoah anticipated.

'But, when she retraced her steps two hours later, he was still there, still sitting as though he was waiting for a bus, just staring into space. Or another neighbour would tell me she'd seen him sitting on a bench in the park in the middle of the working day, just sitting there ... and all the while we'd be getting hate mail from the bank and building society about the overdraft and the mortgage arrears. Then, once in a while, he'd come home with the briefcase bursting with cash, used notes, and he'd hand it to me and say, "Don't ask questions, just pay what we owe and buy food, and bank anything that's left over." And I'd think, "Ask no questions so I don't get told no lies", as my mother used to say. So the next day I was shovelling hard cash over the counter of the bank and the building society, buying food, and buying lots of tins of food so we wouldn't starve in the lean times, and putting a bit in the savings account but that never lasted long, not long at all. So that's how we lived for ten years. It was no life, no life at all, but Linda, my daughter, didn't know that, all she knew was that her daddy went to work each morning before she left for school and came home at five p.m. just like all the other daddies, and when she asked what her daddy did, all I could say was that he worked for himself. So, when I reported him missing, I said he was an accountant because that is what he told the neighbours he was, but accountants do well in life, they earn big money, they don't live in the sort of little house we lived in, so I just said accountant/self-employed and the constable didn't ask me to elaborate, they were very busy, the floods you see...'

'Yes, we thought as much,' Carmen Pharoah explained.

'So that was our life. A small semi on an estate in Hutton Cranswick, looked neat and perfect but inside it was hand-to-mouth, desperately short of money, real fear of the future, for weeks meals were created from the contents of tins, main meals, and then occasionally there'd be a bag full of cash on the kitchen table. We'd pay off the wolves at the door and then we'd start all over again and all the time, putting on a jolly face for the benefit of the neighbours. No life at all. I often thought that we'd be better off on the dole because then I'd know what was coming in, little as it might have been. So in the middle of the floods, twenty years ago, he didn't come back. One evening the door didn't open at five o'clock, he didn't come home and I knew in an instant that something was wrong. Then the next morning I sent Linda off to school and went to the police station in Driffield and reported him as a missing person, with the police station full of folk in a panic about this and that and the phones ringing like they were going to melt. All the officer could do was to take details and give me a case number and suddenly Oliver wasn't a person anymore, he was a "missing person", and you know, I had an identity for the first time in ten years. Up to then I was the wife of "I don't know what he does for a living" and then I became the wife of a "missing person". Imagine a wife of a "missing person" being better than what had been before, but that was the truth.' She shook her head. 'But then things got better for me and Linda. I went on the dole for a while and so had a regular income and then I got a job. A real job. I had office skills but Oliver would never let me work, even when we were penniless, my place was still in the home. But then I went out to work for a small company in Driffield, very unsatisfying and I never liked the idea of working to make someone else rich but I did a good job, I got good references and eventually I got a job as a receptionist in a medical centre. That job gave me a sense of purpose and I was there until I retired and all that time me and Linda had a steady income. It wasn't much but it was regular as clockwork – heaven ... I mean, after Oliver's idea of providing, it was heaven and I got on top of things, slowly but steadily, a little like climbing Mount Everest. I found that the trick was not to look at the peak but to look at your feet, the "one day at a time" principle, and it worked. Just keep 'em going, one foot in front of the other, then one day, lo and behold, I was at the top. Done it, all by myself, mortgage paid off. My daughter was twenty-two by then, and two years later she got married and she and her husband asked if they could buy my house because I was looking for a small flat to end my days in.'

'Neat,' Pharoah commented, still thinking that Penny Hill was uttering as an eighty-year-old might utter. 'But what can you tell us about Mr Hill's ... Oliver Hill's friends and acquaintances? Any that you know?'

'Friends, none, no family either, all predeceased him. Well, I never knew what he did, so I knew none of his friends.'

'In a marriage of what, ten years? I find

that so difficult to believe that I can scarcely credit it,' Carmen Pharoah pressed Penny Hill with restrained anger.

'Neither can I,' Ventnor growled supportingly, 'there must be some contact. Who sent you Christmas cards? Who called at the door demanding money?'

'How did you know that happened?' Penny Hill wailed desperately.

'I didn't.' Ventnor remained stone-faced. 'I guessed that happened, going by the description of your husband's lifestyle. Such men borrow unwisely, and make enemies – so who were they?'

Penny Hill began to move her head rapidly from one side to the other as if looking for an escape route but remained silent.

'So,' Carmen Pharoah pressed, 'name names.'

'You could be in trouble with the police if you withhold information,' Ventnor added, still growling. 'This is a murder investigation.'

'Is it?' Penny Hill glared at him. 'You have not found his body.' She spoke almost as if in protest. 'You can't have a murder investigation without a body.'

'Not wholly true,' Carmen Pharoah replied in a calmer tone of voice. 'It's difficult, but it's not wholly the case. A lady reported her daughter and grandchildren missing once and reported her suspicions about her daughter's husband who was known to be violent. The disappearance of the mother alone might have been insufficient, but mother plus two young children was sufficient, to suspect murder that is, and the jury found against him and he collected three life sentences. So it is not strictly true that we have to have a body in order to prove murder. In this case we are looking for a gang of four, well three now, one of whom had a green van at the time of Mr Hill's ... disappearance. The "one" of the gang we are no longer looking for is now deceased. He had the unlikely name of Walpole Moulton, and gave his son the unlikely name of Ebenezer.'

'Ebenezer!' Penny Hill gasped. 'Did you say Ebenezer?'

'Yes ... why? That name clearly has some significance for you. What is it?'

'Ebenezer, how many children are called by that ridiculous name? I mean how many in England, let alone the Vale of York? Just the one, I'll be bound. He's about Linda's age. Mid-twenties?'

'Yes.'

'Ebby, he was called Ebby by Linda, my daughter, and her friends. He was a bit of a hanger-on I thought. A stone.'

'A stone,' Carmen Pharoah echoed, 'a stone? I am sorry you have lost me.'

'The name Ebenezer, I looked it up, just out of curiosity. I thought it sounded biblical, very Old Testament sort of name; it is the name of a stone set in the ground to commemorate a battle – the stone Ebenezer. If I recall the line it is, "Then Samuel took a stone and set it between Mizpah and Jeshanah and called the name of it Ebenezer". It's in the book of Samuel in the Old Testament.'

'Interesting,' Carmen Pharoah pressed, 'but tell us about the living Ebenezer.'

'Well, yes, Ebby, a young lad, lived in Driffield then moved to York with his father. What is he doing these days? Married with a family?'

'No, but other than that, I can't tell you. Sorry.'

'I see. I learned the value of confidentiality when I worked for the doctors at the health centre. They were very strict about that, so I can understand, but Ebby ... it's all coming back to me now. He went to be a footballer then went off the rails, so I hear tell.'

'Something like that.'

'Well, so that was his father, one of the men who killed Oliver ... the family name was Moulton ... knew that. Their address, it was, twenty-four Larkrise Lane, Driffield. Yes, twenty-four Larkrise Lane, Driffield. Odd house, I saw it once, always overgrown, the front garden I mean; probably the back garden as well, but I only ever saw the front. So, Moulton, that was the family name.'

Penny Hill paused and glanced out of the window towards the town square. 'You know, my husband knew Ebby's father.'

'He did?'

'Yes,' Penny Hill nodded slowly. 'Yes, he did.'

'So, tell us. This is what we want to know. You see if Walpole Moulton and his friends did murder your husband, then the more we know about Walpole Moulton the better, the easier it will be to trace his friends of twenty years ago. Although Walpole is no longer alive, his friends might still be, and justice will catch up with them.'

'That would be satisfying.' Penny Hill looked at the carpet, smiling.

'So...?'

'Well, one of the few times and I mean one of the very few times I saw my husband when he was supposed to be at work was when I had to go into Driffield for some reason. I needed something I couldn't buy in Hutton Cranswick. We must have had a bit of money at that time and I saw him smartly dressed and carrying his briefcase, which would have been empty. It was for show and only for show because that was Oliver Hill, all image and no substance. Anyway, I saw him and Ebenezer's father talking to each other in the centre of Driffield. Oliver looking so smart and Ebby's father looking so down at heel, they did look an odd pair, a bit like a lawyer talking to his client who was a petty crook.'

'That's very interesting,' Carmen Pharoah murmured. 'Not arguing or fighting?'

'No, chatting as though they were on the same side, or like they were good friends.'

'Very interesting,' Ventnor commented.

'Is it?' Penny Hill looked at Ventnor.

'Possibly. What else do you know about Ebenezer's father, Walpole Moulton?'

'Not a lot. Used to see him in Driffield from time to time, walking about with an unpleasant-looking set of characters. I wouldn't like it if my Oliver had got mixed up with them – really shifty-looking, really a rough-looking crew.' She paused. 'So is that what did happen, he got his silly self mixed with that lot; got himself mixed up with folk he shouldn't have got mixed up with?'

'Too early to say, Mrs Hill,' Pharoah replied diplomatically. So thought Ventnor, much too early to say.

Janet Nash looked at the man and held his hand. 'He took a dreadful bang on the head,' she said. 'So his mum told me, he got really violent after that, doesn't make a lot of difference to me why he's violent ... he just is.'

'Well I just need to get close enough.' Alex Mower stroked the barrel of the gun. 'If I can just get close enough...'

'I can help you there.' Janet Nash smiled. 'I can tell you where he'll be, and when he'll be there.'

'Good,' Mower said, smiling. 'Then Shaw will be no more.'

Carmen Pharoah curled up on the sofa in the living room of her flat on Bootham, wearing jogging bottoms and a man's rugby shirt which she occasionally smelled, searching for a scent. She thought of the day, the smelly, unwashed and ludicrously named Ebenezer Moulton and thought further how right he had been that life could change so quickly and so permanently. One day your life path ahead of you is this, and in an instant it becomes that. Just as she had grown up as Carmen Bennett in Leytonstone and had married and become Carmen Pharoah, she a detective constable in the Metropolitan Police, and he a chartered accountant, both happy to live in London where he had been born, and then she was a widow, while still in her twenties ... and felt the only thing she could do after the shock, and the funeral and the grieving, was to come north, as if the hard, grim North of England which had never held any appeal for her, had become the place where she must live for her sins, and York was as good a place as any.

In bed by ten p.m. because she felt tired and in need of rest. She lay listening to the sounds outside, the laughter and rapid speech of university students; the clicking high heels of a woman walking slowly, calmly home; the whir of the diesel engines of the buses and the 'ee aw' sound of an intercity train arriving, or leaving the nearby railway station. Sleep took her before the Minster bell chimed midnight.

It was Monday, 23.40 hours.

The man lay staring at the ceiling, listening to the heavy breathing of his sleeping cellmate. He thought that pleading guilty to manslaughter hadn't helped, hadn't helped at all. The judge still sent him down for fifteen years. He knew he had to get out before ten years. You can't survive more than ten years, after ten years you just didn't recover. All he had was the butcher's knife, covered in the guy's blood with the 'Field Marshall's' prints on it – all over it – in the blood, he could use that to reduce the time, shave a few years ... more than a few, and given to him to get rid of while they were in the 'Field Marshall's' house having a drink to celebrate topping the guy, and didn't he get rid of the knife? Didn't he just. In the 'Field Marshall's' garden, not the way the 'Field Marshall' thought he'd got rid of it. But it's out of sight. Safe. In case it's needed.

It was Tuesday, 01.43 hours.

* * *

'Do you think I'm stupid?' Norman Budde snarled down the phone. 'Give my name? You can guess it. I've told you all I'm telling you and I am not going to repeat it 'cos I know you tape emergency calls. Just go to the address, look for a yellow scarf hanging from the front window. The bloke inside is dead – I mean dead – not old and croaked in his sleep dead, but hole in the head dead, that sort of dead. I was there yesterday, he'll still be there. I'm well away.' Budde hung the phone up with a gloved hand and walked home. Yesterday had been a good day, hard cash in four figures and good stuff he could unload to contacts who will get rid of them in car boot sales or through junk shops. A very good day's work, and the best part was he had observed thieves' honour, only stolen from those who could stand the loss, not done needless damage to any property. He'd warned another blagger that he was calling the law to report something well off-side ... really well off-side. It had been a good mission. His grandfather was so right, 'Only fools and horses work.'

It was Tuesday, 09.47 hours.

Three

Tuesday, 28th June, 10.33 hours –
Wednesday, 29th June, 02.35 hours

In which an isolated family is described, the cause of a death is determined and Thompson Ventnor is at home to the courteous reader.

Louise D'Acre rested her hands on the side of the inflatable dinghy as it was slowly pulled along the street by a constable wearing waders. She could not help a wry smile at the strangeness of it all, especially as the dinghy was manoeuvred into the driveway of the house and up to the front door where another constable stood. She also noticed how silent everything seemed, a road, houses, yet all was silent save the occasional lapping of a wave created by the constable's legs as he moved forward, no sounds of family life from within the houses, no sound of road traffic. The street, she thought, was like a ghost town. At the door of the house she, tall, slender, an observer would note, with excellent muscle tone, short, close-cropped hair and just a trace of lipstick as her only make-up, handed her Gladstone bag to one of the constables and shared their good humour as she stepped out of the dinghy into the water which came up above her knees. The waders which had been found for her were a few sizes too large but they would suffice for the short journey from doorway to stairs. Finding her feet in the still but unclean water, she then followed the constable into the house. She found walking in two feet of water surprisingly difficult and she knew then why even a few inches of water moving at speed would be sufficient to cause a person to lose their balance if trying to walk in it. She thought that water is like snow: it has a deadly beauty about it. She reached the stairs and began to climb them and was again surprised at the effort required to lift her foot up to one stair and then the next. Eventually she emerged fully from the water and climbed the remainder of the stairs encumbered only by the heavy waders which she found hot and uncomfortable but realized were far, far preferable to having to wear soaking and reeking clothing. Once on the landing, she was drawn to the front bed-room of the house by the soft murmur of voices, the sense of activity and the flash of a camera. She entered the room where her eye was caught by George Hennessey to whom she nodded and observed that he seemed to be a controlling, masterful presence in the room even though he was just standing and saying nothing. He was the man in charge. He knew it and all others present also knew it.

'Good morning, Chief Inspector–' Louise D'Acre smiled as she crossed the threshold – 'a double first for me this morning.' She took her bag from the constable who had carried it up the stairs for her and did so with a word of thanks.

'Oh?' Hennessey smiled.

'Yes, a double first. The first time I have attended a crime scene by boat and the first time I have come to work wearing jeans.'

'Indeed, double first as you say, ma'am,' Hennessey replied for want of something to say. 'Dare say there is a first time for everything.'

'Yes ... as you say.' Louise D'Acre glanced around the room, familiarizing herself with her surroundings before focusing on the corpse. Neat, clean, smartly kept, quite a normal bedroom in a lower middle-class house in suburbia. She noted the double bed in which the deceased lay, not central, she saw, but on the side closest to the window, the right-hand side, the usual male side of the bed, so that a female would lay to his left. It had been the pattern in her marriage and was the pattern with her present partner when they had the opportunity to share time together. The bedroom furniture was as she would have expected, a set of drawers and a wardrobe, both lightweight and inexpensive looking. With the SOCOs, one constable, the Chief Inspector and herself, the room was, she felt, quite crowded. 'Have you taken all the photographs you need to take?' she asked of Hennessey, hoping to sound diplomatic.

Hennessey glanced at the portly scene of crime officer, who replied, 'I believe so, sir, both colour and black and white. It's a badly contaminated crime scene, as you said, having been burgled and so it's impossible to tell what is relevant to the murder, so I photographed everything. Wouldn't you say, Sid?'

Sid, the second SOCO, who stood behind the first, nodded and in a laconic, very Yorkshire way, thought Dr D'Acre, said 'Aye.'

'So all done that can be done, sir,' the first SOCO added, he being clearly more wordy than Sid, his assistant, 'in this room anyway, we still have the other rooms and the attic to photograph. The thieves went there, that's plain. Imagine finding a corpse and then calmly burgling round it. Sometimes I just can't understand some folk, really can't. Anyway, we'll make a start of the other rooms, sir, give the doctor room to breathe.'

'Yes.' Hennessey glanced at the constable. 'If you could wait on the landing, please, give Dr D'Acre more room to work.'

'Yes, sir.' The constable followed the SOCOs out of the room.

'A contaminated crime scene did he say?' Louise D'Acre pulled on a pair of latex gloves, looking all the while at the corpse.

'Yes, ma'am.' George Hennessey stepped back against the wall opposite the bay window. 'It could have been days before the body was discovered, but a vulture of a burglar found it and phoned us ... nice of him really.'

'A vulture of a burglar?' Dr D'Acre turned and glanced at Hennessey with a brief grin and a sparkle in her eyes. 'An interesting turn of phrase, Chief Inspector. What do you mean?'

'Just the way I think, ma'am, just the way my mind works,' Hennessey replied, also with a slight grin. 'You see these houses have been evacuated, as you know.'

'Yes, an awful experience to have your home flooded like this and it isn't as though it's clean water ... the smell.'

'Yes, but upon being evacuated, the burglars descended, vulture-like I thought, looting, a very low crime.'

'Ah, looting is scavenging and a vulture is a scavenger. I understand your thought process. This entire estate is like a stricken animal and the vultures descend, tearing away at the flesh. So yes, quite an apt image, but this corpse does not seem to be at one with this house. It's a young corpse, I mean. He was a young man when he died. This seems to be the home of a middle-aged couple ... the decor ... the furnishings.'

'Yes, our observation also.'

A silence descended, broken by Dr D'Acre, who said, 'You mean the corpse was brought here?'

Hennessey opened his palms outwards as if to say 'Who knows?' 'He seems not to be a part of the house, early days yet, of course, but a puzzle to be answered, but this is police work. We don't get paid much but we see life. It appears that a felon burgled the house yesterday, as many of these houses will probably have been burgled. Sadly, a lot of homeowners will return to find their houses have been burgled, valuables missing as well as valuables being damaged by flood water. It's upsetting, how folk can turn on each other.'

'Yes.' Dr D'Acre paused as she took a thermometer from her bag. She remained silent as she pondered whether or not to tell George Hennessey something. She eventually decided to tell him. 'You know, there is a story in our family, passed down from generation to generation. I haven't told my children yet but two teenagers and one pre-teen, it's about time I told them the story.'

'Oh?'

'Yes, relatives on my mother's side. They

lived in the Channel Islands, on Guernsey, when the Nazis invaded.'

'Oh, dear.'

'Yes, not a good time. They were a young couple then and selected for deportation to Germany as forced labour. They were taken from their house and carried across the island by lorry and arrived at the port in time to see the boat that they were to be put aboard disappearing over the horizon on its way to occupied France. Anyway, the Nazis told them to return home and so they set off and walked back across the island, arriving at their home about eight hours after they had left ... just eight hours ... and they returned to find that in those eight hours their home had been stripped of all its contents by their neighbours. People who they had lived with in the same community, people they numbered amongst their friends. Those people clearly didn't think my relatives would return – ever – and so they descended on their home and helped themselves. So I probably shouldn't have smiled at your description of the burglars of this house as "vultures" because ... well, it has personal resonance.'

'I'm sorry.'

'Well, I wasn't alive then and my bloodline did not depend upon them, so even if they had been deported and not returned, I would still have been born and also my children and my children's children still to come, but it is harrowing to think how fickle people can be, if that's the correct word.'

'Well, I'd put it stronger, but I know what you mean.'

'They got the substance of their belongings back over the next few weeks. Nobody ever knocked on their door and said, "I am really sorry but it was I who stole ... whatever ... and I'd like to return it." No one said that but they'd wake up one morning and the dining table and chairs would be on the front lawn having been placed there during the night and on another morning, the wardrobe for the bedroom would be on the lawn, the mahogany desk which was an heirloom, was left at the gate and a canvas bag hanging over the front hedge contained their jewellery and other small possessions that had been stolen, but they didn't recover all their belongings and for the rest of the war their neighbours just could not look them in the eye. I suppose it's good that the neighbours felt guilt about what they did, but they shouldn't have done it at all. Sometimes I wonder what I would have done had I been one of the neighbours. I like to think I would have done one thing, but I fear I may have done the other, especially if I saw a free-for-all going on.'

'I know what you mean.' Hennessey glanced across the room, out of the window, at the yellow-painted house on the opposite side of the street and at the dark cloud gathering above and behind it. 'Society has a fragility about it. It is delicately held together and the pack instinct is very strong.'

'Yes,' Dr D'Acre said softly, 'that is a good way of putting it. After the war they left the island and settled in Devonshire, where my cousins were born and they, not I, they and their children are only with us because their parents missed the boat.'

'Frightening.'

'Yes, it would keep me awake at night if I were they, and at least the people in this street are being burgled by strangers ... slim compensation I know, but it's better than having your house raided by your neighbours.'

'Indeed,' Hennessey growled. 'That was not a funny story.'

'No, but to the matter in hand, the deceased is male, Northern European or Caucasian by racial extraction. I observe a gunshot wound to the middle of the forehead and a second to the rear of the skull just behind the left ear.'

'Two!'

'Yes.'

'We only noted the one but we didn't examine the body.'

'Well there are two ... both small calibre, .22, I'd say.'

'An assassin?'

'Well, that really is more your department than mine Chief Inspector, but a small calibre gun and a point of entry just behind the ear. It has a neatness about it. This is not the outcome of a marital squabble. To misuse a word, this is very "professional", no exit wounds, so I'll be able to recover the bullets for you but they will have turned his brain to porridge. The small calibre bullet would not have had the momentum to punch an exit wound through the skull and would have whizzed round looking for a way out. It would be a bit like beating up the brain matter with an egg whisk, that's why the .22 is the weapon of choice for the hit man, so I believe. One clean entry wound and no messy exit wound and the bullet goes round and round and round inside the head.'

'So I have heard. A hit man has more kudos the closer he gets to his victim, or so I believe ... the knifeman, he's the top dog. The fella who uses a .22 and stands within a few feet of his victim, he's second division, but the guy who uses a rifle with a telescopic sight, he's bottom of the league ... so I am advised.'

'Well, I'll take your word for it, Chief Inspector–' D'Acre continued to examine the head of the deceased – 'but I can well believe it.' She peeled back the duvet covers. 'Now, you are going to ask me about time. Oh ... how interesting.'

'Oh?'

'Wearing jeans and naked from the waist up, jeans – but no socks or shoes, hot weather, and a flood alert. He might be too young for the house but he is in a state of semi-undress that I would expect someone to be in if they were removing furniture upstairs and someone interrupts him and bang, he's dead, well, bang, bang, he's dead ... possibly.'

'Possibly, we'll keep an open mind but you think he might be a younger relative of the homeowners?'

'Well, a thought, although I am straying from my area of expertise.' She paused. 'He is ... he was a very muscular man. Rigor is established, legs are beginning to rise. Well, it was a double tap for him and a double first for me. Time of death ... sometime between when the house was evacuated because of the flood and the time it was reported. I don't like being pinned down to time of death, no pathologist does, it is the invention of writers of those awful detective novels and screenplays, but more than twelve hours ago, less than forty-eight hours ago. Well, I'll take a rectal temperature and then I'll have the body removed to the York District. Will you be attending the post-mortem for the police, Chief Inspector?'

'Yes, yes I will. I will go and organize the stretcher party and a mortuary van. I think the van could get within half a mile of here.'

'Very well. Could you ask the constable to come in, please, I'll need help to turn the body over?'

'The Moultons?' The man had a protruding stomach which seemed to the officers more square in profile than beer-belly round and thus spoke of a serious medical condition more than an overfondness for beer. He stood in the front garden of his house, hoe in hand, beads of sweat rolled off his brow which he mopped frequently with a hand-kerchief. 'I remember them, mother, father and son. They lived in that house there.' The man indicated the adjacent property. 'It was a right mess when that family were there, garden all overgrown, then they got a trans-fer of tenancy to York, got tired of Driffield I suppose. Got some nice folk in there now, as you see. The garden is pristine, better than mine and I put all my hours into mine but that fella took a real dip in life, the new tenant, a real dip.'

'A dip?' Ventnor asked.

'Well, I call it a dip. He was a career soldier and had to retire at forty-two. He was a frontline soldier so he explained to me when he moved in. An infantry man, a sergeant major, even the junior officers were frightened of him, so he told me. Now ... well, now he drives a taxi with women in the back seat giving him directions; right here, left here, it fair gets under his skin being ordered about like that when just a few weeks ago an entire regiment snapped to attention at his command. It's quite a dip. He's looking for something better, so he won't stay driving a taxi for long. He wants what my brother has. My brother was in the parachute regiment for a good number of years and when he was time expired the regiment took him back as a civilian outdoor instructor. He loves it, teaching the new entrants basic fieldcraft, map reading, climbing, rough country hiking, camping. He loves it. Everything he loved about the army without the bull and he found out that he was a natural teacher that made it even better for him.'

'Sorry–' Ventnor held up his hand – 'good for your brother, but we are here about the Moultons and we are under a little time pressure. What can you tell us about that family?'

'The Moultons, aye.' The man mopped his brow. 'The soil's wet, it's hard work turning it but the Moultons? Well what can I say? They were ... dunno really. What can I say about them? Not antisocial but not social either. You see round here on Christmas Eve night you'll see folk going from house to house putting Christmas cards through each other's letter boxes. Always has been like that, but we never got a card from the Moultons. We put one through their letter box each year but never got one in return, no one did. We also watch each other's houses when folk are away on holiday but we never watched the Moultons because they never went away. They just seemed happy to hide behind their huge front hedge and overgrown garden. The hedge was an eyesore, it must have been well over six feet high and the garden was just ... a mess. You'd see mice dashing in and out of the grass it was that tall. Tom, the present tenant, he's turned that garden round and it's as neat as any now, as you see, but he had his work cut out and a couple of us pitched in to help him get on top of it. He has a wife and a daughter, they were not able to help him, it needed the strength of about four or five men to clear up the garden. That was what the Moultons left behind them. I helped as much as I could but this gets in the way of heavy work–' he patted his stomach – 'so we helped Tom and helped ourselves because we were getting rid of a local eyesore. So there was a bit of "what's in it for us" about helping the new neighbour.'

'Nonetheless, I am sure he was grateful for the assistance–' Carmen Pharoah was impressed by the man's honesty – 'no matter what your reasons for helping. But, tell us about the Moultons.'

'Oh ... yes ... well, not a lot to tell, they hid behind that huge privet hedge of theirs. Never gave any cause for complaint, never had fights or rows, never played loud music. Their boy Ebenezer, what a name to hang on a lad in this day and age, but their lad, he wasn't a nuisance, never vandalized anything, didn't get involved with the local gangs. There was some damage done to cars by that gang when they were all about fourteen or fifteen, car tyres let down and aerials snapped off, windscreen wipers bent back but Ebby wasn't part of that. He liked to play soccer. He was often to be seen kicking a ball about and in fact I heard he signed for York Town Football Club, but that was all the mixing he did. They were just—'

'Isolated?' Carmen Pharoah suggested. 'Would you say what is known as an "isolated family"?'

'Yes–' the man smiled – 'that's a good way of describing them, like on a desert island they were, for all the contact they made with folk on the estate.'

'Alright. So what do you know about Mr Moulton's source of income?'

'Nothing.' The man shook his head. 'I never asked and he never said. We know what each other does, no regret. I was a long-distance lorry driver before I got me stomach, Tom, like I said, ex-soldier and now he drives a taxi; Lenni, he's a bus driver, and Will, across the road, self-employed gardener, cigars in the summer, rollups in the winter. Loves his work, Will does, out of doors all the time. Even the bit of work he gets in the winter is outdoor work ... that keeps him going; you'll never get Will in a factory or an office. Miss Davis down the street, she teaches in primary school but Walpole? We never knew what Walpole did. He did go out to do something, something for money, so it was more than just the dole, but this is a high-amenity estate, one of the best in Driffield, if you don't pay your rent you get kicked off the estate into a low-amenity housing area, so they paid their rent but I always thought Walpole was a bit of a shady character, a bit dodgy ... a bit iffy.'

'Now you interest us,' Ventnor said. 'This is what we want to know.'

'I don't want to get done for slander.'

'You can't slander the dead.' Carmen Pharoah spoke in a matter-of-fact tone.

The man's jaw dropped. 'Walpole? He's dead?'

'Yes, a few days ago. The funeral was yesterday, in York. Not very well attended, we believe, but if they were an isolated family, you wouldn't expect a large attendance.'

'No–' the man mopped his brow – 'no, you wouldn't.'

'So, no danger of slandering anyone. So,

100

tell us what you know,' Carmen Pharoah pressed the man. 'Tell us what you suspect.'

'All goes into the pot,' Ventnor added. 'All information gratefully received.'

'Well, he has ... he had a record. You must know that.'

'We do.'

'He was done for receiving stolen goods. We found out because the local newspaper reported it.'

'Quite a long time ago, a few other minor offences as well, but we really want to know the sort of thing that is not in police files.'

'Such as?'

'Well, at the time that Ebenezer was about seven years old, we believe that Mr Moulton had a friend who owned a green van, so we are talking about twenty years ago ... about—'

'Twenty years, that was before my stomach ... I was working. Well, I never saw him with friends at home. What's that word? Isolated? Never seemed to have visitors. A green van?' The man turned and shouted towards his house. 'Meg ... Meg ... you there, pet? Are you there, lass?' He returned his attention to Pharoah and Ventnor. 'Meg, she was always the one to stay at home. She never worked. I mean was never employed. The housework is enough for her. I mean it's enough for any-one and our house, always so neat and clean and spick and span.'

'Hello.' A female voice, quite high-pitched, thought the officers, was heard coming from within the small house.

'Meg,' the man yelled as he mopped his brow again. 'Have you got a minute pet, the police is here.'

'The police!' There was a clear note of alarm in the voice. The voice, initially high-pitched, became shrill.

'They just want information, pet, nothing for us to worry about.'

But by then Meg had emerged from the side door of the house and advanced on her husband and Pharoah and Ventnor, in an arm-wringing, bustling manner of great anxiety. Her face drawn with worry, she wore an apron over a blue dress and had swollen legs and puffy ankles. 'Police ... police ... police,' she chanted.

Carmen Pharoah said, 'Nothing to worry about, Meg,' for she saw that Meg, who kept a pristine house, was clearly a highly strung personality, and she knew from experience that such people can be volatile and difficult to deal with.

'Nothing?' Meg looked at Carmen Pharoah in a yearning, needy way. 'Meg Dawkins, miss,' she said. 'This is my husband, Eric.'

'Yes, we have met.' Ventnor smiled what he hoped was a calming smile. 'I am DC Ventnor, this is DC Pharoah.'

'Like in Egypt?'

'Spelled differently,' Pharoah explained, 'so, no, not like the ancient Egyptians.'

'The police are asking after the Moultons,' Eric Dawkins explained.

'Oh...' Meg Dawkins glanced skywards.

Out of interest, Ventnor followed her gaze. The sky was a strange mixture of summer blue and winter grey; it seemed to him to be heavy with rain.

'Strange old family,' Meg continued, once again looking at the officers. 'I used to feel sorry for Ebby, growing up with parents like that, so strange. Never did harm or cause trouble, just strange.'

'So your husband has explained,' Ventnor replied calmly.

'A soldier has that house now.'

'As we believe.' Ventnor continued to speak calmly. 'Did you ever see a green van at the house? This would have been about twenty years ago?'

'Twenty?' Surprisingly to the officers the highly strung and excitable Meg Dawkins laughed loudly. 'I think I have a good memory ... I think I have, I have been told I have, but twenty years? A green van?'

'Ebby would have been about seven,' Eric Dawkins added. 'I would have been driving for Vale Coaches then ... away a lot at that time.'

'Oh, yes, you liked that job, I remember that. Fourteen-day coach trips all round

Scotland and over to Ireland, stayed in some lovely hotels, sent me postcards from all over. Away for two weeks, one week off, then off again, May to September.'

Eric Dawkins smiled. 'Aye, lovely little job. So you'd be alone for long periods, just you and the girls.'

'Yes. Kept seeing Walpole leave the house, be off of a morning, walking briskly away but he'd never say what he'd do and I tell you, sometimes I wondered if his wife knew. I'd see him sometimes getting off the York bus at the end of the day. I also used to see him with a dodgy-looking bunch from time to time.'

'Dodgy?'

'Looked wrong ... not honest working men, more like hunters.'

'Hunters?' Pharoah repeated with a surprised tone in her voice. 'You mean poachers?'

'No ... no ... I mean–' Meg Dawkins paused as if struggling for words – 'I mean they seemed to use their eyes a lot, always looking around them but not moving their heads or their bodies very much but not in a nervous sense, not like they were hunted, more in a sort of "I am in control" sense, looking for victims, that sort of using their eyes, a whole team of them.'

'Our Meg has always been good at seeing folk for what they really are.' Eric Dawkins beamed with pride. 'And she's always been proved right. Time after time she's been proved right. Haven't you, Meg? If she says they looked dodgy, then they were dodgy.'

'Time after time,' Meg repeated, clearly having calmed now.

'So, you'd best listen to her,' Eric Dawkins added.

'Oh, we will,' Ventnor replied. 'I assure you we will. Where did you see this ... this ... gang of no-goods?'

'Outside the Zetland Arms.'

'We're from York, we don't know Driffield.'

'It's on Flamborough Road.'

'We'll find it.'

'Roughest part of Driff,' explained Eric Dawkins. 'Every town has a rough side and Driff has the Flamborough Road Estate.'

'Used to visit my sister who lived on that estate, she's moved now but I often used to see Walpole hanging about outside the Zetland Arms with a gang of men, just loafing about on a summer's day, but a green van, sorry, didn't see any car ... or van.'

'So you never talked to Walpole Moulton?'

'Never, not even in passing.'

'So he never mentioned anyone called Oliver Hill?'

Eric and Meg Dawkins both shook their heads. 'No, never.'

'It's a name I'd recall,' Eric Dawkins added, 'because I once knew a bloke called

Charlie Hill, we were good pals, so the name Hill would ring bells with me.'

Carmen Pharoah glanced about her. The estate was still and quiet. Above, the grey clouds looked to be more menacing than they had looked just a few seconds previously.

'Calm before the storm.' Eric Dawkins saw what Carmen Pharoah was looking at. 'Even the birds are quiet, that's always a sign of bad weather. Get plenty of birds here, plenty of shrubs and a wood behind our house, but no birdsong now. I'll be getting my tools in; it's going to pour down.'

'Well, thanks for your time,' Pharoah said smiling, 'you have given us something to work on. Did the new tenant know anything of the Moultons?'

'Doubt it, the house was empty for a few weeks before Tom moved in and the council had to clean the building out. The Moultons just turned the key and left. The council took skip loads of junk out of the house and I mean skip loads.'

'And even Tom had to fumigate it. He lit a fire inside the house.'

'A fire!'

'Yes. He knew what he was doing, a single lump of coal, on a metal grill, over a metal plate, surrounded by airbricks. You know, the bricks with the holes in them that allow walls to breathe.'

106

'Yes ... yes.'

'A sheet of metal over the bricks to contain the flame. It filled the house with smoke – got rid of all the bugs.'

'Still, a bit dangerous.'

'Tom knew what he was doing.'

'Did it twice,' added Meg Dawkins. 'Then he and his missus attacked it with detergent, took it right back to bare walls and floor-boards, but they took over from the Moultons, they had to do that to clean the house. That was what they were like, nothing of the Moultons in that house. I'd try the Zetland Arms. If the landlord is the same, he'll remember Walpole Moulton and maybe even a green van. I'd try there if I were you.'

Louise D'Acre adjusted the microphone that was attached to a stainless steel angle poise arm which in turn was bolted to the ceiling of the pathology laboratory so that it was central to the dissecting table and at head height. She pondered the corpse of the youth as it lay on the table with a starched white cloth draped over his genitals. 'The body,' she began in a clear, unhurried tone for the benefit of the audio typist who would later transcribe the tape, 'is that of a well-nourished muscular male and is Northern European by racial extraction. The deceased kept himself clean, clean fingernails, clean hair which was neatly cut.' She turned to Hennessey.

107

'This man had a very high self-esteem, a high level of self-respect.'

'Could help us identify him,' Hennessey responded. 'Thank you.'

Dr D'Acre continued after a brief pause. 'Rigor is established, so we can turn to cause of death because I won't be pinned down on time of death. The cause of death appears to be either one of, or both, gunshot wounds to the head. The first gunshot wound is located in the very centre of the forehead, a little above the bridge of the nose. The second is above and a little way to the posterior of the left ear. Both are small calibre and no exit wounds are in evidence.' She turned to Hennessey. 'We have had the skull X-rayed,' she said as she walked over to the X-ray display. 'Would you care to look at it, Chief Inspector?'

'Love to.' Hennessey, clothed in green coveralls from head to toe, padded silently over the industrial grade linoleum that covered the floor of the pathology laboratory and stood beside Dr D'Acre, who was similarly dressed.

'You see.' Dr D'Acre indicated the X-ray of the skull of the deceased on which were two white objects, small and pointed at one end, flat at the other, each one no more than half an inch long. 'If they appear to be floating in the brain that is because that is what they are doing. As I said at the scene of the crime,

108

they entered at great velocity and whirred around inside his head looking for a way out, turning the brain into mush as they did so and eventually they ran out of momentum and came to rest. One would have done the job, but two made sure. Somebody wanted this young man dead. He trod on the wrong toes alright. So, let us return.' She walked back to the dissecting table, and Hennessey returned to his appointed place by the wall of the laboratory.

'A photograph, please, Eric.' Dr D'Acre addressed the youthful-looking pathology laboratory assistant, who obediently picked up a 35 mm camera with a flash attachment, which was still preferred despite the development of digital cameras. Hennessey had grown to like Filey. He found that, unlike most of his profession, Filey had an exuberance, a sense of humour, and managed, very skilfully, to tread the fine line between appropriate humour and irreverence.

Dr D'Acre placed a stainless steel ruler against the bullet wound to the forehead and then withdrew to allow Eric Filey to take a number of photographs of the injury. She then said, 'And just here, please, Eric', and placed the ruler beside the bullet wound to the rear of the left ear, and again withdrew to allow Filey to take further photographs of the second bullet wound.

'Well,' Dr D'Acre continued, 'the next step is to remove the bullets. Do you have any idea of his identity, Chief Inspector?'

'None, ma'am.' Hennessey raised his voice a little so as to ensure his reply carried across the laboratory. 'The Voters' Roll gives the occupants of the house as a Mr and Mrs Hewitt, Albert and Belinda Hewitt. We are tracing them now but by their given names, they sound to be more elderly than youthful. So, unless the deceased is their son or other relative...'

'I see. Well I'll keep the name as unknown until you can determine the identity.' She paused again and once more pondered the corpse. 'He's just too young to be in here, too young, far too young. The young ones always seem to reach me. I suppose when they stop reaching me, then that's the time to give up and go and plant potatoes.' Dr D'Acre took a scalpel from the instrument trolley and drew the cutting edge round the circumference of the head, above the ears, and peeled back the scalp to expose the skull.

'We have to fear for the Hewitts' safety until we know otherwise,' Hennessey added, looking at his feet and wondering at the calm manner in which Dr D'Acre could dissect a human corpse – as calmly as he might dissect a roast leg of lamb on a Sunday lunchtime.

Dr D'Acre glanced at him. 'Of course, that issue had not occurred to me.' She paled slightly at the thought.

'Well, we have to be concerned,' Hennessey explained. 'Where there's one body, there may be more.'

'Of course. Well, I'd better stay on my side of the street. Oh—'

'Something?'

'Yes, a linear fracture of the skull ... quite old. This young man took an almighty blow to his head earlier in his life which left a four- or five-inch-long fissure. Eric, could we get a picture of this, please?' Again Dr D'Acre stepped a little way from the body as Eric Filey approached, camera in hand, and manoeuvred himself into the optimum position for taking a photograph of the fracture.

'It could easily have been fatal.' Dr D'Acre spoke to Hennessey as Filey took a succession of photographs. 'But, fortunately for him, he has a thick skull. Bone thickness of skulls is variable. I once did a post-mortem on a little boy who died because his father smote him about the head with the flat of his hand and what parent hasn't done that? But it was sufficient to cause the boy's death. He had a so called "eggshell skull". You see, no outward sign of it at all. The father was suicidal with guilt and grief. I had to explain that it wasn't his fault; his son's skull was so thin that an ordinary bump into a door could have proved fatal and no one would know he had such a condition until he bumped his head. The coroner ruled the death as being accidental and no charges were brought against the father.'

'I am relieved to hear it.'

'Yes, so was I. No purpose would be served by prosecuting him but no eggshell skull here. There will likely be medical recording of this injury somewhere ... possibly a police record as well.'

'Well, Albert Hewitt of that address is not known to us. The fingerprints were lifted, of course. No results had come back when I left the police station to attend here.'

'I see. Strange though, lying in the main bed in the house clothed in jeans and under-pants only, without the appearance of a squatter or burglar. It is as though he has some connection with the house. You know, lying on the bed, as if for a rest is one thing, we've all done that, but *in* the bed, under the sheets and blankets, very strange – but I encroach on your territory.'

'Oh, please, encroach all you like, all help gratefully received and appreciated, ma'am. All appreciated.' Hennessey smiled. 'Really, all help and all other perceptions always welcome.'

'Your open-mindedness does you credit, Chief Inspector.' Dr D'Acre picked up an

112

electrically powered circular saw. 'Much credit'. She switched the machine on and began to saw round the circumference of the skull, following the line she had just drawn with the scalpel, cutting just above the line of remaining flesh.

Hennessey winced inwardly and glanced at the ground as the high-pitched sound of drill against bone set his teeth on edge and he once again wondered at Dr D'Acre's ability to address such tasks, to take them in her stride. He found the sound just as uncomfortable as having the dentist's drill whirring inside his mouth. He had never had a bad experience at any dentist, yet still dreaded the summons for his six-monthly check-up and he felt it little wonder that dentists, unlike doctors, are never plagued with 'heart sink' patients.

The sawing complete, Dr D'Acre lifted the top of the skull from the head, causing a sucking sound as she did so. Once again, George Hennessey flinched, and once again, Dr D'Acre showed no reaction at all. Just another skull top lifted from just another head.

'The skull fracture did not cause any brain damage,' Dr D'Acre observed, 'and as I thought, the skull is quite thick, not abnormally so, but more than the normal thickness of the human skull and sufficiently thick that it probably saved his life when he sustained the skull fracture.' Dr D'Acre glanced up at the X-ray display and then, taking a long, thin, stainless steel instrument, used it to probe into the brain, delving for the first of the two bullets, and finding it, then used a long pair of tweezers to extract it. She placed the bullet in a small metal tray and began to delicately search for the second which she, upon locating and extracting it, also placed in the tray with the first bullet. 'Yes, .22 calibre, I think.' She picked up the tray and handed it to Eric Filey. 'If you could bag and tag them please, Eric, and have them forwarded to Wetherby...'

'Yes, ma'am.' Filey took the tray and laid it on the bench that ran the length of the further wall of the laboratory, for his further attention.

'So–' Dr D'Acre pondered the corpse – 'let us move on ... or down. Before we leave the head, we'll look in the mouth. Always a goldmine of information is the mouth.' Dr D'Acre prised open the jaw of the deceased, causing it to break with an audible 'crack'. 'Dare say that would have been quite painful for him in life–' she grinned, half turning to George Hennessey – 'but that is the great advantage for we poor pathologists.' She loosened the jaw sockets and peered into the mouth. 'We might not be able to command the salaries of leading surgeons or senior consultants, but our patients don't feel pain

114

and are unlikely to raise legal action for negligence or malpractice. We are mercifully free of that pressure and stress. Ah, recent dental work, British dentistry and quite expensive-looking work as well, so he was monied. There will definitely be dental records in respect of the deceased which will be able to be used to confirm his identity, dental patterns being unique to each person. Your DNA profile might be shared by ten other people in the UK, but no one in the world has your teeth pattern and dental records have to be kept for eleven years by law. Since he visited the dentist within the last few months, somewhere there are dental records of this ... too early deceased, deceased. He also looked after his teeth, not the sort of patient to leave it all to the dentist. They're free of plaque, he flossed daily, his gums are healthy, he clearly knew the importance of brushing his gums as well as his teeth.'

'Brushing his gums?'

'Oh, indeed ... indeed.' Dr D'Acre continued to look into the deceased's mouth. 'I hope you brush your gums as well as your teeth, Chief Inspector, you too Eric.'

'Yes, ma'am,' Eric Filey replied quickly.

'Well, I confess...' Hennessey by contrast, stumbled his reply.

'Well you should ... you should, Chief Inspector. Don't be afraid to make them bleed because that stimulates and strengthens them. It's your gums which hold your teeth in place and if you brush them as well as brushing your teeth, then they won't shrink so quickly. You know that phrase "long in the tooth" which is used to mean an aged person, should really be "short in the gum" because the teeth do not grow as you get older, your gums shrink and thus expose the teeth, making them appear longer.' Dr D'Acre held up the short stainless steel rod which she had used to prise the jaws of the deceased open, in a mock gesture of admonition. 'So remember that, gums as well as teeth after each meal from now on.'

'Yes, ma'am,' Hennessey replied with a smile.

'Good. You too, Eric.'

'Yes, ma'am.' Eric Filey also replied similarly with a smile.

'Good.' Dr D'Acre turned her attention to the deceased. 'Well, a health-conscious young man in life, very clean, as I said, and very clean orally as well; a good muscle tone about his body, arms, torso and legs. He was a sportsman or a man who pushed weights, the sort of young man who would have been a regular attendee at the gym and probably, but only probably, a steroids user, the blood tests will confirm that, or otherwise. In fairness to the deceased because physiques like this can be achieved by hard work, not by

116

cheating by use of pills, but he certainly liked himself. So, to continue...' Dr D'Acre took the scalpel and held it poised over the deceased's stomach. 'Deep breaths, gentlemen. Are the extractor fans on, Eric?'

'Full on, ma'am.' Filey took a deep breath.

Dr D'Acre inserted the scalpel into the stomach of the corpse, turning her head away as the gasses escaped with a clearly audible hiss. She waved the air above the stomach and when she opened her mouth again it was to say, 'Not as bad as it could have been. Quite on the mild side really.'

'Indeed, ma'am.' Hennessey managed to reply just as the smell of putrefaction reached him. He had indeed smelled much, much worse, much worse indeed.

'Not as bad as the body we took from the river a few weeks ago. Remember that one, Eric?'

'Never forget that one, ma'am.'

'The body was at that stage where it was about to burst of its own accord.' D'Acre half turned to Hennessey as she explained the reference. 'I evacuated the laboratory of Eric and the observing police officer, ensured all extractor fans were going full blast, and then I took a deep breath, stabbed the stomach and ran for the door. We didn't return for an hour ... even then it was still difficult to breathe—' she shook her head slowly – 'but that was extreme, and we never

117

found out what happened to that man. I mean, in the sense of how he came to be in the river. Did he fall or was he pushed?' Dr D'Acre drummed her fingers on the side of the stainless steel dissecting table and breathed deeply of the formaldehyde-laden air. 'He was a down and out, that poor wretch, as I recall, had a lot of alcohol in his bloodstream. He was just the sort of person who could have fallen and stumbled into the river and drowned by accident, but such people are also easy and inviting victims of random and gratuitous violence and so could equally have been pushed to his death. Never found out his name either. Gave him a name and buried him in a pauper's grave. He would have had his hopes and aspirations, as we all do, and then ended his life like that, very sad.' She paused, peering into the stomach cavity of the deceased, having enlarged the original penetration by use of the scalpel. 'This gentleman, hardly surprisingly, was a meat eater. Heavens, you wouldn't ever find a vegetarian with a muscular development like this ... and he was shot a very short time after eating what appears to be a cold meat salad, healthy and season appropriate. He didn't masticate well, swallowed before he had properly chewed his food and so I can still identify boiled egg, lettuce, ox-tongue and ham. Interesting, don't see much ox-tongue these days, very popular when I was growing up, very tasty too. Folk seem to have become very delicate in their taste these days.'

'Never known a war,' growled Hennessey, 'and not I, give me a plate of liver and bacon on a bed of fried onions and I am a very happy camper indeed.'

'Good for you, Chief Inspector. Well, the stomach contents are quite interesting from a police point of view I would have thought.'

'Oh?'

'Well, digestion will continue for a little while after death but I feel it strange that someone would eat this sort of carefully prepared meal and then, within an hour, be wading in two feet of water. I also did not notice signs of food having been recently prepared in the home. Heavens, who would prepare salad while standing in two feet of polluted water?'

'As you say, and there was no recently washed or unwashed plate in the house, so someone brought a meal to him in the house as he was moving what he could upstairs away from the flood water, and then took the unwashed plate and tools away again, prior to him being shot,' Hennessey pondered aloud, 'or he ate locally and returned with a full stomach to carry on working and was shot shortly thereafter?'

'Or–' Dr D'Acre turned to Hennessey – 'he was conveyed to the house already deceased, and clad only in jeans and underwear. There was, after all, no sign of a shirt or socks or footwear in the house ... not that I saw.'

'There wasn't, was there?' Hennessey replied quietly.

'Well, that is your department and I always hate to encroach. I do know the value of keeping in my own box.'

'Oh, as I often say, ma'am, encroach all you like,' Hennessey replied softly, yet enthusiastically. 'All encroachment welcome.'

'More than one suspect I would think. He's a big fella, it would take two or three others to carry him upstairs and lay him on the bed, then place the duvet over him. Also of note is the absence of any defence injuries ... he didn't know what hit him. A good way to go I have always thought, so long as your affairs are in order but not quite so young in life.'

'Indeed, ma'am. He was not ready for the cemetery ... not in himself.'

'No, though few of us are. So that will be the finding of the post-mortem, that is unless the toxicology report comes back positive which I very much doubt it will. I would have noticed telltale signs of poison had they been present. So, death by gunshot wounds to the head, small calibre weapon, to wit .22, shortly after he had a meat salad meal and death was in the last few days, not going to tie myself down any closer. My report will be faxed to you within twenty-four hours.'

'Appreciated, ma'am.'

'Yeah ... yeah...' The landlord of the Zetland Arms pursed his lips as he wiped a freshly washed beer glass with a starched white towel. 'Moulton, Walpole Moulton, yeah, I remember him, a not so notable local. Except perhaps he was notable in the wrong sense, you know, infamous, not famous.' The man placed the glass under the bar and then leaned forwards, resting two meaty hands between the handles of the beer engines. He was clean-shaven; both Thompson Ventnor and Carmen Pharoah thought him breathtakingly clean. Like the glass he had just wiped dry, as though he had spent an hour under the shower that morning, scrubbing himself and cleaning under his fingernails, before putting on his clothes which were as clean and as fresh as he. His shirt was varying shades of blue and seemed expensive. He wore no jewellery but a watch which similarly seemed an impressively expensive item. 'He was not one of my favourite characters, neither him nor his friends, but what can you do? I had to make a living. I still have to do so and they never caused trouble, but this is going back a long time, I mean a long time. I hear Walpole moved to York.'

'He did.' Carmen Pharoah held eye con-

121

tact with the man and added matter of factly. 'He died very recently.'

'Really?' The landlord raised his eyebrows as his eyes widened. 'Sorry to hear that.' He shook his head. 'Well, I am sorry ... comes to us all in time, I suppose, that bit, but when it's someone you have known, it's always an impact. So Walpole is no more? Well, I'll light a candle for him, of course, but I won't miss him. Haven't seen him in a good ten years, but well, Walpole is gone. I'll drink to his memory and light a candle.'

'We are interested in his friends.' Ventnor glanced around the pub, small, cramped, a hard-seeming environment, functional rather than welcoming. Dimly lit, natural light limited by a high brick wall close to the windows, as though the Zetland Arms backed on to another building with barely sufficient room for a man to walk between the two. One or two aged patrons sat alone drinking small measures of beer. 'Do you recall his drinking partners of about twenty years ago?'

'Twenty years?' Again the landlord raised his eyebrows. 'Now you are going back a long way. I was new here then; I took over from old Bernie North. He had let the place go. He just hadn't the strength to keep the underage drinkers out ... and the undesirables. It's a rough estate; it would be easy to let this pub slide. I've made enemies, banned people and had the windows broken, had acid thrown on my bar, but I've got a clean pub. Walpole and his mates were ... what can I say? The lowest I would tolerate, so yes I remember them – the Wild Bunch – not original but that's what they were called and Walpole was part of that crew, but more of a hanger-on.' The man paused and glanced to his left. 'No ... no, that's not fair. He was one of the team, a full-time player, he just wasn't the captain.'

'Who was the captain?' Ventnor took his notebook from his pocket. 'Do you remember?'

'Let me see ... there was a fella called Dangall, "Big Andy" Dangall. He was "Big Andy" because another member of that crew was "Little Andy" Barnes. Hmm ... then there was "Mid" Dave Hartley. Don't know why he was called "Mid" Dave but I think it was because they also knew two other Davids, one taller and one shorter than him. So he was "Mid" Dave, so I believe. Then the boss, the captain, was a guy called Bowler, "Two Tone" they called him because he had a patch of ginger hair growing out from the black hair he had.'

'Ginger?' Carmen Pharoah asked. 'Sure?'

'Yes,' the landlord nodded, 'sure I am sure. It was very striking, big patch of ginger on his right side, almost too big to be called a patch, nearly enough to say he had a scalp of

123

two different hair colours ... so he was called Two Tone.'

'Ginger,' Carmen Pharoah turned to Ventnor.

'Ginger,' Ventnor nodded. 'Could be, could be.'

'So I have helped you?' The landlord asked.

'Possibly. Any other names?'

'See ... "Titch" Riley ... short but a hard man, something to prove, like he always had to compensate for being small – vicious thug. It would take one of the others to put somebody on the deck but once somebody was down "Titch" Riley would be in there with the boot. He always wore shoes with pointed toes, "winklepickers" as they were called. Well out of fashion by then but you could still get them and they could do a lot of damage, especially Riley's. He had had them fixed with metal toe caps, very nasty.'

'Ugh!'

'Yes–' the landlord's jaw set firm – 'and he didn't keep them shiny, always kept them black, like you wouldn't know they were metal until they started knocking lumps out of the side of your head. Pleasant sort of individual. And then there was Walpole. The six of them, Bowler, Riley, Dagnall, Barnes, Hartley and Moulton. Bowler was a loudmouth and a cause of trouble when he was drunk – you'll know Bowler, if he's still alive.

He was always popping in and out of the magistrates court and going down for a few months from time to time, but that made him part of the gang, leading by example. They all did time, you'll have records on all of them. They'll all be in the fifties or even sixties now ... they were guns for hire.'

'Guns for hire?'

'Not literally, of course, never used guns, but the rumour was that they were on the wrong side of the law and were for hire, extra hands, any dirty job needs doing, no questions asked, that sort of rumour.'

'I see, not the best sort of customer as you say.' Pharoah's eye was caught by an elderly patron who eyed her with hostility. She glared back at him forcing him to avert his gaze.

'Yes ... well, as I also said, I had to make a living and they didn't cause trouble, they were just low-grade foot soldiers of the criminal world.'

'Did any have a green van that you recall?'

'A green van? Not that I remember but as you see you can't see the street from here, and this is an estate pub, the punters walk here, all regulars, don't get any passing trade at all. Try the Royal Sovereign, it's the other pub on the estate, I think they drank there as well, probably more than here.'

Pharoah and Ventnor walked out of the Zetland Arms into a very light shower of rain which fell like fine mist from a blue sky and in bright sunlight. The inevitable rainbow, a very fine example, thought Pharoah, arched over Driffield in the south-southwest.

'So, we reckon we know where Walpole Moulton went when he walked out of his house in Hutton Cranswick each day–' Ventnor took his car keys from his pocket – 'the bus to Driffield and thence to the Zetland Arms to work for "Two-Tone" Bowler, doing this and that and no questions asked.'

'No wonder he never would say where he was going.' Carmen Pharoah stood by the passenger door. 'Just need to know the same thing about Oliver Hill now. Where did he go each day, and at what point did his path cross with the "guns for hire"?'

Thompson Ventnor returned home later that day. He showered, changed his clothes and ate a meal of instant food which he had purchased from the supermarket and which he heated in the microwave. He then drove out to a large Victorian-era building set in large grounds on the outskirts of York. He parked his car close to the door of the building between two other cars. He pushed open the door of the building, entering without ringing the doorbell and signed his name in the in/out book in keeping with fire regulations. Once again he was struck by the degree to which the heating in the building was turned up; it was, he thought, akin to walking into a sauna without the steam being present and far, far too high to be healthy. The interior of the building was quiet, utterly silent. He walked up a wide carpeted stairway. A woman in black slacks and a white tunic passed him, descending as he ascended and smiled briefly at him but otherwise paid him no heed. On the first floor landing he entered a room in which a television set stood in the corner, where people sat in chairs around the walls of the room but did not interact with each other. As he stepped over the threshold of the room, an elderly resident sitting in the far corner smiled in recognition of Ventnor. Ventnor crossed the floor of the room and knelt beside the elderly person and said, 'Hello, Dad', but already the old man's recognition had vanished as he was staring blankly into space and occasionally grinned to himself. Ventnor stood and talked about his father's welfare with the senior care officer and then returned home.

He parked his car outside his house and walked to the bus stop and took a bus into York. He visited three pubs, had two beers in each and then at about ten p.m. he fetched up at Caesars.

'Divorced,' he said to the woman in the too-small, too-tight dress who allowed him to buy her a drink.

'Me too–' she raised her glass – 'cheers, Darlin'.' Her accent was foreign, Birmingham he thought.

She bought him a drink.

He bought her another drink.

They had a dance when the dance floor was full and they did not feel self-conscious.

They had more drink.

Eventually he went home alone, in the rain, walking the whole way because at two a.m. there were no buses, and because that night the Almighty had swept all taxis from the streets of the 'famous and faire'.

Nice. Dark. In a dark street. Plenty of shrubs in the front garden ... always useful to hide in. The gate had a latch which he opened and let fall, making a loud 'click' which sounded clearly in the still night air, amid the houses which still glistened from the recent rainfall. No sound came from within the house, no barking of an alert dog. Nice. No burglar alarm. Very nice, very nice indeed. Especially no dog.

Norman Budde prowled the streets, sighting up likely houses.

He had found his next mark.

It was Wednesday, 02.35 hours.

Four

In which an overview is made, Inspector Hennessey visits a nineteenth-century pub, and Yellich and Webster visit a school.

George Hennessey sipped his tea and held eye contact with each person in the office very briefly in turn, moving from his left to his right, Sergeant Yellich nearest the window, then Carmen Pharoah, then Reginald Webster and finally, nearest the door, Thompson Ventnor. Each he thought to be alert, fresh-faced, eager, all that is except Thompson Ventnor whose eyes appeared to Hennessey to be more than a little bloodshot, his voice a little gravelly, his 'Good morning, sir', a little too low-pitched and with a slight, very slight cynical tone about it. It was as though Thompson Ventnor seemed to want to be elsewhere, as if he were not wholly comfortable in the meeting. It might, pondered Hennessey, it might be an issue, something for him to keep his eye on. He sipped his tea again. 'Can we bring this meeting to order, please?'

In front of his desk the four seated persons shuffled and raised their heads and looked in Hennessey's direction, at him, attentively.

'We have this week not one but two murder investigations that are going to stretch our resources, though one murder is significantly older than the other and so, if we find ourselves overstretched, we will focus our efforts on the most recent of the murders, which is still really only a few hours old, though it is now outside the all important first twenty-four hours, but only just, and is still very fresh. The other murder is a very cold case.' Hennessey glanced out of the small window to his left and saw a tightly bunched group of tourists walking the walls, bundled, it seemed, in response to the unseasonable threat of rain, although at that moment the walls were basking in a ray of sunlight, courtesy of a gap in the cloud cover. 'So,' he continued, 'I'll keep with the chronological order of the two murders for the purpose of illuminating the team. So, DC Pharoah and DC Ventnor, perhaps you could bring us up to speed with the case you have been working on, a brief overview.'

Pharoah and Ventnor glanced at each other and Pharoah said, 'Shall I?' to which Ventnor opened his palm as if to say 'Please do' and in doing so displayed what seemed to be a certain relief on his part that Carmen Pharoah was going to do the work for them both.

'Well–' Pharoah glanced to her left and right as if addressing Yellich and Webster, but then looked for the main part towards Hennessey's desk as she spoke – 'our investigation started in a very unusual manner. A young man with the unlikely name of Ebenezer Moulton, son of the late and equally unlikely named Walpole Moulton, walked into the station direct, and I mean direct, from his father's funeral to report that twenty years ago he watched as his father and a bunch of other lowlifes pushed a man to his death, Ebenezer being about seven years old at the time. I interviewed him and he described how he had buried the memory for a long time and then it surfaced, as such memories tend to do, when he was having a quiet drink alone one night. It surfaced piecemeal over the next few days and it was also received out of chronological order, to use a word that Mr Hennessey used a couple of moments ago. So he spent some time putting that ... what's the word?' She looked down at the brown linoleum floor.

'Sequence?' Hennessey suggested.

'Yes, sir.' Carmen Pharoah smiled. 'Thank you ... sequences. It took some time before he put all the sequences in the correct order. Then he had to decide whether he was recovering a dream or actuality and when he realized that what he remembered had really happened, he ... he—'

'Came forward?' Webster suggested.

'No,' Carmen Pharoah shook her head. 'No, just the opposite, he kept mum, said nothing, told no one or perhaps to his father ... perhaps ... but otherwise said nothing and it was only when he had cremated his father's body that he reported the incident.'

'Really?' Yellich gasped.

'Yes, really, but not just out of loyalty to his father but also because it seems that he was intimidated into keeping quiet. He cuts a bit of a sad figure, a young man who walks with a crutch because his right leg, I think it is his right, but anyway, one of his legs was fractured in many places when he was rolled in the street one night just outside his father's home. The attack put him in hospital for a long time and he reported one of his attackers said to him, "You saw nothing".' Carmen Pharoah paused. 'He blames the attack and the injury he sustained for ruining a promising career as a professional footballer, but enquiries reveal that he was not going anywhere in that direction anyway. He has found a way to blame someone else for his loss of ball-kicking career opportunities but that attack and his father being extant led him to keep quiet about the murder he saw his father commit, at least partly commit.

132

But when his father was deceased, then he came forward and did so speedily, driven, he said, to do something useful in his life.'

'Good for him,' Yellich commented.

'Yes, his father pushed someone to their death from a bridge during a period of flooding – as now.' Again she paused, collecting her thoughts. 'No one can survive water in a state of flood, it's the power of the surge.' She shuddered. 'Sorry, it's just that drowning is a form of death I happen to fear. Anyway the floods of twenty years ago were spring floods, a lot of snow-melt as well as excess rain and so the water must have been very cold. He would not, could not have survived. He was knowingly pushed to his death and was apparently punched powerfully in the stomach before being tipped backwards. That would have made swimming impossible, they were making sure alright. The victim was described as tall, bearded and wearing a suit, unlike his attackers who were described as shorter and casually dressed. We trawled the misper reports for that time and came up with Oliver Hill, who fits the description and his body was never found. We believe that once in the water he would have drowned and his body carried away, possibly, in fact probably, sub-surface, from the Ouse to the Humber and possibly out into the North Sea with the ebb tide and ... then he was crab meat.' She allowed herself another brief moment of silence. 'We traced his widow, now older than her actual years in terms of her attitude and lifestyle, now living in Ripon, she being one Penny Hill. Interestingly she is not sure what her husband did for a living but he kept the mortgage payments up with erratic and irregular income not dissimilar to Walpole Moulton's similarly irregular income in fact. It did sound like their financial life was like a cork being bobbed up and down in a stormy sea. Oliver Hill seemed to have been a bit of a wide boy in his own right with some very unhealthy connections and he might, just might, have stepped on the wrong toes. He loosely described himself as "self-employed" and professed to have accountancy skills ... but wrong toes ... somewhere.'

'Sounds like it,' Yellich growled. 'Being pushed to his death like that – that was an execution, gangland style. Somebody ordered that.'

'So we also believe,' Carmen Pharoah replied. 'That is our belief.' Pharoah glanced at Thompson Ventnor who nodded in agreement but said not a word.

'So it seemed we needed to know more, considerably more about Walpole Moulton,' Pharoah continued, 'so we went to the address the family had at the time. We talked to the neighbours who were most helpful and cooperative and who painted a picture of a socially isolated family who lived quietly behind a tall privet hedge, now cut down and neatly trimmed. We were pointed towards a pub called the Zetland Arms and the publican remembered Walpole and his gang or rather the gang he belonged to because he was a foot soldier, by all accounts, not a leader, and the publican gave us the names of the others in his crew. He described them as "guns for hire". We have given their names and approximate dates of birth to criminal records but the results have not come back yet. We were also referred on to another pub called the Royal Sovereign that we have yet to visit. If any one of the gang had a green van twenty years ago we will be very keen to speak to him.'

Ventnor struggled to speak and managed to say, 'Ebenezer Moulton reported that Oliver Hill was pulled out of the back of a green van before being bundled over a bridge into the river.' As he spoke the heavy smell of strong mints reached Hennessey.

'Hence our interest in the green van, or rather owner thereof.' Carmen Pharoah spoke quickly, as if to save Ventnor from having to speak further.

'Alright.' Hennessey gave Ventnor a puzzled and a worrying look. 'So you'll be pursuing those leads, the Royal Sovereign and the names of Walpole Moulton's associates?'

'Yes, sir, if you wish it?'

'Yes.' Hennessey turned to Carmen Pharoah. 'Yes, I wish it. Your names are against it.' He turned to Yellich, to Yellich and Webster.

'Sir?'

'Your names are against the other murder inquiry in which I have played a small part because of our shortage of manpower. So I'll tell Pharoah and Ventnor what has transpired. We must keep each other up to speed on both cases. I'll be handing the second case to you two, Yellich and Webster. The second investigation concerns the report we received from a burglar who was looting a home that had been abandoned due to the floods. He found a dead body neatly tucked up in the main bedroom. Enquiries have not identified the deceased as yet, but he was also executed gangland style this time with two small calibre gunshot wounds to the head. Such bullets whizz and bounce around the inside of the skull because they are not powerful enough to blow an exit wound, so Dr D'Acre informed me at the post-mortem. They criss-cross inside the skull mashing up the brain until they run out of momentum. One is enough to do the trick, two makes sure, makes very sure indeed. Somebody wanted this boy dead. He was only in his early twenties, very muscular build, very fit and wearing only jeans. The puzzling thing is that the Voters' Roll gives the householders as one Mr and Mrs Hewitt. The decorations and clothing et cetera in the home indicate the house belongs to a couple in their late middle age, not early twenties, so the first priority for you two is to find Mr and Mrs Hewitt.'

'Yes, sir.'

'See where you get. See if they had a son, or grandson who remained behind to lift stuff upstairs for them and who knew his killers well enough to allow them to get very close inside the house and put a gun right up to his forehead. You don't use a point-two-two from a distance.'

'No, sir.'

'That is, of course, if the Hewitts are still alive. They might also be deceased, we just don't know.' Hennessey paused. 'I have prepared a press release, which will make today's lunchtime news on regional television and radio and the early editions of the newspapers. So that's the state of play there, that's where you pick it up, Sergeant Yellich, you and DC Webster.'

'Understood, sir.'

'I must keep the overview. As you may recall, the commander is very worried about my health, good man that he is. Though he is a little officious at times, he is determined that I will live to enjoy my retirement. He is haunted by an incident in his boyhood, quite an unfortunate incident in which one of his schoolteachers was told to take on work he was incapable of. A very good lower-school teacher but not senior school material, yet he was given the senior class to tutor to national exams. So instead of letting him coast to retirement, they piled on the pressure. He was a heavy smoker, so the commander told me, and more than a social drinker ... a red nose, a reddish complexion, overweight ... and the extra pressure must have made him drink and smoke even more, a heart attack waiting to happen, and happen it did. Returned home one night complaining of feeling ill and then keeled with a massive coronary. A man of false good humour too, by all accounts, being another symptom of stress. Anyway, that incident has clearly made a big impression on Commander Sharkey and he is determined that the like will not happen in his nick and so I am clearly instructed by the commander that I will be less "hands-on" than hitherto, hence the expansion of the team, though still insufficient bodies, but that is how the commander wants it. But do notify me of any and all developments and let me and your colleagues know where you are at all times.'

'Yes, sir.' Yellich spoke and, by doing so, by implication, also answered for Pharoah, Ventnor and Webster.

'Good. So, Yellich, I suggest you and Webster go to St John's Community College.'

'Sir?' Yellich raised his eyebrows. 'That's a school.'

'Yes.' Hennessey smiled. 'I have ascertained that it is closed, much to the delight of the pupils and probably the staff also, in order to provide emergency accommodation for people who have been evacuated from their homes due to the flooding. If you can't find the Hewitts, then find their neighbours. You can obtain their names from the Voters' Roll.'

'Yes, sir.'

'In the meantime, I am going to do something to aid your inquiry, Pharoah and Ventnor.'

'Sir?' Carmen Pharoah inclined her head questioningly.

'Yes.' Hennessey smiled. 'I am going to talk to a gentleman who has been very useful in the past and I am sure he will be very useful to us in the future, and he won't talk to anyone but me, for my sins. I am deeply touched by the trust he places in me, though it can be a nuisance at times ... can't ever send anyone in my stead.' He paused. 'Well – to horse!' He patted his desk with both hands as the officers rose from their seats. 'To horse, to horse!'

'Doors to manual,' Yellich responded.

'Is an alternative way of putting it.' Hennessey also stood and reached for his coat. 'More up to date as well, "doors to manual", though that sounds like we are landing ... but ... action!'

The man, slightly built, slender, middle-aged, looked at first glance as he always looked at first glance, to be well dressed, but then upon closer inspection his clothing revealed itself to be threadbare and ill maintained. The Italian-cut lightweight jacket in a very gentle shade of green had pink buttons – that sort of threadbare; off the shelf at the charity shop. He pushed an empty glass across the table top towards Hennessey with what, thought Hennessey, was a desperate, pleading look across his eyes. It was a look which Hennessey had oft-times seen and which he always felt to be pathetic, but there was no doubt about the man's proven usefulness in times past, nor, Hennessey also believed, about his continuing potential usefulness in times present and future.

'Not so fast, Shored-Up. Not so fast.' Hennessey sipped his fruit juice, savouring the liquid, feeling his body's craving for vitamin C. 'Mind you that whisky went down as though it didn't touch the sides of your throat. Have you been dry for a while?'

'Three whole days, Mr Hennessey, three days ... three ... I confess I could use a few "Adam Smiths" at the moment.'

Hennessey smiled, 'Dare say we all could, dare say none of us ever has sufficient money. It's a fact of life.'

George Hennessey had left Micklegate Bar Police Station dressed in his Panama hat and a summer jacket and trousers but expectantly carried his raincoat over his forearm, the threat of rain being ever present. The sun may well, at that particular time, have been warm and shining brilliantly but it did so via another rent in dark and mountainous clouds. The local floods seemed to have stabilized, the waters might even have begun to recede, but the forecast was clear: more rain was expected. Hennessey had walked briskly, purposefully, up to the brow of Micklegate and pondered, as he walked, upon the famous 'Micklegate run' in which participants start at one end of Micklegate and progress to the other, taking just half a pint of beer at each pub along the route. No one has ever been believed to have achieved it and hence the alternative names of 'The Micklegate Challenge' and also 'The Micklegate Crawl'. That is the nature of York, the 'famous and faire', Hennessey further pondered, the York 'within the walls' where there is a pub for every day of the year and a church for every Sunday, and all crammed into an area of about two and a half miles in circumference, or about three-quarters of a mile across at its widest point. He had crossed the fiercely flowing Ouse at the recently constructed Ouse Bridge and saw, as Carmen Pharoah had earlier reported, how the vast body of forging water held a fascination for many people who lined the parapet of the bridge gazing at the river in flood. He had also seen how astute had been her observation that, if Oliver Hill had been swept to his death in similar river conditions some twenty years earlier without being seen, then his body must have been carried beneath the surface. The wretched man, thought Hennessey, must have known great terror before unconsciousness offered its own form of anaesthetic and peace of mind. He had then turned into High Ousegate, thence into Piccadilly and, having cut through Merchant Gate, entered the pleasantly medieval Walmgate at the bottom of which he turned into Navigation Road, being a street of nineteenth-century terrace housing, and then took the first right into Speculation Street, at the far end of which stood Ye Olde Speculation. The pub was, it seemed to Hennessey, to be little changed from when it had been built in the middle years of Victoria's reign, with electricity instead of gas lighting and power-pumped beer being the main changes, so far as Hennessey had been able to ascertain. In all other respects it seemed original, with hard horsehair-filled benches running round the edge of the snug, solid tables, and equally solid chairs. The weather was kept at bay by frosted glass which still had the name of the long defunct brewery of 'Sander's and Penn's Fine Ales' etched upon it. Hennessey had lowered his head to enable him to enter the doorway of the Speculation and he had turned immediately left and entered the snug. He nodded to the man who sat in the corner in front of an empty glass and whose face broke into a smile upon seeing Hennessey. Hennessey had walked across the floor of the snug to the serving hatch, there being no bar in the snug of the Speculation, and ordered a whisky with ginger and an orange juice from a young barmaid who spoke with a pleasingly familiar local accent. The middle-class students at the university had still to discover and 'occupy' the Speculation, which is just how Hennessey and, he guessed, the locals and regulars liked it. It was their pub, and not for the delectation of plummy-mouthed southern counties, youth who might find the building 'quaint' and come to dominate it. Hennessey carried the drinks over to where Shored-Up sat, thin-faced, neatly cut grey hair and a pencil-line moustache. He placed the drink on beer mats on the highly polished top of the circular table. Shored-Up grabbed the drink and sank it in one thirsty, desperate gulp.

'Three whole days,' he complained, 'and then today, I had enough shekels to buy that one.' He pointed to the empty glass which had stood before him as Hennessey had entered the pub. He pushed the second, recently emptied glass across the table towards Hennessey.

'Not so fast.' Hennessey spoke firmly as he sipped the orange juice feeling the vitamin C course through his veins as he did so. He clearly was deficient in the vitamin. The humid weather was clearly taking its toll on his body. He made a mental note to address the issue, more, much more orange juice over the next few days, he thought. 'Scrimp and save, make do and mend,' he said.

'And make full use of charity shops.'

'Yes, I noticed your jacket; it helps you cut quite a dash – from a distance.'

'Oh–' Shored-Up inclined his head towards Hennessey – 'you are too kind, Mr Hennessey, but you are correct. There lies my problem ... there does so lie my problem. You see, if I could just afford a little more quality in terms of my clothing...'

'Then you'd be able to con more wealthy widows, but as it is you have to confine yourself to those who are deficient in terms of their eyesight and often they have sharp-witted nephews who in turn have twenty-twenty vision. Yes, I see your problem, Shored-Up, and as a police officer I can only say "long may it last".'

'You do me a disservice, Mr Hennessey.'

'I do you a great service, Shored-Up, I keep you away from committing further

144

offences and I do you a great service by ignoring the number of warrants that have been issued for your arrest.'

'But only for trifling offences, Mr Hennessey.'

'But outstanding warrants nonetheless and persuading a succession of probation officers not to breach you for failing to observe the terms of your probation order, but fortunately for you, I am the only police officer in this division who knows where to find you, and fortunately for you I ... we ... the police, need your help from time to time and this is one such time. I need to pick your brains, Shored-Up and if you help ... well, I'll see what I can do about those Edwards you seek and see that the warrants are overlooked.'

'My rent, you see...'

'I see, that's unfortunate.'

'And my new probation officer, Mr Hennessey, oh my, she's very keen, very young and very keen. My last probation officer, Mr Swan, he was more mature, we talked more about his forthcoming retirement than about my offending and search for employment and he minded not at all about the occasional missed appointment. I believe the time he set aside to talk to me he spent reading books about fly fishing. *There* was a probation officer who understood my needs. I do so dislike pressure. But young Miss Pratt, oh my...'

145

A ray of sunlight suddenly flooded into the room and illuminated specks of dust floating in the air before it faded. Drops of rain began to fall upon the window pane.

'Twenty years ago...' Hennessey felt cold, the 'more rain expected' had arrived.

Shored-Up pursed his lips. 'Mr Hennessey, I sometimes cannot recall what I did yesterday.'

'Which is often a sign of a busy life, nothing to worry about. So, twenty years ago. You were living in York then, I believe?'

'Oh yes, never in my life have I moved from the city.'

'And getting included in every scam that you could, though now you'll be telling blind widows that twenty years ago you were serving Queen and country in the Green Howards.'

'Devon and Dorsets, Mr Hennessey. I changed my act some time ago when I realized I was in danger of running into the real thing up here in Yorkshire ... at least the widow of the real thing, so I changed my history a little. I served with a southern counties, regiment don't you know.'

'Sensible I dare say, wholly reprehensible, but I can see the logic therein.'

'Well, one has to survive, Mr Hennessey, and the income of Lieutenant Colonel Smythe does come in fits and starts.'

'So I can tell. Not been a good summer for

you, I see.'

'Well–' Shored-Up shrugged – 'I have had better times, much better times.' He glanced up at the low ceiling of ornate plaster work. 'I have had times of real plenty, times of such bounty, so yes, this year has not been good for me ... but–' he held up a long index finger – 'the good times will come again, of that I am certain, and half this year is still to come.'

'Ever the optimist but times of plenty for you are times of loss for your victims, so you'll understand why I am not very sympathetic. You ought to consider changing your line of work.'

'What do you mean, Mr Hennessey?' Shored-Up frowned and looked puzzled.

'Well...' Hennessey leaned back in his chair and rested his meaty hands on his knees. 'How shall I explain? You see, Shored-Up, people network, like finds like. The cops in the Vale of York all know each other, the blaggers like you in the Vale of York all know each other, and the wealthy and elderly widows in the Vale all know each other ... attend the same tea parties, the same bridge clubs and by and large the same funerals, and you have been at it a while now. Perhaps it is the case that they are wise to you. Perhaps they are telling each other about the most charming gentleman of the old school, one Lieutenant Colonel Smythe (retired) late of the Devon and Dorsetshire regiment and who just needs a little cash to finance a "can't lose" business venture ... or perhaps to invest in a recently discovered seam of silver ore in Bolivia, and silver ore of unheard of richness ... or to help in raising the treasure-laden Spanish galleon and of which only he knows the exact location. The loan would only be for a short term and the interest offered is generous. You see, Shored-Up, the word gets around.'

'That indeed might explain...' The man's voice trailed off. 'But what else can I do? The act of genteel poverty that arouses sympathy in the right sort of person—'

'You mean right sort of victim.'

'Whatever. But the act has taken a long time to polish and I can't turn my skills to anything else. I couldn't steal from the poor. I am possessed of some sense of integrity.'

'I am so pleased to hear so,' Hennessey growled. 'It gives me hope for the world.'

'But the thought of acquiring a new skill, that is an obstacle, especially for a man of my advanced years, and the one thing you forget, Mr Hennessey, the one advantage I have—'

'Oh?'

'Yes, the one advantage is that of Britain's ageing population. There are always plenty of recently widowed ladies seeking companionship, always new members of the golf club, new faces at the church socials, many are heavily laden with jewellery, or driving a Bentley with two little dogs in the rear seat as their only source of companionship, ladies of such aching loneliness who have "target" written all over them and also right through them as though they were a stick of Bridlington rock.'

Hennessey sighed and shook his head.

'And I can't relocate, York and the Vale is my home, never lived anywhere else.'

'Except inside one or the other of HM guest houses.'

'Temporary addresses, Mr Hennessey, temporary addresses but not particularly pleasant. All those rough boys and so noisy at night, a fella can't get a wink, and when I have to share a cell ... oh,' Shored-Up put his left hand up to his forehead. 'Horrible, a shared cell, the conversations I have to listen to ... the privations.'

'Bit of a comedown for a retired Lieutenant Colonel.' Hennessey sipped his orange juice.

'Well, one gets used to a certain lifestyle, Mr Hennessey. Whether or not it is at someone else's expense, it is still a lifestyle: fine dining, silver service, the occasional weekend in a large hotel overlooking the sea; sharing a bed with a lady who would normally be a little old and a little large for my tastes, but it is all part of the job – an investment. The trick is to keep your mind on the purpose and get through the here and now as rapidly as possible. Switch off and do the job, like the ladies of the night have to do with their Toms.'

'So the snoring when she removes her full set of false teeth is the price you pay to obtain the contents of the jewellery box, and the balance in the deposit account, all of which will be repaid when the Spanish galleon is raised?'

'But of course, Mr Hennessey. Plus interest. Though I have learned not to touch if I can help it. The possessions I mean.'

'Yes, it was a little careless of you to leave your fingerprints all over the lady's collection of antique silver prior to driving away in her Rolls Royce.'

'It was a Bentley actually and I collected three years for that little exploit. Annoying really, someone in the Middle East or Eastern Europe where no paperwork is required, got his Bentley, I lost three years and the lady lost her late husband's favourite car. There should only have been one loser not two and she was able to claim for the theft from her insurers. She had compensation. I didn't get a penny and still did time.' Again he held up his index finger. 'The police got a conviction, all good for your statistics, Mr Hennessey. So my life is one of swings and roundabouts. So I ate for free for three years and paid no rent for that time. Then I emerged and found a new target but she was wary ... paid for the meals and the stays in the upmarket hotels but she clung to her money like a drowning man clings to a piece of straw, so I didn't get anywhere. My present lady friend is looking more hopeful but her late husband was an army officer, a real one. I think her suspicions are being aroused ... I confess nothing else is.'

'Well, take my advice and get out for everybody's sake. If we catch you bang to rights you go down. I can't help you and I won't. You'd be better making an honest living on the dole.'

'Oh, the dole queue is as bad as prison, the smell in the queue–' Shored-Up shivered – 'it's too bad for one like me.'

'Well, I want some help, I need some help, and it's very appropriate you talk of a drowning man clutching at straws because it is about a drowning man and I am straw-clutching.' Hennessey glanced at the rain, by then falling heavily on the windowpane.

'Oh?' Shored-Up pushed his empty glass further towards Hennessey.

The glasses replenished, Hennessey told Shored-Up about the death of Oliver Hill.

'Twenty years ago,' Shored-Up mused.

'Yes. Practically the whole of the Vale was underwater and the death toll rose as the bodies of down-and-outs and heroin addicts were discovered when the water receded.

151

Very unfunny. Very unfunny indeed.'

'Yes ... folk still talk about those floods.'

'As they would. They'll talk about those floods for years, long after they have stopped talking about these floods; these floods are mild by comparison ... the flood defences are working.'

'So it seems.' Shored-Up seemed to Hennessey to be lost in thought for a moment. 'You know, I do remember the Driffield crew, that name Two Tone. What was it? "Two Tone" Bowler. He was the gang leader. Unpleasant set of street turks. Not heavy-duty criminals, just a gang of boys, well, young men, but each one was a nasty piece of work. Yes, I can really see them shoving somebody into a river of icy water in a state of flood. I met Two Tone once ... inside ... we were in Full Sutton together, his stay and mine overlapped by a few weeks. I was doing the pre-release course when he was a new arrival. He'd take food from my plate and do so with a gleam in his eye. Not a tall man, but very wide, "stocky" is the word. I really can't see how I can help you, Mr Hennessey; though I do need a little help in the folding blue department and I fear my probation officer, it's like being hunted by a peregrine falcon. I could make enquiries. I do see "Two Tone" Bowler from time to time, just pass in the street. Last time was a good few years ago, so it's not a frequent sighting. He has that straight ahead stare of the psychopath. Now he's bald though and walks with a stick.'

'Really?'

'Yes. He is still a dangerous person. He didn't seem to recognize me without my prison clothes but I recognized him. Always wearing a hat to cover up this two-tone hair, now wears it to cover his bald head, but it was his look, I mean the look in his eyes, always focused straight ahead.' Shored-Up nodded. 'Yes, he'd push a fellow to his death without a second thought but he's very small time.'

'So we understand. You see our thinking is that he and his gang—'

'The Driffield Crew that was their name. The other gang in Driffield at the time was the Driffield Fleet.'

'As in a fleet of ships?'

'Yes. Good name for a gang but they were also low-grade, small-time criminals. Met one of them recently, now in his forties, doing well as a second-hand car dealer and sends his daughter to a private school.'

Hennessey laughed. 'Yes, strange isn't it, once the system starts to work for you your attitude changes. But it seems to us that the Driffield Crew was hired by someone to murder Oliver Hill. They have been described as "guns for hire".'

'That is a good description, Mr Hennessey.

"Guns for hire", yes, I like it ... "guns for hire", it sums up the Driffield Crew very well.'

'So someone had money, because assassins don't come cheap. Someone had clout. We'll nail the Driffield Crew for the murder, if we can, but we really want the man who ordered it, that person has real clout.'

'Yes, I see your reasoning, Mr Hennessey. I can but make enquiries but I have to be discreet. Asking the wrong people the wrong questions, well ... all this flood water about, I don't want to disappear as well.'

Hennessey stood and opened his wallet and put a twenty-pound note on the table. 'Well, do your best, Shored-Up. If you come up with the goods, I'll see what I can do about those troublesome warrants and your keen-as-mustard probation officer. You are clearly very useful to us when at liberty, despite the way you earn your crust.'

'I was hoping for a little more.' But Shored-Up snatched up the 'Adam Smith', speedily so.

'Well, if you can come up with the goods, then there will be more. You know how to contact me.'

George Hennessey stepped out of the Speculation and turned his coat collar up against the rain, but he warmed at the sight of blue sky in the west.

* * *

The school assembly hall contained the majority of the evacuees, so Yellich and Webster noted. They saw how the people had arranged themselves into family groups separated from each other by some form of demarcation of territory, usually their suitcases. The people slept on canvas and wood-framed camping beds that seemed to have been loaned by the army or perhaps obtained from the Civil Defence stores. The sound in the hall was that of a low hum of conversation interrupted occasionally by the clatter of something dropped or an infant's wail. Here a man lay on his side on a camp bed engrossed in a thick novel, there a husband and wife sat opposite each other on their beds sharing a newspaper, having divided up and separated the pages. By the door two women, clearly well known and liked by each other, stood in conversation. In the corner two children squabbled and two older children were immersed in a game of chess. Other people were less active, a middle-aged woman with no obvious family and a very small amount of personal space, lay still and silent on her camp bed staring at the ceiling as if getting through the ordeal of temporary homelessness by thinking herself somewhere else, a long way away perhaps, thought Yellich, and possibly back in an earlier phase of life. The officers were both pleasantly surprised at the absence of stress and tension in the air, which they thought was due to the fact that the evacuees knew that this, their present arrangement, would last for a few days only. Any longer and the adults would probably start squabbling as well as the children but, at present, there was still a sense of adventure about it, but dampened by the knowledge that all would be returning to flooded houses.

'Don't wish to be a snob—' the housing official stepped over a child's toy that had been carelessly discarded in one of the walkways between two lines of beds – 'but I am so pleased that the folk here are professional middle-class people, at least in the main. If another part of the city had been flooded, then the people taken into refuge would be drunk each night and fighting each other from the word go, clothing and bodies would go unwashed, but I dare say you two gentlemen know what I mean.'

'Yes.' Yellich glanced around him and saw a woman light a cigarette, only to have another woman indignantly say something and point to one of the large 'no smoking' signs. Perhaps things were a little more tense than he realized. 'Yes,' he repeated, 'I know what you mean.'

'Interesting too—' the official spoke in a low hushed tone – 'some neighbours seem to have sought each other out and others have seized the opportunity to move as far away from each other as possible but by and large, the folk are very good, coping with the washing facilities, being the sinks in the children's toilets. A morning strip wash in front of each sink keeps the body odour in check and the folk have organized themselves well. Families with young children go first, then the adults who have no children. Doesn't do for little Johnny to see granddad naked, soaping his body all over.'

'I'll say.' Yellich watched the woman storm out of the halls with her lighted cigarette, leaving a trail of blue smoke behind her, making her point.

'And you get to know them, the good and helpful ones, the bad and uncooperative ones, one or two by name, but the rest remain as nameless faces.' The official led Yellich and Webster up the steps on to the stage of the hall where more beds had been set up, all, it seemed, for single persons. One camp bed then one suitcase then a camp bed, only adult reading material, only adult artefacts, only adults of either sex laying or sitting on the beds or standing chatting in small groups. The official took a whistle from his pocket and blew a very brief note, the briefest of brief notes, any longer and it would have been a tyrannical gesture, so thought Yellich, and would not at all have been well received by the professional middle class that the official was so grateful to

157

have to accommodate. Tom Marshall, by his name badge, smiled upon the sudden silence and said, 'Thank you. Can I have your attention please, ladies and gentlemen? These two gentlemen here are from the police.' Marshall indicated to Yellich and Webster, who stood beside him. 'Perhaps ... sir...'

'Thank you.' Yellich stepped forward. 'I am sure it is nothing to worry about but we are looking for a Mr and Mrs Hewitt, Mr and Mrs Albert and Belinda Hewitt–' his words carried clearly within the hall – 'of Chester Avenue. Could they please indicate and make themselves known?'

One man in his late middle years cautiously raised his hand, as did, at the same time, another man at the opposite side of the hall, both could not be Albert Hewitt. Yellich guessed that both must be neighbours of the Hewitts and both belonged to that group of folk who had seized the opportunity to get away from each other. Yellich nodded his thanks to both men. He and Webster stepped off the stage and, as they did so, the low hum of conversation resumed. The two officers made their way to the closer of the two men who had raised their hands who stood from his bed as Yellich and Webster approached.

'Mr Hewitt?' Yellich asked.

'No. We are Mr and Mrs Keeling–' he gestured to the middle-aged woman who sat opposite to where he had been sitting and

158

who was listening intently – 'and he isn't either, the other fella who raised his hand, he's Mr Buchanan. The Hewitts live between us. We are to their left; the Buchanans are to their right. Albert and Belinda are in one of the classrooms. I'll take you to them.'

'If you would.'

'They are with the other elderly people.'

'Elderly?' Yellich queried.

'Yes, they are getting on in years. The Housing Department thought it better to separate them. They believed that the elderly need a bit more peace and quiet than the rest of us so they gave them a classroom and they use the staff toilets for washing et cetera.'

'I see. Perhaps you could introduce us?'

'Delighted.'

Keeling, in his fifties, but dressed youthlike in jeans, tee shirt and sports shoes, led Yellich and Webster out of the hall and turned right into a narrow corridor with a brown parquet floor and yellow-painted plaster walls upon which were posters of an educational nature: the planets, the different species of whale, plants of the desert regions of the world. There were also photographs of the school trip to Wharram Percy which Yellich thought, in passing, was a little adventurous for nine- and ten-year-olds. He had visited Wharram Percy and even as an adult had been hard pressed to be able to identify

159

the street pattern of the village that had been abandoned many hundreds of years previously. All young children would have seen was a green area nestling between two steep hills in a remote part of the Vale. A pleasant day out no doubt, he thought, but more appropriate for university students to visit than for primary schoolchildren. Keeling turned from the corridor into a classroom from which all desks and chairs had been removed and replaced with similar camp beds to the camp beds in the hall, but in addition, a series of upholstered and upright chairs had been provided, in which sat elderly, frail-looking people. A sense of peace and quiet reigned in the room in contrast to the noise and clattering in the hall. Some of the elderly people dozed, others watched a television which had been found and installed though the picture was, observed Yellich, a little cloudy. Other people sat in a state of calm wakefulness, just sitting in silence, staring ahead of them. One elderly couple played cards, both very content in each other's company, as if still very much in love after fifty or sixty years of union, the sort of couple, Yellich thought, where it would be said, 'When the first one goes, the other won't be far behind.' Keeling approached another elderly couple who also seemed to be happy together, though this couple simply sat side by side.

'Albert, Belinda–' Keeling knelt in front of them and indicated Yellich and Webster who stood behind him – 'these gentlemen are from the police, they wish to speak to you.'

'Oh.' Albert Hewitt smiled. He seemed alert and, while elderly, was younger than the majority of people in the room. 'Welcome to Death Corner.'

'Death Corner?' Yellich raised his eyebrows.

'Yes, that's what we call it in here.' Hewitt grasped both arms of the chair and levered himself into a standing position. 'They got a TV as you see and some upright chairs from an old folks' home and put the oldies in here. They thought we'd be better off in our own little room, where things are quieter.' Hewitt nodded to a raggedy-looking man with a long silver beard who sat in the corner of the room close to the window. 'Don't know his name but he's Welsh, going by his accent and he came in here and looked around and said, "Oh, it's Death Corner, thought I'd got away from that, thought I'd left that well behind." Turns out boyo from the valleys lived pretty well all his life in the same village in the Rhondda Valley where there is just the one pub with just one room, and it seems that when you are a young man you stand at the bar in that pub and as you get older you move further and further away from the bar and nearer and nearer to the door, finally ending up an old boy sitting with all the other old boys in the corner near the door, that being "Death Corner", so we adopted the name, we quite liked it. Well, how can I help you? There's no trouble I hope?'

'Is there somewhere we can talk?' Yellich asked, still smiling at the anecdote about 'Death Corner' in a pub in a valley in South Wales.

'Yes, yes–' Hewitt stepped forward – 'we can go outside, the rain's stopped. Nice grounds here, a stand of crack willows provide shade, a pond with frogs and newts ... vast playing fields.'

'Yes–' Webster stepped to one side – 'we saw the playing fields, extensive, as you say.'

'And a yard with a climbing frame, it's a very well equipped school a damn sight better equipped than the inner city thing Belinda and I attended–' he smiled at his wife – 'but we met there so we can't complain. First set eyes on each other when we were in Miss Bates' class, six years old we were, that was nearly seventy years ago. Anyway, let's go and join the smokers.'

The smokers, it transpired, stood in a group in the schoolyard all smoking cigarettes, save one who smoked a pipe. Yellich noticed the woman who had lit a cigarette in the hall and had then had the 'no smoking' sign pointed out to her was by then standing by herself, leaning against the wall of the building with her arms folded in front of her looking at the ground as if in a state of indignation at some real or perceived slight. The group of smokers complained in loud and angry voices about the insurance companies who 'won't pay out anything like we'll need to cover the loss' and 'they'll take their sweet time about it too', being the comments Yellich and Webster overheard as they followed Hewitt across the yard, which glistened and shimmered in the sun. Hewitt led the officers to a group of ash trees, three in number, which grew in an area of uneven and stony ground. 'These trees are older than the school,' he said as he stopped by them. 'Seems that the builders used to tip spoil round the trees then covered it with soil. Anyway, the stones make it an unpopular place to sit or stand so we'll get privacy here and I don't want to leave Belinda alone too long, she's putting on a brave face but all this is very upsetting for her, for both of us really but more so for her, she wants to be back home as we all do. So how can I help you?'

Yellich told Hewitt the reason for himself and Webster calling on him. He did so as gently and sensitively as he could but he still saw colour drain from the old man's face as he did so.

'In our bed?'

Yellich nodded. 'Yes, I am afraid so. The

front bedroom ... a double bed.'

'Yes, that is our room. But who is he?'

'We thought at first it might be yourself, sir, the Voters' Roll doesn't give the age of the adults registered to vote at each address just their names.'

'Yes, and that is reasonable of you to think that but as you see, I am alive, as is my wife, but it will all have to go, this will destroy Belinda, our house has not just been looted, our valuables gone, we were only allowed to bring a change of clothing you see ... one suitcase per person but ... but a dead body has been put in our bed.' Hewitt turned away. 'This is, I don't know, it is ... something ... something awful.'

'Do you know who the youth might be, sir?'

Hewitt shook his head. 'No, we know of no one in York of that age. We have a grandson of that age but he lives in Australia. Our daughter and her husband emigrated to Australia where their children were born. Our son lives in Bristol, he has two daughters. So not a relative and not a personal friend, not of his age. Twenties you say?'

'Yes ... early twenties.'

'In our bed!' Hewitt raised his arms in protest and disbelief. 'So a stranger came and entered our house, our bed and died there. I can hardly believe—'

'No,' Webster interrupted Hewitt. 'Sorry,

we didn't make it plain – he was murdered. Shot. Twice. In the head.'

Hewitt steadied himself against one of the ash trees.

'So ... oh, this gets worse. Just how many people have been in our home? The burglar and the dead man and the man or men who murdered him. When does it end?'

'We are sorry.'

'We have been violated. We knew of the danger of being looted but somebody murdering someone in our house, and total strangers to us, this will destroy Belinda. Mind you, in a sense it could have been worse, we could have found him, if the burglar didn't have the sense of decency to phone you and tip you off. He could have kept quiet and we would have returned home and discovered ... oh ... that would have been worse.'

It was Wednesday, 12.10 hours.

Five

Wednesday, 29th June,
12.20 – 21.40 hours

in which the same name is mentioned by separate sources and Reginald Webster is at home to the most charitable reader.

It was, thought Ventnor, a criminals' pub; darker even than had been the Zetland Arms despite its regal-sounding name. The Royal Sovereign seemed to Ventnor to be a bar for all the blaggers, wide boys, wrong 'uns, ex-cons and the downright 'iffy' con artists in the Vale of York, those on the way up, those settled in and those on the way down ... and out. All of them would have passed through the doors of the Royal Sovereign and would continue to do so just as long as the building stands and is open for business. It was, Ventnor observed, and as Carmen Pharoah also observed, just one of those pubs.

'Did you bring that list?' Carmen Pharoah hissed, with a smile and a twinkle in her eye.

Ventnor's chest heaved with suppressed

laughter as his eyes focused in the gloom. It was the middle of the day yet the pub was dark within, for, like the Zetland Arms, it had windows on only one wall opposite the bar and also like the Zetland Arms, those windows were close, very close, to the side of another building, but unlike the Zetland Arms the publican did not like artificial light. It was as if his eyes had adjusted to the gloom over the years and that was all that mattered. If that meant the patrons, especially visiting patrons, had to grope about in semi-darkness, then it meant that. The gloom seemed to suit the pub which for both Ventnor and Pharoah said 'crime', low income, irregular money, dole, men being put in touch with other men for purposes known to very few and parcels being passed under the tables in the shadows, also known only to those who need to know. There had been, as both officers noticed, no large front entrance to the pub. Entrance, they found, was to be gained via a small door set in the side of the building, a door so small and of faded and peeling green paint, a door so inconsequential of appearance, that it could be mistaken for the door to a small outdoor cupboard where coal or brushes might be stored. The door had no sign above it but the officers pulled it open and found themselves in the shadowy bar of the Royal Sovereign and had felt as though they were entering a dark cavern. The pub clearly catered for local trade and so a sign which might read 'entrance' or 'bar' was not needed. Within, the bar was illuminated only by the thin natural amount coming in through the windows and equally thin artificial amount coming from the glow of the beer engines and from the spirit rack behind the bar. The tables were, at that part of the day, all vacant and all were small, circular and surrounded by small wooden chairs. An old and worn pool table stood at the far end of the rectangular-shaped floor area, beyond which was a door on which a barely visible sign in white paint read WOMEN. A door at the opposite end of the floor area had no sign upon it but, thought the officers, if it had a sign then that sign would read MEN.

Pharoah and Ventnor stood in silence in the empty pub, both making out more and more detail as their eyes adjusted to the gloom. When the publican eventually appeared, he seemed to emerge from the shadows behind the bar with a disinterested, slothful attitude. He viewed Pharoah and Ventnor with clear suspicion and disdain, staring at the officers as he stood square on to them, as if, had the bar not been between them, he might be preparing himself to fight them. He was a publican whose business was evidently kept going for him, nicely ticking over, by his regulars. He did not need to be warm and welcoming to strangers, particularly strangers who were neatly dressed, well dressed, especially as one was black and the other white. Clearly lawmen. 'Yes,' he snarled with a heavy local accent.

'Police.' Ventnor showed his ID.

'I know–' again that unblinking snarl – 'I can tell.' The man was bald, strongly built, in his sixties, thought the officers, with a barrel-like chest with silver hairs pushing out of his open-necked shirt, his shirt sleeves were rolled up neatly, cuff over cuff, military style, and thus revealed powerfully-built, muscular and heavily tattooed forearms. He rested two large paw-like hands on the bar, revealing that each of his fingers had a ring upon it, sometimes two, the sort of jewellery, Ventnor pondered, that would be very useful in a punch-up. 'You have it tattooed on your foreheads, just here–' he tapped his own forehead – 'you don't need warrants.'

'Known to the police, are you?'

'I have had a run in with the like, aye, you could say that. You took a lump out of my life for something that I didn't do.'

The officers remained silent. They wanted the man's cooperation but both thought that the landlord was of the ilk that had committed many offences for which he had evaded justice and then once was sent down for an offence he probably did commit despite his protestations.

'And I've been expecting you.'

'Oh?'

'Yes. Barry Last phoned me, he's got the Zetland Arms, he said you'd called, he said you might be calling here.'

'We're looking for information.'

'I can't help you.' The landlord turned away and seemed to the officers to be consumed by the murk, an impression aided muchly by the man's black shirt and trousers.

'We could return,' Ventnor said into the blackness.

'With a warrant,' Pharoah added, 'to search your cellar. We have received information, you see.'

'Oh.' The man's face reappeared.

'From a very reliable source.' Ventnor held eye contact with the man.

'About the duty-free tobacco and alcohol you allow to be stored in your cellar, van loads of the stuff brought up from the channel ports, having been purchased in France or Belgium,' Pharoah commented with a smile.

'Guys distribute it on the estate and pay you rental for use of your cellar and sell you some to sell over the counter with a little profit ... all cash in hand ... declaring nothing.'

'Cheaper than the corner shop, or the mini market, even cheaper than the supermarket.'

Pharoah continued to smile, knowingly so.

'Highly illegal, of course–' Ventnor also smiled – 'cheating the Exchequer out of all that revenue, that's your licence up in smoke if it was to be exposed by a police raid.'

The man took a step forward and once again rested his two hands with their ring bedecked fingers on the bar and hung his head.

'Something that the brewery would want to know,' Ventnor continued. 'I mean, it's difficult enough for an ex-con to get to be a licensee of a pub. You have to be clean for a lot of years and even then you get not the plumb and posh pubs owned by the brewery you get the likes of the Royal Sovereign, but if you were to be prosecuted for selling and storing duty-free goods in very large quantities...'

'I don't believe you have an informant,' the publican replied icily, 'none of my customers would grass me up. The estate is tight like that; this is more like a private members' club than it is a pub. Everybody knows everybody else; they'd just be harming themselves. A lot of my customers are on the dole so I sell stuff a little cheap, it's a public service. I do it, it keeps them going.'

'I see you still have ashtrays on the tables. Smoking is illegal in pubs.'

The man shrugged. 'No one would come in if I stopped them smoking. We never have strangers in here and I don't serve food so no one complains.'

'And you serve all hours,' Ventnor continued, 'I mean, no front windows, no front door, from the street it'll look to be in darkness and shut up at eleven p.m. sharp.'

'I am saying nothing–' the landlord avoided eye contact – 'nothing.'

'Well...' Ventnor paused and then said, 'information received is still good enough to get a warrant and you'll be out of work and out of a place to live and in the circumstances that would be seen as you being intentionally homeless.'

'You'll get one offer of the worst housing the city has to offer,' Pharoah explained.

The landlord sank back against the shelf beneath the spirit rack and by doing so he was hardly visible, appearing to the officers like a disembodied head floating in space. 'So what do you want to know?'

'Whatever you can tell us about a gang that was active twenty years ago.'

'Twenty years ago!' The landlord smiled.

'Yes. We are not interested in what it is that is going on now, unless we stumble across it then that's different, then we will be interested.'

'But right now,' Pharoah added, 'right now we are going back two decades. You were the publican here twenty years ago?'

'Yes ... yes...' The landlord continued to

smile, still clearly very relieved. 'Nearly thirty years in fact.'

'You were a young con?'

'Youth custody, but it was still five years out of my life.'

Ventnor and Pharoah remained silent. Five years in youth custody, that sort of sentence, they both knew, was not given for nonpayment of a library fine or littering, but they remained silent.

'We have names,' Ventnor continued, 'they might mean something. "Tich" Riley, "Two Tone" Bowler, "Big Andy" Dagnall, "Little Andy" Barnes, "Mid" Davy Hartley, Walpole Moulton.'

'Do they ring any bells?' Carmen Pharoah asked.

The landlord continued to relax, visibly so. Carmen Pharoah thought he must have his hands in a very dirty pie. There was evidently something he did not want the police to find out about, something probably a lot more serious than the sale of duty-free tobacco and alcohol.

'You are going back a few years now,' he commented.

'Well ... twenty, as we said.' Carmen Pharoah found herself beginning to be intrigued by whatever the landlord was involved in. She determined to check with Criminal Records when she returned to the station.

'Names from an earlier age, but yes, names

I recognize. Surprised they are of interest to you, they're spent. Never were anything much, fancied themselves as hard men. They've all done a bit of time but wouldn't last long in high security, just street turks with big ideas.'

'I see.' Ventnor spoke softly. 'Does the name Oliver Hill mean anything to you?'

'Oliver Hill? No ... sorry, they did bring a few mates in with them for a drink once or twice, he might have been one of their mates, but no one of that name was ever a regular.'

'Alright, so what do you remember about them? We understand "Two Tone" Bowler was the boss?'

'So he thought, but they just played at it you see. They always sat at the table over there by the men's toilets and we have always had trouble with the men's toilets, no matter what we do, every time the door opens there is a blast of drain smell, really bad odour that gets through two doors and that table gets the first and worst of it.'

'And that's where they sat?' Ventnor gasped.

'Got it in one,' the landlord smiled. 'The weakest of the regulars sit there. I mean there are boys in here, retired Hull trawler men, boys that would have sorted them out in the blink of an eye. I mean it would have been a big-time massacre in the yard at the side of the pub. Even when they were at their peak, if "Two Tone" Bowler or one of his gang had looked at the wrong guy in here … just once…'

'I see.' Ventnor smiled. 'So it all happens outside?'

'Yes, they take it outside to sort it out, I insist on that, always have. I don't try to stop them, but if something, or somebody, kicks off, well I've got a loud voice and I can handle myself and I just yell to them to take it outside and they do usually, just one comes back but sometimes they both come back with battle scars and buy each other a drink, but I never step in and stop it.'

'Too dangerous?' Carmen Pharoah asked.

'Yes, that's how I lost my brother-in-law – my wife's brother. He was ex-Merchant Navy and he could look after himself. He was with a mate having a drink one Sunday before lunch, that was the way in their house, he didn't drink at all except on a Sunday lunchtime while his wife cooked the meal. Anyway, it got to about the time that he was expected home and there was a knock on her door and she, his wife, thought he'd forgotten his key, opened the door and it was two coppers, two uniforms come to tell her her husband's dead. Turned out he and his mate tried to break up a fight between two thugs and he got a knife in his chest for his reward, straight into his heart.

He stopped the fight alright and the boy was out in three years bragging about his victim, carrying himself like a hard man ... that was in a pub on Preston Road Estate in Hull. Rough place, makes this estate look like part of the stockbroker belt down south, Surrey, or wherever it is. So, no, I don't break up fights. Too dangerous. If someone is hurt bad I lift them up and put them on the pavement and then phone the law and say I saw nothing, let it seem like a street fight which took place outside the pub and the pub is usually deserted by then, the punters just melt away, go home early, leaving a wounded soldier on the pavement for the police or the ambulance crew to pick up ... best that way.'

'I see,' Ventnor growled. 'So, the names, local but not hard men?'

'No, never were and now they are wasted. Walpole was a bit of an outsider, lived outside Driffield but he was part of the gang, all the others were on the estate.'

'Alright, so if they were not real hard men, what did they do?'

'They were wide boys, a bit of graft ... moving stolen goods, got into the large-scale duty-free racket before anyone else, running the stuff up from France, but when it became clear how much money they were making, their vehicle got torched and they knew better than to retaliate or even try to stay in business. Mind you, they were stupid enough not to heed the warning, and they got fair warning.'

'Oh?'

'Yes, they were sitting round that table by the men's toilets as usual and a couple of very heavy boys walked in and just dropped a match on their table – that was the warning – they didn't heed it, brought up another load of tobacco and their van and all the tobacco inside it went up in flames. Then they stopped. If they had carried on then there would have been blood spilt and bones splintered.'

'What did they do then?'

The landlord shrugged. 'They kept together as a crew and had money to buy booze so they had some action going but what I couldn't tell you. Sorry.'

'Could they be violent?'

'Suppose. Somebody's always stronger than you and somebody is always weaker than you, so, if there was money in it and the other person was weak enough, then yes, I wouldn't put it past them, not that crew, didn't have many scruples ... not that crew. Didn't then, probably still won't have many scruples even now, not the "Two Tone Boys".'

'The Two Tone Boys.' Ventnor smiled. 'Is that what they were called?'

'Yes, and one or two less flattering names

behind their backs and sometimes to their faces if it came from a heavier crew. That made them worse really, after that they needed a victim.'

'I see.'

'So, like I said, they could be really vicious, but only if the victim was weak enough, and they were all small men with a chip on their shoulders.'

'I think we get the picture.' Carmen Pharoah glanced at Ventnor. 'Lowlifes.'

'Yes.' The landlord nodded in agreement. 'Very low life ... even for a pub like this they were the scrapings.' He shrugged. 'So what? I have no problems with what this pub is ... it was, it is, the best I can do with my record and I understand that it's the punters not the governor that controls a pub. Any landlord that thinks he controls his pub is a landlord that has a problem, he's the gaffer that has a violent pub, quite true, it's like the slammer; it's the cons that run the prison, not the guards. They couldn't control the prison if the cons didn't let them.'

'True enough,' Ventnor growled. 'So, the question now is, who did they work for? Selling duty-free stuff is easy and they don't sound to have been the sort of crew who could organize themselves to do anything significant, the "guns for hire" label seems to be accurate.'

'Well, whoever was hiring for any job that

178

wasn't too heavy, a little reminding here and there, a little debt to be collected here and there, if the victim was small enough.'

'Do you know of any person in particular?' Pharoah pressed.

'You'll forget the stuff in the cellar?'

'For the purposes of this enquiry, like I said.' Carmen Pharoah held eye contact with the man.

'What does that mean?'

'It means that in respect of this enquiry we won't request a warrant to search your cellar but if we come across evidence of anything, we can't ignore it. So for now you are safe, so long as it is only contraband that is down there.'

The landlord took a deep and audible breath and leaned forwards, resting his huge hands on the bar, causing the row of rings to glow in what light there was. 'Yes, you may as well know, I let my cellar to a few boys. I don't get involved myself other than taking rent, but they run booze and tobacco up from France and store it below, then sell it locally. This pub struggles, it isn't a licence to print money like some pubs, but I made it clear that nothing goes down there apart from duty-free – nothing illegal – no control-led substance, no illegal immigrants, especi-ally illegals, I don't like illegals. Crims can make as much money by smuggling people as they can from smuggling heroin and the penalties are much lighter, just a slap on the wrist compared to the ten or fifteen stretch that you can pull for smuggling the powder. But that's the cellar, mostly tobacco because it's lighter to transport and people on the estate don't ever read the sign about "smoking kills" on each packet of hand rolling tobacco. A few bottles of wine and a few cartons of beer but tobacco in the main.'

'OK, so if we agree not to grass you up about the tobacco in the cellar, then you give us something that will make us go away happy?'

'Well, I never knew who they worked for, but I heard rumours that whoever it was, was a very heavy boy, a very serious criminal, like so serious he is unknown to the police. That means a lot of protection among the crims.'

'Yes, we know the type.'

'So ... well, I know someone they did a favour for once, she'd have to be connected to have the favour done for her. She's in her forties now. She's the headmistress of Sandbank Primary School in York.'

'Sandbank Primary,' Ventnor repeated.

'Yes, Sandbank something ... Sandbank Road Primary, Sandbank Drive, something like that.'

'Alright–' Thompson Ventnor wrote the name in his notebook – 'I dare say we can find it.'

'I'd be obliged if you wouldn't tell her that it was me that gave you her name.'

'We'll do our best.'

'Your best!'

'It's all we can promise,' Carmen Pharoah replied firmly. 'Come on, you're doing well, you're keeping HM Customs and Excise out of your pub and you know that they have more power than the police. They won't stop at your cellar if they visit you, it will be the full weights and measures package. So tell us what you know about the lady who is now a headmistress of a primary school.'

'It was about the time you are interested in,' the landlord said with resignation, 'twenty years ago as I recall. The Two Tone Boys had just had their van torched, so no more duty-free money for them, and they were looking for work and this young woman was getting harassed. She lived on the estate and went on to university and did well, but this guy she got in tow with would not accept it when she broke things off with him, so the harassment began ... damaging her car, following her everywhere ... you know the sort of thing.'

'Yes.'

'Well, it got her into a right state, a real nervous wreck, but the guy was a nobody and he was visited by the Two Tone Boys and she was left alone after that. Left the estate to go to university, became a school teacher and is now a headmistress of a school in York, but she had to have connections for the boys to do that.'

'Alright, we'll visit her. Do any of the Two Tone Boys still live on the estate?'

'Yes, I see Two Tone himself hobbling about from time to time and "Titch" Riley comes in here in the afternoon sometimes, both shadows of their former selves.'

'Still at the same addresses?'

'I would think so. They don't get into trouble with the law anymore but they haven't moved on in life either. That's the way of it on the estate. If you don't leave and make good like the woman who became a head teacher, you stay on the estate, you grow old while life goes past you, but do me a favour will you?'

'Another favour?' But Carmen Pharoah was smiling warmly.

'Yes. Don't go straight from here to their homes. The estate has eyes and ears. You'll have been seen coming, even at this time, and you'll be seen leaving and you'll be recognized as the law. I reckon about ten people on the estate will know that you are here. By six o'clock this evening all the estate will know and about eight o'clock tonight a very heavy boy will lean on the bar and say, "I heard you had a visit today?" That could make things difficult for me. I mean very difficult.'

Thompson Ventnor nodded. 'That's reasonable and it's a cold case anyway but shut down on time tonight because that's why we called, didn't we, quiet word, quiet warning about staying open after eleven p.m.? Good enough?'

'Good enough, and appreciated.'

'Well, you scratch our back and shut down on time each night for a week, then start to push the boat out again. That will keep everybody happy.' Ventnor turned to go; Carmen Pharoah also turned and followed him out of the pub.

Somerled Yellich halted the car in front of the house. He and Webster looked at the building for a few seconds in complete silence and growing suspicion.

'It reminds me of that case in Liverpool,' Webster said softly, breaking the silence. 'Do you remember it? It got a lot of publicity. A home in a prestigious suburb, Rolls Royce in the drive, a high fence all around it, bristling with burglar alarms and movement-activated spotlights. It attracted the attention of the Merseyside Police because it just didn't look right. Kept it under observation and saw that occasionally the bloke who lived in the house would drive into the city, to a small office block which had the name of an import/export agency on the door.'

'But no listing for the agency in the Yellow

Pages?'

'That's the one. so they kept the house and the bloke under close surveillance and brought down a massive heroin importation organization, all because a house in Liverpool's stockbroker belt just didn't look right.'

'Which just goes to show—' Yellich kept his eyes on the house – 'that as is said, if something doesn't look right, it invariably isn't right.' He pondered the house. It was set on the edge of the fashionable village of Much Bewley in the Vale of York, in a rich farming area within the spill of Malton, very green wellie brigade, very Range Rover country. It was tucked away behind the main road and had a very precise neatness about it to the point that it seemed that every leaf on the shrubs that lined the driveway and in the front garden, every blade of grass, was in its proper and designated place. The black-painted wrought-iron gates, with the spikes picked out in gold, had a letter box attached to them so that the homeowner was evidently obliged to walk from his door to the top of his drive to retrieve his post, but clearly that was a price he was prepared to pay, rather than allow the postman and deliveries of junk mail flyers on to his property. The house itself was at a lower level than the road, so that from their vantage point within the car, all that was clearly visible to Yellich and Webster beyond the front garden was the red-tiled roof of the building, glistening in the sun after the last rain shower.

'Well–' Yellich turned to Webster – 'we know that at least one member of the house is or rather was, a criminal, and given that, as is also said, "the apple never falls far from the tree", we'd better—'

'Proceed with caution, Sarge?' Webster smiled.

'Exactly–' Yellich returned the smile – 'the very words I was going to use, proceed with caution, much caution.'

The two officers left the car and walked to the gate. They located the bell above a metal grill which was clearly a 'squawk box' set in the left-hand gate close to where the two gates met, though without any form of sign indicating its purpose. Yellich pressed the bell. Twice.

There was no response as he and Webster waited. Yellich pressed again, twice more, allowing his finger to linger longer on the bell button.

'What!' The voice, male, ill-tempered, shouted at them through the 'squawk box'. The voice spoke of an indignant as well as an ill-tempered personality. It was not the voice of a man who needed new friends, or indeed, Yellich pondered, needed any friends at all in his life.

'Police.' Yellich put his mouth close to the metal grill.

'What's it about?' The voice replied after a pause, and was by then quieter, more cautious.

Yellich and Webster glanced at each other and raised their eyebrows. The voice, its new wariness, said much to the officers. It said 'active criminal with something to hide'.

'We need to talk to you, sir.' Yellich's voice was calm, soft, but also insistent.

'I'll come out.'

'We'll need to come in.' Yellich's voice tailed off as a distinct 'click' came from the grill, telling him that his protest and insistence was going unheard.

Yellich and Webster waited and as they did so they turned side on to the gate and glanced about them. They found Much Bewley to appear to be a wealthy village. There were bungalows and large houses and each property, certainly in that part of the village, sat solidly it seemed to the officers, in a generous parcel of land. Many seemed to be whitewashed and with some sort of distinctive red tiling on their roof. Smaller, second-looking sort of cars, stood in the driveways and were of the ilk of BMW and Audi. The gardens were similarly neatly trimmed as the garden of the house on which Yellich and Webster were calling, though none seemed to exude the same

186

repressive attitude. The gardens about were neat, but still gardens with a life of their own. The garden of the house in front of which the officer stood seemed to indicate that if a blade of grass stood just one half inch higher than all the others it would be instantly snipped back to size. Yellich glanced up at the sky and saw dark clouds approaching low over the landscape: rain would soon fall to ease the closeness and humidity.

When the householder and presumably the ill-tempered owner of the voice appeared, he revealed himself to be a short but strongly-built man, casually dressed, but smartly so, even when clearly not expecting visitors. He had a full head of hair which, like his garden, was kept short and neatly combed. He walked confidently from his front door up the incline that was his driveway, bristling with cleanliness, and looked Yellich squarely in the eye and said, 'What?' He didn't disguise his hostility and Yellich felt that any visitor, whether police or not, would receive a similar reception.

'Mr Halverson?' Yellich asked calmly. 'Mr Roger Halverson?'

'You know it is.'

'We don't know it is. Are you Mr Roger Halverson?'

The man sighed with a forced display of patience. 'Yes, I am he.'

'You have a son ... also Roger Halverson?'

'Oh, no–' the man relaxed a little and looked down and to his left – 'what has he done now? I told him to keep his nose clean. He's accumulating too much track. I told him to be careful. I told him to keep himself covered.'

'No,' Yellich said calmly, 'he's not in trouble. I'm afraid it's a bit more serious than that. Can we come in, please? You really don't want to have this conversation through metal bars and in the street.'

Colour rapidly drained from Roger Halverson's face as he stepped smartly to one side and pressed a button on the inside of the gatepost which caused the left-hand of the two gates to spring open and then swing loosely on its hinges, allowing Yellich and Webster to step through the gap between the two gates. Halverson then closed the gate shut, causing the lock to 'click' loudly, holding the gate in place.

Halverson turned and walked down the drive towards the house, which was a bungalow of large proportions, extending widely either side of the door. Unlike the other houses, Roger Halverson's house was not whitewashed but of exposed brick, neatly pointed. At the door Halverson wiped his shoes on the matting despite only having walked to the gate and back and entered the house. The officers also wiped their feet and also entered the house. The interior of the house was similar to the garden, so the officers noted, and did so with no little surprise. It all had an air of 'ideal home neatness', with an 'everything-in-its-place' rigidity. The house smelled strongly of furniture polish and air freshener. Halverson walked down a long hallway, past a number of doors, all closed, and turned right into a room that was clearly the lounge and of similar generous proportions as the remainder of the house. It was, Yellich guessed, probably fifteen feet wide and twenty feet in length. The fireplace was of stone and beside the fireplace was a wall-mounted plasma TV screen. A four-seater settee stood against the further wall, and also in the room was a pair of matching armchairs. A glass-topped coffee table stood in the centre of the room on which were copies of *Country Life*, *Yorkshire Ridings* and *Motor Sport*. The carpet was fitted and was of a red Axminster design and probably, thought Yellich, the genuine article. The wide window looked out on to the rear garden, where one lawn, nearest the house, gave way to a second lawn accessed by steps and on a higher elevation. The borders of the garden and the dividing border between the lawns were, as the officers had by then come to expect, precisely trimmed. The upper part of a wooden gazebo, highly varnished and glinting in the sun could be seen at the bottom right-hand side of the further lawn. Roger Halverson turned and faced Yellich. He wore a blue tee shirt and white summer trousers, blue sports shoes. 'Just tell me,' he said calmly, all aggression and ill-temper, all hostility, having evidently evaporated.

'Mr Halverson,' Yellich said softly, 'I am afraid that we have some bad news for you.'

Halverson stood his ground. He showed no emotion and remained completely still, motionless, statue-like, clearly waiting for Yellich to finish speaking, waiting for Yellich to tell him what he had to tell him.

'A body has been found and fingerprints taken from the body have identified it as being Roger Halverson, aged twenty-eight years, and this is his last known address.'

Still no response.

Yellich had always found breaking news of this nature difficult, very difficult, but the man's lack of reaction in this instance proved doubly difficult to deal with than anguish or extreme grief reaction and denial. Yellich continued, 'His body was found yesterday. There was some delay in making the identity because we ... the police ... thought initially that the body was that of the owner of the property in which he was found. That proved not to be the case. We then took fingerprints, we found the deceased had a criminal record and ... we are here. I am very sorry.'

'How was he killed?' It was Halverson's first reaction, his first question, and still he showed no sign of emotion, no denial, as Yellich had come to expect, no 'are you sure?', 'no, it couldn't be', just an expressionless request as to the cause of his son's death.

'Murdered,' Yellich replied and found himself falling into Halverson's clipped way of speaking. It seemed that Halverson was controlling the pace just as he had once read about sending and receiving of Morse code, the quicker of the two will always slow to the other's pace.

'How?'

'Shot.'

Halverson remained silent, as if waiting for more information.

'Twice. Two bullets. Both to the head. Close range.'

Halverson nodded.

'You seem to know something, Mr Halverson?'

'Know nothing.'

Again there was a period of silence and Yellich longed for some sign of life in the room, an animal, a vase of flowers, a plant pot, even a fly buzzing against the windowpane he would have found welcome, anything to compensate for Halverson's emotional void.

'His body was found in a householder's bedroom, in the bed, the householder and his wife having been evacuated because of the flooding. That's why we at first assumed the body was that of the owner or one of his relatives.' Yellich told Halverson the address at which his son's body had been found. Halverson said that the address had no significance for him.

'No significance to me,' Halverson added. 'Possibly it had to Roger.'

'Well, the householders are both elderly, not at all of Roger's age group. It's unlikely your son knew them. What is more likely is that their house was chosen at random. They could have left him in any house on that street. All the houses are still under two feet of water and all evacuated. Your son's body was found by a looter who phoned the police, but not until after he had a good root round the property, so he had contaminated the crime scene and our job was made more difficult. We now depend more on you.'

'Me?' Halverson looked at Yellich and then Webster and then Yellich again.

'Yes.' Yellich allowed himself to glance around the room for a second time, reading it as a police officer is trained to do. It was, he thought, a hard, cold, soulless room. It was the sort of house, he thought, which might contain a collection of tropical butter-flies, each in a glass cage, each with a large pin through its long-deceased body, but it would not contain a model railway. It was the sort of house that might hire a private shooting gallery for .22 target practice but it would not have a library in which each wall was softened by shelf upon shelf of books.

'Me?' Halverson demanded again. 'Me?'

'Yes. Do you know of anyone who would want to murder your son? Or have him murdered? It has all the hallmarks of an underworld shooting.'

'It has?' Halverson's cold eyes seemed to bore into Yellich's.

'Small calibre,' Yellich explained, 'so the bullets didn't exit the skull. One bullet to the middle of the forehead. The other behind the left ear.'

'Underworld execution—' Webster spoke for the first time – 'close range. He was not shot accidentally.'

'No. I don't know of anyone.' Halverson spoke strongly but his reply came too quickly to sound sincere to the officers.

'Was your son living here?' Yellich asked.

'No. He moved out a few years ago. He really left home when he was sixteen. He moved about a lot in the early days, from flat to flat. He wasn't actually living here when he was convicted but it was his permanent address ... it was his home address. He'd receive any mail that was sent to him here. Usually I'd post it on to whatever flat he was in at the time, or if he was due to visit in a day or two, I'd leave it for him to pick up.'

'Alright. Where was your son living?'

'With a girl. Not married. No kids. I think she wants ... he doesn't.'

'What is her address?'

Halverson paused.

'You could be prosecuted for obstruction,' Yellich growled.

'93 Hall Place,' Halverson snarled in response, grudgingly so.

'Where is it?'

'York ... Heslington.'

Yellich glanced at him with widening eyes. He did not attempt to conceal his surprise. 'A house in Heslington, at his age?'

'Yes.' Halverson smiled. 'He did well.'

'Doing what?'

'Used cars.'

'I see.' Yellich smiled briefly, knowing that the used-car trade is often a conduit to the underworld, an interface with criminality and for a used-car dealer to be able to afford a house in Heslington at the age of just twenty-eight, then he was likely to have a finger in some very suspect pies that his used-car dealership would have concealed, some very illegal activity. 'We'll have to call on her.' Yellich folded his notebook.

'I'll phone her.' Halverson spoke flatly. 'Let her know that you are on your way. And why.'

'Rather embarrassing that you folk had to

come here.' The woman was short of stature, short of hair, grimly thought Carmen Pharoah and Thomson Ventnor alike, conservatively dressed. She had a small desk in a small office which she kept neat and efficiently tidy, allowing herself no homely photographs or posters. The small window of her small office afforded a view across a small car park to a low metal fence and then to a line of trees which obscured the narrow lane along which Pharoah and Ventnor had travelled. The sign on the desk read, Ms Sandra Crookes BA (Hons) BEd Headmistress. The room possessed a heavy fragrance of scent.

'Yes, sorry we had to arrive unannounced, we were quite discreet at the reception desk. We didn't say why we wanted to see you,' Pharoah explained.

'Well, probably no harm done. Please do take a seat.' Sandra Crookes indicated vacant chairs in front of her desk. 'The catchment area of this school includes a tough council housing estate; we are often visited by the police about the antics of the children as they travel to and from the school. We are responsible for their behaviour from the moment they leave home to the moment they return. The receptionist will assume that this is just another such visit, so the news of it won't make the staff room gossip and I'll make a point of seeing you out when you leave saying something like, "anything we can do to help" or something similar. But, yes, you are going back a long way, so long ago that all that seems to be as though it belongs to a different lifestyle, that estate in Driffield, the Zetland Arms, the Royal Sovereign ... what a pair of dives, especially the "Sovereign". The estate was the underside of what is really quite a prosperous little town. I am so pleased I got out.'

'I can imagine.' Pharoah settled into the low plastic chair.

'Yes–' Sandra Crookes took a deep breath – 'I realized I had to get out when I found myself sitting in the Zetland Arms with my girlfriend drinking strong cider realizing I was looking at the men and trying to work out which one I was going to marry, looking for my future husband. If I stayed much longer I'd be on the estate now, overweight and varicose-veined because of the dole queue diet and endless hours of housework and an evening job polishing school desks. I'd just be repeating my mother's marriage ... a small-time crook and a big-time unemployed man for a husband and a father and role model to my children, just an action replay of my parents' marriage – no thanks. I never remember going hungry, not once ever, but there never seemed to be enough either. You know, we thought we were rich if we had a packet of twenty cigarettes in the house. I studied in the evening after work then went to York University. So I am here, not a great success in the scheme of things.'

'Oh, you did well.' Pharoah smiled. 'You overcame many, many barriers. You deserve your success, modest as you think it to be.'

'Thank you.' She glanced out of the window. 'Confess I got a bit angry when I met privately educated women who knew they were going to go to university from the age of five years. One of them once said, "I believe in adversity". Can you believe it? I really had to swallow my words then, sometimes I wish I hadn't. Anyway, that's why I chose to teach at a series of tough schools, try to give the underprivileged children a leg up and one or two have done well and I have had reports of them reaching university, so I have done some good, but ... that's not why you are here?'

'No. We believe you had some trouble once and turned to the publican of The Sovereign for advice?' Thompson Ventnor asked. 'Could you tell us what happened?' He opened his notebook.

'Well yes, it's one of those instances ... that's the wrong word; it wasn't an instant at all.'

'An episode?' Carmen Pharoah suggested.

Sandra Crookes smiled. 'That's the very word. It was an episode that I won't forget. Myself and this boy went out for a drink on

197

a few occasions. It didn't take long to realize we were ill-matched. All I saw in him was long-term unemployment and a life watching the seasons change until we both went to a premature grave. Of getting children up and away to school and then going back to bed again to escape from a life in a sort of half sleep, and as a means of staying warm without burning fuel, then getting up at four p.m. in time for the children to come home. That's how a lot of parents still live today. A lot of these children's parents are doing just that at this very moment – sleeping, dozing in the middle of the day. Anyway, I stopped the relationship before it went any further and I was right to do so because that's exactly how he ended up, long-term unemployed, married a lass from the estate, children in trouble from a very early age, in trouble with the police I mean, antisocial behaviour orders from the age of twelve. But he was obsessive, just wouldn't accept that we were not going to be an item, kept calling on me, kept phoning me, writing letters, sending flowers, but then things got worse, the letters became poisonous in their content, really sour and vitriolic, hoping all sorts of evil would befall me. The flowers stopped arriving and all sorts of unpleasant substances would be posted to me. Then he became threatening, describing the unpleasant death that would happen to me if I didn't return to him and he even threatened my family: my parents, my brothers and sisters. It was really horrible.'

'Did you go to the police?' Pharoah asked.

'No ... no ... no.' Sandra Crookes shook her head vigorously.

'You didn't? Why not?' Ventnor was genuinely surprised. 'That amount of evidence, we would have had a successful conviction, a definite "result" as we say.'

'It wasn't allowed on the estate. It wasn't allowed to involve the police, not even for something like that. Any family who involved the police to sort out a dispute would have the entire estate turn against them. It was just the way of it, probably still is. In fact it is still the way of it; a code of conduct which has to be honoured. The law would only be called in if the situation became really serious ... murder, arson attack, very severe assault that left someone permanently injured, but a dispute between two people? That sort of thing is kept within the estate. Differences were settled in the street with the other residents providing the audience and witnesses as to the fair play of it – no weapons – and determining who was to be the victor. My sister still lives there. She tells me it is still like that. So, no police for my little problem.'

'I see.'

'Confess I am a bit disappointed that

Bernie Truro should have pointed you in my direction, that was a breach of estate rules.'

'We—' Ventnor glanced at Pharoah – 'let's just say we had something to hold over him.'

'We had a bit of leverage,' Carmen Pharoah added with a smile.

'I see.'

'And we are going back a long time. He probably thought it was grey enough to be safe.'

'Grey enough?'

'Not wholly wrong, but not wholly right either. In the middle of the black and white of it,' Ventnor explained. 'Sorry, it's just the way my mind works.'

'Alright.'

'So, do carry on,' Pharoah pressed. 'A young man was harassing you?'

'Yes, as I said, things got really, I mean really, really bad with this man. He began to vandalize my car. It was only an old VW but it was mine, a lovely motor, so reliable. I had to leave it parked on the road because we had no drive. It was damaged, paintwork scratched, tyres slashed, aerial snapped. I knew it was Tony ... the boyfriend. Anyway my dad, he mentioned it to Bernie Truro. I don't know the ins and outs but understand that Bernie had a word with Two Tone and they agreed to take care of it because what Tony was doing was bang out of order, and like I said, it was against the rules to call the police, the estate takes care of things like that. Things like that are settled with a cat-fight or a punch-up but Two Tone said he'd need some more muscle because Tony was seriously fit, into bodybuilding with steroids, so Two Tone had a guy he worked for, fella called Halverson—'

'Halverson?' Ventnor wrote the name in his notebook.

'That's the name I recall, an unusual name so I remember it, sort of Scandinavian sounding. He also had to clear the action with Halverson because Two Tone was on Halverson's books or something. It sounded like this fella Halverson owned "Two Tone" Bowler.'

'Owned?'

'In a criminal sense. I thought it meant that Two Tone couldn't work freelance ... that's what I assumed. Anyway, that was my problem over and Tony even now walks with a limp and still suffers from double vision, from time to time anyway. Suppose they gave him the excuse he needed for long-term unemployment.'

'Halverson, you say?' repeated Ventnor.

The young woman was ashen-faced under long lemon-coloured hair. She held the door wide open for Yellich and Webster, allowing them to enter the house. 'You'll be the boys in blue?' She spoke with a Southern accent.

201

'We'll be the boys in blue–' Yellich stepped over the threshold – 'except we'll be the plain-clothed variety.'

The woman stepped to one side. She was slender, Yellich noted, as did Webster, and looked attractive, they thought, in a green tee shirt and faded, threadbare, figure-hugging blue jeans. She was barefoot and revealed toenails painted in a loud scarlet nail polish.

Yellich and Webster entered the house, which smelled sweetly of rose-scented air freshener as if recently sprayed in anticipation of the officers' visit. The young woman ushered them, in a gentle, feminine manner, into the front room of the small terraced house and which was clearly the "lounge" or "best room", neatly kept with a three-piece suite and a modest television set on a table in the corner of the room furthest from the window.

'Please.' The woman indicated the chair and settee. Yellich sat in the armchair closest to the window. Webster chose the settee. The woman gracefully folded herself into a cross-legged position on the floor in front of the television set.

Yellich took out his notepad. 'How do you wish to be addressed? I mean, we were advised that you were not married to Mr Halverson junior?'

'No,' she said, as if with some relief, as if

she had survived a close shave. 'My name is Nash, Janet Nash. I'll be going back to that name now.'

'Miss Nash? Alright.' Yellich wrote on his pad. 'You don't seem upset?'

'Probably because I am not upset, probably because I feel suddenly very free of something. Probably because I didn't realize how trapped I was until I was liberated.' There was an angry sounding edge to her voice. 'I had always thought that when someone is bereaved they are supposed to feel surrounded by darkness, but me ... me ... I kid you not, me old flower, I feel surrounded by white light. A weight has been lifted from my shoulders. A really, really stressed-out feeling has gone from inside my head and all because of a single phone call. I still feel a bit numb, still a bit shocked, but for me the news is good, not bad.'

'Not a happy relationship?'

She shook her head. 'One big, bad, stupid, stupid mistake. You know once not too long ago, when I was fifteen and beginning to go out with boys, my father and I had a talk. We never did talk much but that wet Sunday afternoon we did and he said ... he asked, "Is money important to you, Janet? Is it important to you that a man is rich" So I said "yes" 'cos it was. I mean, who wants to scratch pennies all their days? And my dad, you know, he said that was the correct answer, which surprised me a bit. Then he explained that a man has to provide for his own, so he has to have money. He needs an income, to do that, a good income and then my dad, he said but the thing is ... the issue is ... how is that money earned? That's the question. There is moral money and immoral money. Then he asked me if I would prefer to be the wife of the headmaster of a primary school who earns enough to keep his family's head above water or would I prefer to be dripping with wealth and consumer goodies as the wife of a second-hand car dealer? So I said, of the two I'd go for the primary school headmaster and that reply pleased my dad, and then what do I do five years later but become the common-law bit of a second-hand car dealer? I mean, love a duck–' she looked up at the ceiling in an exasperated manner – 'and as if that wasn't enough, he was only one of the Halverson team, wasn't he? I mean that is one tribe of crooks and wide boys and all-time blaggers and once their tentacles are around you, once their old hooks are in you, they don't let go.'

'Oh?'

'Yeah. Roger told me what to expect if I ever left him, and his father was there when he laid down the law, looking at me, nodding his head and later that day his mother took me on one side and said, "Don't annoy them dear, it's best not to do that. I have learned that's the best way".' Janet Nash fell silent and pondered the deep-pile carpet of deep blue. 'So I am just so pleased that I have the chance to get out of here, to get out of this house, out of that family and out of York and get my tail home. London.' She spoke the name of the city with a clear mixture of longing and affection, of hunger and passion.

'Yes, I didn't think you were Yorkshire.'

'Oh, it shows does it?' She smiled and spoke with an exaggerated London accent. 'Lavender 'ill, darlin', Clapham, SW11, we live just off Lavender Hill. Just want to see the red buses and black taxis, go into a pub for a pint of London beer, a pint of IPA, read the *Evening Standard*, go up the West End for a bit of a laugh, listen to Radio London, hear the accents, walk over Chelsea Bridge and look at the Old Father gliding by underneath with the boats on it. I just want to go home now, that's all I want to do, put all this behind me. You know, I am the first one of my family to venture north of Potters Bar and I mean that includes grandparents and cousins as well as parents and both my big sisters ... and what a mistake. I feel really sorry for those people trapped in foreign gaols. I mean if this is what it's like living two hundred miles north of "the Smoke", what must it be like doing years of bird in the

Bangkok Hilton? Ugh–' Janet Nash shuddered – 'just think of all that bird ... years and years and years.'

'So how long have you known Roger Halverson junior?' Yellich was pleased for Janet Nash that she was soon to be returning home but the interview had to be focused.

'Three years. He was so charming at first, he made me feel special, but when I brought him home for the first time and introduced him to my family it felt so wrong. It felt like I should not have brought this person into this house and as we left the house to drive north a few days later, the look my mum gave me, the fear and pity in her eyes. Then we drove up the A1 in his Porsche ... but now I'm going home, up in a black rocket, down in a bus, but that's no problem so long as it's heading south. I'll stay for the funeral, I'll have to do that. Mr Halverson said he was shot, was Roger—?'

'Yes, he was. Would you know anything about it?' Yellich thought the question was a bit of a gamble. The impression he had rapidly gained was that Janet Nash had been kept well separate from the Halversons' affairs.

'Who would?' She shook her head, covering her face with her lemon-coloured hair as she did so. 'No. No, I don't, sorry ... and that's the truth. I was kept well out of it, all the time, the little woman to come home to.

I was kept captive here, no money, none at all. He bought everything, food, everything, but I can imagine plenty of people would want to chill him. He was a nasty piece of work. Always so smartly dressed but eyes as cold as the old North Sea on a winter's night. Cor blimey, how could I? He had a garage full of shiny second-hand motors but it was a front for something. He was the only used-car merchant I ever knew that didn't move the metal, as they say. Got to be seen to move the metal. I knew a few dealers in the trade before, you see, so when he put me on display in the front seat of his car once and stopped off at his business I checked the metal on the forecourt, then saw the forecourt again a few weeks later.'

'Same cars?'

'Yes. I mean, nothing had moved. Nothing. But he still had fists full of hard cash to throw around. I mean it didn't take no rocket scientist – it doesn't take no old Philadelphia lawyer.' Janet Nash ran her slender fingers through the carpet pile. 'His dad is called the "Field Marshall",' she added.

'But you were not part of that?' Yellich probed gently.

'No.' Again a vigorous, face-covering by long hair shake of the head. 'Not allowed, was I? And that was something else his old mum once said to me, she said, "Just keep your home neat and shipshape. They like

207

things just right ... and keep him satisfied and don't ask no questions, 'cos then you'll get told no lies ... I've heard that." So I didn't ask no questions and I didn't get told no lies.'

'We don't know the Halversons, not really, a few petty offences. They sound bigger than that.'

Janet Nash threw him a despairing glance. 'Well, don't hardly surprise me that don't. The really clever blaggers never see the inside of a police station, never mind the slammer. I'd like to have seen Roger Halverson do a ten stretch. A bullet is too quick, a bit too much like his life, quick, clean and painless.'

'So how many are there?'

'Two ... well one now. Father and son each like clones of each other, all charm masking viciousness, real smile-as-you-kill merchants – and then there was one ... that's nice ... one down.'

'They murder?'

'Well–' Janet Nash shrugged – 'wouldn't know, would I? Remember, me job, keep the home clean and him satisfied and don't ask no questions. So I'm the last brainless bird to know about anything as heavy as murder. So far as I was led to believe, Roger Halverson was a second-hand car dealer, but I'm not such a dumb blonde – blonde maybe – but my teachers at school said I had it in me to go to university ... if only...'

'Not too late for that,' Yellich said, smiling.

'No?' Janet Nash glanced hopefully at him. 'I'm twenty-two; I thought you had to be eighteen.'

'No hard and fast rules at all. Folk better themselves by starting university when they are a lot older than twenty-two, believe me.'

'They do?'

'I assure you.'

'Well maybe. When I get home.'

'Yes, make some enquiries, sounds like you deserve a fresh start ... but back to the Halversons?'

'Yes ... well, don't know what they did but so far as I picked up, their family motto was, "If there's money in it, and you can get away with it, then do it."'

'So where is Mr ... your partner's—'

'Late partner.'

'Yes, his business premises, where are they?'

'Out on Shipley Road, Clifton area, "Shaw's Used Cars".'

'Shaw?'

'It's a name they use. I think they just plucked it out of thin air. They use the same name for all their business, Shaw's this ... Shaw's that. Shaw's Hotel which they pack full of homeless people for which the city pays, that's one of theirs. It keeps their real name out of the public eye and that's how they like it.'

'I see.' Yellich wrote Shaw's in his notebook. 'Is there anything of his in this house, that is, anything relating to his business?'

'Here?' Janet Nash laughed. 'Where I could read it? Not a chance. I mean–' she extended an open palm – 'do look round, you don't need a warrant but you'll be on a hiding to nothing. No, he kept business and home as separate as separate can be. He learned that from his old man. I have picked up a few things in three years of marriage in all but name.'

'Well, perhaps we might come back at a later date if we have something specific to look for.'

'Well, I'll be here for the funeral, then I'm off south. I'll post the keys of the house to his old man, the house is his anyway, it didn't belong to Roger junior. I am going to phone home and ask my mum and dad to send me some money. There's nothing left in the fridge and I'll have to ask them to send me the bus fare but all I've got is what I stand up in after living in a comfortable home with a man who drives a Porsche. I'm going to walk home.'

'To London!'

'No, silly–' Janet Nash smiled – 'I mean from Victoria Bus Station to Clapham. Take me about ... dunno ... couple of hours if I take it steady, which I will, savouring every step. I'll phone home later today, when my dad gets back home. Have to reverse the charges from the call box at the end of the street. The phone here has a lock on it. I can answer but I can't phone out. I mean control freak is just not the expression for R.H. junior. Anyway, I'll wait until my dad gets home. He works for London Transport, just normal office hours though; he'll be home at just gone six. Be nice to hear his voice ... love my daddy.'

'Not bad.' Carmen Pharoah stirred her tea and replied to Yellich's enquiry. 'Not a bad day at all, went to a couple of pubs, a primary school ... led to an iffy sounding character called Halverson.'

'Halverson?' Yellich echoed. 'Halverson did you say?'

'Yes.' Carmen Pharoah nodded. 'Why, is that significant, sarge?'

'Could be–' Yellich glanced at Webster, who had also responded to the surname – 'could very well be, something Mr Hennessey ought to hear about anyway.'

Reginald Webster drove home favouring, as he always did, the quieter B1222 and B1223 route through Cawood rather than the more hectic A19 York to Selby Road. He drove slowly through the housing estate and halted in front of a neatly kept post-war three-bedroom semi-detached house. He sounded the horn twice. Strictly speaking it was a traffic offence to do so, but he believed extenuating circumstances allowed it and doubted that any of his good neighbours would complain. As he left his car, the door of the house opened and a long-haired Alsatian bounded out to meet him to be greeted warmly. He approached the door as a young woman stood on the threshold wearing a long summer skirt in white cotton and a blue blouse. She extended her arms as he approached and, finding him by touch, embraced him. Later that evening they sat down together for a salad that Joyce Webster had prepared for her husband, being the only meal that he would permit her to prepare. She had repeatedly pleaded to be allowed to prepare hot foot but Reginald Webster was adamant: it was too dangerous. In the cold months he prepared the food, but in the summer, she prepared salads.

Still later that evening, as dusk settled over yet another brief shower of rain, Webster took Terry for his evening walk, allowing the working dog a period "off duty" to wander at will, exploring moist and sweetly smelling woodland near his home, and as he watched the dog move lightly, yet majestically among the trees, he again wondered at his wife's courage ... studying fine art at Edinburgh when she was involved in a car crash at the age of twenty and she alone was the only occupant to survive the accident, but at the expense of losing her sight and despite that, considering herself lucky and displaying such enthusiasm for life, such courage, such resilience, such virtues that he doubted he would be able to muster. Reginald Webster felt more than all-enveloping love for his wife; he felt awe, respect, honour, admiration and considered himself the most fortunate man in all England.

It was Wednesday, 21.40 hours.

213

Six

Thursday, 30th June,
09.32 hours – 23.42 hours

*In which the kind reader is privy to George
Hennessey's demons, and is later at home with
the Yellichs, and in which further information is
obtained.*

George Hennessey had awakened that morning as the sun rose amid a shower of clean-
looking rain which fell gently, lazily even, he
thought, more in the manner of a very light,
refreshing drizzle than a hard, driving winter
rain. He felt refreshed and fully satisfied
after a full eight hours of solid sleep. He
turned away from the window and lay on his
back with his hands clasped behind his head
and focused on a small stationary spider on
the ceiling who, upon further study, revealed
itself to be a blemish in the plaster. As he
surfaced fully into wakefulness his thoughts
turned to the previous evening and he
recalled those few hours fondly.

He had returned home shortly after the

rush hour had died its usual peaceful death and saw, as he approached his home on the Thirsk Road, a silver BMW had been parked half on and half off the grass verge outside it. His heart leapt at the sight and his chest had swelled with pride as he turned his car into the driveway. The tyres on his car had crunched the gravel and the sound, as usual, had caused a dog to bark excitedly within the house. As if triggered by the barking of the dog, the front door of the house had opened to allow the small brown mongrel to run out of the house and leap up at Hennessey with an excited tail-wagging dance. The person who had opened the door was a smartly dressed man in his thirties who stood upon the threshold, smiling. He had waved one hand in greeting; the other holding a mug of hot liquid, tea most likely, had assumed Hennessey, knowing his son's penchant for the fluid and his equally strong dislike for coffee. George Hennessey had left his car and greeted dog and man, in that order, but with equal warmth.

Later, a fresh pot of tea infused, father and son had taken a seat in the wooden chairs that had been a long time placed upon the patio at the rear of the house as the sun was still high in the sky, and Oscar criss-crossed the lawn, having picked up a rain released scent which clearly interested him.

'Where are you this week?' Hennessey

senior had asked, noticing a cloud edging up from the south-east, threatening yet more rain, though it was still a long way off and moving slowly.

'Bradford,' Hennessey junior had replied softly and as if with some distaste, or so had thought his father.

'Problems?'

'I'm defending a felon who is a long-term criminal, a career criminal, who is insisting on going NG despite overwhelming evidence. I mean, talk about same old, same old ... I mean, "I definitely didn't do it, not me, not me at all."' Charles Hennessey had sighed. 'What can you do? We have to act upon instruction. This bloke, I can't fathom him, I can't fathom him at all, the attitude, continued denial despite contrary evidence is something you expect of teenage defendants. After a while they learn to put their hands up to reduce sentence but this man, he's fifty-seven years old and he's genuinely frightened of going back inside but what does he do but insist on making it worse for himself. You know an admission of guilt and he might even avoid custody. I could plead for probation and a fine ... a community service order, I like them.'

'So do I, offenders feel them but it avoids prison and they put back into society ... two hundred hours community work at six hours a week tidying up the gardens in the old people's homes. They feel that and it's better than prison, better for them and better for us.' Hennessey watched Oscar as he went through the narrow gateway set in the privet hedge which ran widthways across the rear garden, dividing the lawn from the orchard beyond.

'But this fella, he could swing non-custody because he's up before Judge Walsingham – the merry old soul – not known for harsh sentencing to put it mildly, but will my man be persuaded? And I don't think he's insane either, it's as though when he's confronted with his guilt he switches into a state of denial and eventually believes it himself. The Crown's evidence is overwhelming; fingerprints everywhere, loot found in his flat. Well, he'll be inside for a Christmas or two.'

'Sounds as though he learned the wrong lesson early in life,' George Hennessey growled.

'Well, he's that sort, learns only what he wants to learn and listens only to what he wants to listen to. So, what are you doing?'

'We have two major cases running parallel,' Hennessey had replied, continuing to keep a cautious eye on the seemingly stationary rain cloud. 'We've been stretched, just one would tie up all our resources but two together ... other investigations just have to go on hold.' He had then commenced to relate to his learned son who had taken silk impressively early in his career at the Bar, the state of play in respect of the twenty-year-old murder of Oliver Hill and the more recent murder of Roger Halverson.

'Well, as you said yourself, many times,' Charles Hennessey had replied, 'you might not get paid much but you see life.'

'Aye,' George Hennessey had said with a smile. 'That was said to me when I was a young copper and it has turned out to be oh so true. So, when do I see my grandchildren again?'

'Ah–' Charles Hennessey had raised an admonishing finger – 'the answer to that is, whenever we meet your new lady friend. I mean, fair is fair.'

'Oh–' Hennessey had laughed softly – 'you can't hold that over me.'

'We can and we have decided to do so.' Charles Hennessey had also laughed softly. 'So we had better make some arrangements, you and I.'

'Alright–' Hennessey drained his mug of tea – 'soon ... soon. Shall we have another mug of tea, there's plenty in the pot?'

'Well make it an early meeting because they are clamouring for another visit to Granddad's. Mind you, I confess I think it's the ice creams and we'll-do-whatever-you-want-to-do sort of day in York or at the coast they really look forward to, so be advised.'

'Spoil them rotten then give them back. It's

lovely being a granddad,' George Hennessey had said warmly.

When the fresh mugs of tea were being sipped Charles Hennessey had said, 'Couldn't have been easy for you, Dad.'

'It wasn't but Mrs Welland helped, couldn't have got through without her.'

'Yes, but it's not the same as a wife ... and mother to me. She was a lovely woman but it wasn't the same, for either of us. Only now do I realize.'

'Do you remember Jennifer?'

'Fleetingly, just one or two very fleeting memories of someone I knew was special in some way and who suddenly wasn't there anymore. I remember being on her lap looking up at her and thinking there was something special about this person but I didn't know what. My continuous memory starts from about four years of age but I have small islands of memory before that, so yes, I do remember mummy.'

'That's interesting.' Hennessey turned to his son. 'I mean, that you recall her not being there ... suddenly so.'

'Oh yes, a summer's day, a sense that something unusual had happened, I picked that up, I sensed that at an early age. Infants are very sensitive to things like that.'

'Yes, so I was told. You were just three months old and your Aunt Jean, she came up to the house from London and said "He –"

that is you – "he will realize something has happened." But she's still here; I know she's still here. I scattered her ashes in the garden, as you know, and then spent the next few years remodelling the garden to her design. The last thing she did in life pretty much was to sit down one evening and design the garden, even down to the frog pond beyond the orchard. When we moved in this out here–' Hennessey nodded to the garden – 'this looked like a tennis court or a football pitch, just a flat expanse of grass.'

'Yes, so you have said, quite a lady, a woman with vision.'

'Yes ... and I know she's here. I talk to her each evening, tell her about my day. I told her about the new lady in my life one evening, last summer, and I tell you Charles, I was surrounded by a warmth which came not from the setting sun. I was facing the sun but I felt the warmth on my back, all over, like I was being embraced by her. She is happy for me.'

'As I am, father,' Charles Hennessey had replied. 'You've been by yourself long enough.'

Later that evening, after Charles had departed, Hennessey returned to the patio and did then tell his late wife of his day, of the two cases, of the body in the bed and the report of a murder some twenty years previously. Later still, after a wholesome casserole, he sat and read an account of the Battle of Inkerman, selected at random from his library of military history, as his supper settled. Yet later still, he fed Oscar and then man and dog took their customary walk, a fifteen-minute walk out to a field and woodland where Hennessey allowed Oscar off the lead for thirty minutes before returning home. Finally he had rounded off his day, again in customary fashion, by strolling into Easingwold for a pint of brown and mild at the Dove Inn, just one before last orders were called. Homeward bound he had caught a glimpse of the Plough between a gap in the clouds and again noted with some sadness that one of the seven stars had begun to flicker: it was dying.

The following morning, after a refreshing shower and a light but healthy breakfast of muesli and tea, and after ensuring the dog flap was fully operational, thus allowing Oscar access to the fenced-off rear garden in his day-long absence, Hennessey drove into York. At nine thirty he was at his desk. By nine thirty-two his team had assembled and sat in his office. He listened to the feedback from Yellich and Webster and then from Pharoah and Ventnor. 'Halverson?' he said, reclining back in his chair. 'Halverson times two. How interesting.'

'Appears so, sir.' Yellich sipped his tea.

'It's too much of a coincidence.' Hennessey turned to his left and glanced out of his office window as rain fell, once again, but this time vertically, as if with a vengeance, out of a near clear-blue summer sky. 'Unusual, not many Halversons in the Vale of York, I'll be bound.' He reached for the telephone directory and opened it. 'You know, I once asked a phone company official how large the phone book would be if all ex-directory numbers were listed. You know what he said?'

'Twice as large?' Yellich offered.

'Three times,' was Carmen Pharoah's guess.

'I'd say four,' Webster replied.

'Four also,' Ventnor coughed, still bleary-eyed, his breath, Hennessey noted was again smelling strongly of peppermint.

'Well DC Pharoah would be right; this would be three times thicker if the unlisted numbers were listed.' He ran his finger down the Ha's. 'In other words, only one in four subscribers allow their number to be listed and at this moment in time, none of them is a Halverson. The nearest is a few listings for Halton, then it goes to the Ham's – Mr and Mrs E Hambe – so no Halverson. So that does indicate the unusualness of the name, in these parts anyway, probably not so much in Scandinavia, but in the Vale, not many Halversons, so it's not a coincidence.'

'It does sound Scandinavian doesn't it,

sir?' Yellich offered. 'To go along with the legacy the Vikings left behind, those blonde-haired, blue-eyed people who live in these parts, few, but significant, in terms of number, and place names like Thorpe and Foss ... all left behind by the Vikings.'

'Yes,' Hennessey replied drily. 'So, Two Tone and his crew were hired by a man yclept Halverson and the body in the bed is also yclept Halverson. I feel for the householders, their house flooded, then used as a depository for a corpse and then burgled. Things come in threes alright. I think that house will soon be on the market. I confess I couldn't settle back into that house.'

'Nor I,' Yellich murmured. 'After that level of violence, that house is no longer a home again, it's back to being just a collection of bricks and timber. And moving house is difficult at times. Bereavement, divorce and house move ... the three most stressful things that can be experienced and that elderly couple are going to experience one. It's so often the case that felons never seem to appreciate the far-reaching effects of their crimes.'

'Yes, but we are satisfied that the house was chosen at random. Can we move on from there?'

Yellich and Webster glanced at each other and nodded.

'Completely at random, sir,' Yellich answered for both. 'I think the householders are victims, very safe to say.'

'Right, this is interesting, so the two inquiries have become merged, probably not a complete overlap but some merging and the link is the name Halverson. So, we have to cross-refer the files to each other, you see to that please, Yellich.'

'Yes, boss.'

'And Halverson junior is known to us, I believe?'

'Yes, skipper,' Yellich replied, 'petty stuff ... drink driving, receiving stolen goods.'

'Interesting, don't you think?' Hennessey smiled knowingly.

'How so, boss?'

'Well, in my experience receiving is a crime associated by felons who don't want to get their fingers dirty, the sort of felon who is busy behind the scene of the crime establishing alibis but pulling the strings of the other felons ... the coalface workers. How old was he when he was done for receiving?'

'Early twenties, sir, though he was only twenty-five when he was killed.'

'Yes, but the point is that he was already moving away from hands-on crime to hands-off crime. He was part of crime management, supervision of crime, and very early on, and if his father is a felon, so far unknown to us ... you get a bad feeling about him, I believe.'

'Yes, sir,' Yellich replied, 'quite an uncomfortable feeling.'

'We both felt it surprising that we didn't already know him when we called. He was ... is ... wealthy but with no visible means of support, no Halverson in the Yellow Pages so no business by that name, though possibly they use Shaw as an alias. We'll check that out but whatever his income is, he wasn't working midday, midweek when we called,' Webster added. 'And he was also wary and hostile towards the police.'

'And remarkably restrained when we told him about his son,' Yellich offered. 'A hard man, emotionally speaking. It was as though he had leapfrogged grief and shock in an instant and was already thinking revenge and retribution.'

'Frightening.' Hennessey leaned back in his chair. 'Tell me about his home. What did you read there?'

'Neat, obsessively so, even the garden didn't look as though it had a blade of grass out of shape. Inside the house was the same, neat, neat like it had been prepared for a photo shoot. Very materialistic, no books anywhere, nor plants. It was just as I said about what that elderly couple's house had become; it was a house but not a home.'

'He was, is, a very controlling person, sir,' Webster offered. 'He was the king of all he surveyed, that's what it felt like.' He turned to Yellich.

'I thought the same too, sir, very serious-minded, humourless individual ... he's got his victims alright.'

'Age? Best guess?' Hennessey pressed.

Again Yellich and Webster glanced at each other. 'Younger than you might think. I'd say mid-forties.'

'Yes,' Webster agreed, 'very fit-looking, casually dressed, that might have hidden a few years. It's remarkable how many years a pair of jeans can take off a sixty year old if he still has the figure for them. But I'd go along with Sergeant Yellich, a man in his forties ... mid to late.'

'So he was still only in his twenties when he was putting out a contract on Oliver Hill. It's remarkable that we don't know him.'

'It is the observation, sir–' Yellich drained his mug of tea and cradled it in his hands – 'that the clever criminals, really clever ones, never see the inside of a police station, let alone a prison, but we might know him as Shaw. It's difficult to see him getting so far in the underworld without doing time inside, a stretch is a necessary right of passage, it seems.'

'But not always. Tell me, any sign of Mrs Halverson?'

'None, sir, none at all.' Yellich's voice trailed off as he realized where Hennessey was going. 'The house was spick and span yet

Halverson did not seem to be the sort of man who'd pull on a pair of washing-up gloves or get the vacuum cleaner out or spray dust polish about. He just didn't seem the type to take kindly to housework ... not at all.'

'So he has a housekeeper or similar?' Hennessey raised his eyebrows. 'Can we assume that?'

'Yes, I think so, sir, and a gardener as well. Just can't see him weeding his garden. Expecting it to be perfect, yes, but he wouldn't kneel down and get soil on his hands, just can't see it.'

'Me neither,' Webster said, 'me neither.'

'Er–' Carmen Pharoah leaned forward – 'excuse me, this may just be stereotypical woman's thinking...'

'Go on.' Hennessey smiled at her. 'It all goes in the pot; it is all kept within these four walls. Only when it goes to the Crown Prosecution Service does it have to be right and proper but in here, anything can be said. It was because of free discussion that we found we had a commonality of the Halverson name in respect of both cases, so ... do say what you wish.'

'Thank you, sir. Well, it occurs to me that a man who is of the type that is being described and who lives in a village, who is not married and is as defensive and secretive as he's been described, then he would not want

Mrs Woman who lives a few streets away to come and "do" for him and take the gossip about him to the Post Office and the pub.'

'Go on.' Hennessey opened his right palm. 'This sounds quite interesting.'

'Well, I would think a person like Halverson would employ contract cleaners, who would be female. There are a few such firms; you see their vans driving about the city and the Vale.'

'Are you volunteering to go undercover?'

'Yes, sir, I am. I might be one of the few Afro-Caribbean women in York and the Vale, and I am certainly the only black female officer but Halverson doesn't know me. I'd recognize his description if we knew each other. So, I could go into his house as a cleaner, I could purloin ... no, borrow an item from the house which has his prints on it.'

'Dangerous and we couldn't use any prints obtained that way in any case we might build.'

'No, we couldn't but at least we'll know if we know him by another name. We could just take the item out of the house if the SOCO boys could be there, in the road ... lift the print ... and I could replace the item.'

Yellich drew breath between his teeth. 'It's a bit iffy, sir. There'd have to be backup close at hand and he could use it against us.'

'He may well be out of the house.' Carmen

Pharoah spoke enthusiastically. 'A lot of contract cleaners have keys to access clients' houses. They visit when their client is out.'

'Doubt the Commander will like it but yes, do it.'

'Yes, sir.'

'But make sure you have backup just in case.'

'Yes, sir.'

'Take Ventnor and a couple of uniforms, but tell the uniforms to park out of sight.'

'Understood, sir.'

'Alright, Yellich and Webster.'

'Sir?'

'I want you two to pay a call on Shaw's Motors, see what you see, see what you can find out. Then pick up Pharoah and Ventnor's leads on "Two Tone" Bowler and his team. Push them for any information on Halverson. You'll probably only get what he was like twenty years ago, but it's a start.

'So, well done, Pharoah for finding the Two Tone Boys, but I think it will need some heavy male pressure from now on in. But well done ... you as well Ventnor. So, Halverson has a rank odour about him. We'll review at this time tomorrow.'

'Foxes me.' The man was late middle age, possibly more, thought Yellich, possibly above retiring age yet still choosing to work. His office was a small wooden garden shed which stood not on the edge of a well-tended lawn but on a spread of tarmac which glistened in the sun after the recent rainfall. Puddles seemed to be evaporating rapidly. 'Foxes me like this weather foxes me, I've been hopping inside and outside my little hut all summer. It's got to be the wettest summer I can remember and I can remember a lot of summers. Soon be autumn, I feel cheated out of a summer this year.'

'Yes.' Yellich smiled and looked about him. The site of the business was a built-up area on the cusp of the city centre and the suburbs. Yellich thought that Shaw's Quality Used Cars did not blend with the tall Georgian townhouses on either side of the plot, or the Victorian buildings behind the Georgian terrace, or with the early-twentieth-century development on the opposite side of the road.

'Well, it don't bother me,' the elderly man continued, 'I get paid in cash to sit here in the hut and read the paper or my books or just to sit and watch the world go by. It's extra money for me, a lot extra, and it gets me out of the house. My wife, you see, she didn't take kindly to my retirement. I mean, I provided for her the best part of forty years and I got my gold watch, a company pension as well as the State pension and all she does is nip my head about being under her feet all the time. She just got used to having the house to herself all day every day, except weekends and even then I was out most of the Saturdays and the Sundays too. So I took this old job, it gives me peace. I am doing a ton of reading, westerns mostly. I like a good western: men are men and the women are women; the good are the good and the bad are the bad. It's all so crystal clear, not like this.' He pointed to the vista in front of him. 'Not like life, that's always so complicated.'

'So, tell us about Mr Halverson.'

'Not a lot to tell.' The man, short and slight of build, wiped perspiration from his bald head and replaced the light golf cap. 'No fun being bald—' he grinned – 'you always have to wear a hat. There's only about three days of the year when I can go out without a hat, and that is a luxury. In the winter my head freezes, I mean the cold gets into the bone, right inside your skull and in the summer you get sunburn on your scalp, no more worse place, no more uncomfortable a place to get sunburn. That is really sore, I mean very sore.'

'Mr Halverson?'

'Ah, yes ... well I don't see him too often, he comes to swap the cars round, drives one away and returns with another. Just moving the metal you see, but that's not what moving the metal means. I spent most of my life in the motor trade and moving the metal means—'

231

'Selling,' Webster said. 'It means the same in all trade, to "move" the goods is to sell them.'

'Yes.' The man nodded and smiled. 'Yes, that's what it means but Halverson just swops the cars around to give the impression he's selling them, but he's not. Nothing is ever sold. I mean hardly ever. It looks like he's doing business but he's not. Don't know what his game is but he's not selling cars. Up to no good I reckon.'

'You think?'

The man waited until a white York Rider bus whined past and then said, 'Well what is the explanation? He hasn't sold a car in three months but he drives a Porsche, not just a Porsche but a 911 Turbo, and has a classy-looking girlfriend.'

'Really? The girl I mean.'

'Oh, yes, she sets off the Porsche a treat, sitting there looking like a fashion model, dripping with rings and jewels, long blonde hair...'

'So what happens if someone wants to buy a car?'

'Never happens. Look at these prices. Not one of these cars is worth half the asking price, it's like he doesn't want to sell, it's a barrier to marketing but every week they get swapped round.'

'What happens to the cars?'

'I think he buys them cheaply at the motor

auctions, keeps them for a couple of months or so, then sells them back through the auction to get rid of them and returns with another set of cars and puts them on sale for such ridiculous prices that any customer is deterred.'

'Are you happy with that?'

The man shrugged. 'Me, I don't ask questions. I get paid to sit in a wooden hut to read my books and to get out of the wife's way. Other than that, what goes on here is nothing to do with me.'

'So what does he do all the rest of the time?' Yellich asked.

'Haven't a clue, no paperwork here, that's all somewhere else.'

'Do you know his girlfriend's name?'

'Nope.'

'It's alright,' Yellich growled, 'we do. Ever see him with anybody else apart from his lady friend?'

'No ... never. So what shall I tell him when he comes round? I suppose you want me to keep quiet?'

'You won't see him again. He's been murdered.'

The man's jaw dropped. 'But I haven't been paid for two weeks. He owes me money...'

'We can't help you there.' Yellich turned to go. 'If I were you, I'd cut your losses. Go home and sit in an armchair and read your books and tell your wife she's got some adjusting to do and that your income will only be your pensions from now on.'

In the car, with Yellich at the wheel, Webster said, 'Two Tone?'

'I think so,' Yellich answered, '"Two Tone" Bowler.'

'Don't like it, George.' Commander Sharkey reclined in his chair. 'I don't like it at all and I think the top floor will like it even less.'

'Understood, sir, we knew the risks but I slipped her leash, she's off and running.'

Sharkey allowed himself a rare smile. 'Don't let me hear you say that, George.'

'No, sir, political correctness, but within these four walls, the hound is running.'

'Modern women are very touchy about things like that ... animal references, but the image is clear.'

'I know, sir. I have lived to see attitudes change.' George Hennessey looked round Sharkey's office. As always it was neat, neat, neat, everything in its place perfection. Behind Sharkey on the wall, two framed photographs had been hung, one showing Sharkey in the uniform of an officer in the British Army, the second showing him as an officer in the Royal Hong Kong Police, as was. Of the two photographs, Sharkey would say that he was proud of the first but not the second. The second, he would readily admit was a source of shame. It represented his brush with corruption. He would take bribes, he would admit, not to do something, not to provide information, not to destroy evidence but not to do something, usually not to patrol a certain area at a certain time and in recognition of his corruption then the following morning he would find a brown paper envelope full of money in his desk drawer.

'We are agreed that we can't use anything we find by removing it from the house without a warrant, and we have no grounds for a warrant,' Hennessey explained, 'but it might tell us who we are dealing with, especially since Halverson seems to be an also known as.'

'Yes, I think you are right, George, a little unorthodox as it may be but sometimes the rules have to be bent a little.' Sharkey, immaculately dressed, younger than Hennessey, paused and then asked, 'George, tell me ... I have nothing to worry about do I?' He turned and glanced at the photograph of himself when in the RHKP. 'Something rotten?'

'Nothing, sir, I am sure of it.'

'I hope so. I was never corrupt in the way that individual police officers in the UK have occasionally been corrupt in the past but I just ... well, you know what went on, I have told you. I was only there for a few weeks really. I saw what was going on and got out, unlike other officers who returned after ten years service with enough money to buy a house in north London or an Elizabethan manor house in one hundred acres of grounds.'

'Yes, sir.'

'But I was there, I am tainted. I couldn't cope with anything like that happening here.'

Hennessey stood. 'I can assure you, sir, you have nothing to fear. I can vouch for every officer in this building. Every one.'

The concrete pathway to the door of the house was rough, uneven and deeply pitted in places. The front garden was overgrown, as was the rear so far as Yellich and Webster could tell from the brief glimpse they obtained of it. A wooden ramp led up to the front door from the pathway and both door and ramp were of peeling brown paint. The house though, Yellich allowed, in fairness, blended well with its surroundings, being "the estate", served jointly by the rough Zetland Arms and the rougher Royal Sovereign, being tucked away behind the attractive Vale town of Driffield. Yellich stepped on to the ramp and extended his right arm and knocked on the door and did so using the classic police officer's knock, tap ... tap ... tap. The response was immediate, a female voice called from within the house. 'What?

What? Who is it?' The voice had an alarmed and a plaintive tone.

The door at the side of the house opened. 'What?' the voice said again, but this time was in the open, not calling through wood.

Yellich and Webster stepped to one side and glanced down the side of the house. A middle-aged woman with ruddy cheeks and a mop of black hair leaned out over the threshold. Her eyes seemed frightened, her face lined with worry. She had a full figure which was concealed in a pink dress which hung shapelessly about her, sacklike. Her nylons were rolled down about her ankles; her feet were encased in faded-blue carpet slippers. She looked away from the officers as she spoke, not attempting eye contact, rather, it seemed to Yellich and Webster, she did her best to avoid it altogether.

'Police.' Yellich showed her his ID.

'Never had a problem with the law for years,' she said, as if addressing her neighbours' dustbin. 'Not for years.'

'Is this the home of Mr Bowler?' Yellich began to walk down the path at the side of the house, towards the woman.

'Also known as Two Tone?' Webster added. '"Two Tone" Bowler?'

'Never heard that name for a while, but, yes. He's not Two Tone anymore ... he's not anything anymore.' She continued to address her neighbours' house, but had at least moved from the dustbin and was now considering the roof.

'Anything?'

'He's got no hair at all now, bald as a snooker ball.'

'Is he at home?'

'Aye.'

A pause.

'Well can we talk to him?'

'Aye.' She stepped backwards, moving her body with some effort, so it seemed to the officers, moving much weight with little strength with which to do so; 'front room,' she said as she moved deeper into the small kitchen to allow Yellich and Webster to enter the house and turn to their right, entering the dimly-lit hallway. Yellich walked into the hallway and then into a similarly gloomy and musty-smelling room. He found breathing difficult and yearned for a window to be opened. His feet stuck to the carpet as his eyes adjusted to the shadows, caused largely by a flickering gas fire and the curtains being almost totally closed, which plunged the room into darkness. A man sat in a chair facing the television that was showing racing from a greener and sunnier part of England. He cradled two aluminium sticks by his side. He too was overweight so far as Yellich could make out and, as his wife had said, completely bald. No longer 'two-toned'.

'Mr Bowler?'

'Aye.'

'Roger Bowler?'

'Aye.'

'Police.'

'Aye, I heard you tell the missus.'

'DS Yellich, and this is DC Webster.'

'Aye, and the wife is right, we've not had police at the door for a good few years.'

'Are you ... were you also known as Two Tone?'

'Aye–' the man ran his fingers over his head – 'that also is a good few years back now.' The man coughed deeply, causing his chest to heave. 'Not heard that name for a while, police ... Two Tone, this is like from a different lifetime.' Bowler grappled for a cigarette from a packet that he kept in his shirt breast pocket and then grappled with a blue disposable lighter with fleshy fingers until he had produced a flame. He lit the nail and inhaled deeply. 'The doctor says I have to stop this.' He withdrew the cigarette from his lips and held it in front of his face as if studying it. 'First it was the drink, now it's the smokes. I gave up the drink only because I couldn't hobble down to the Zetland Arms no more, not on these–' he tapped the aluminium crutches – 'though our lass brings me in a bottle now and again, but it's expensive so I usually sit here and smoke, but now I have to give these up too. He tells me I've got to eat healthy. Me and her, we don't eat

239

healthy, well we would if we earned the sort of money a doctor earns, but when you're on the dole, it's burgers and beans and an egg when we have a bit of cash but eggs is expensive. Take a seat.'

'No thanks.'

'Sensible.' He forced a smile which could just be made out in the gloom. 'I wouldn't sit down in the room if I could stand. Our lass, she's not one for housekeeping, never was. This house hasn't been cleaned in ... well, years. So how can I help you?'

'You sound very cooperative, Mr Bowler,' Yellich observed.

Bowler shrugged and drew heavily on the nail. 'Well it seemed that every time I fought the law, I took the second prize. Now look at me, middle-aged, on long-term sickness benefit, arthritis mainly, but get pneumonia a lot in the winter and rheumatics but it's the arthritis that scares me, it just gets worse. So now I have no money. Should have kept my nose clean, there's no future in being a crook, so I have an adjusted attitude to the law.'

'Good for you.'

'Better late than never but I can't see how I can help you. I've been out of the game a long time. Things happen on the estate but I'm not in the know anymore, whole new generation of bandits now. They see me as being past it, I get left alone. I got respect for what I used to be but I'm not in the know, not any more.'

'Halverson,' Yellich said softly.

Bowler froze. The name had a resonance with him.

'Who?'

'You heard. The name meant something to you. We saw it, your reaction, even in this light.'

'Eat a lot of carrots do you?'

'By the ton,' Webster growled. 'So, tell us about Roger Halverson.'

'What is there to tell?'

'A lot. We could ask the others in your gang. I am sure you remember them, "Titch" Riley, "Big Andy" Dagnall, "Little Andy" Barnes, "Mid" Davy Hartley, Walpole Moulton...'

'Well "Big Andy" Dagnall won't be saying much, not in this world anyway.'

'I see, same as Walpole Moulton then.'

'Walpole...' Bowler's voice trailed off as he glanced up at Yellich.

'Yep, earlier this week.'

'Wally ... Wally Moulton, he was a good lad.'

'So, Halverson...'

'So why should I know about Halverson?'

'Because you do, because you worked for him twenty years ago, you and your crew, hired thugs; you did the dirty work for him.' Yellich spoke coldly.

241

'Such as?'

'Such as murdering Oliver Hill,' Webster added, 'pushing him to his death off a bridge into a swollen river during the floods, floods like now except the water was cold. He wouldn't have lasted very long; he wouldn't have been able to swim at all, not after being punched in the stomach before you pushed him over.'

'How?'

'Ebenezer Moulton.'

'Ebby? The little lad?'

'Ebby the little lad. Except that now he's a grown man. He waited until his father died and was safely in the clay and then came and told us what he saw when he was seven years old. I mean, he walked from the funeral to the police station. We worked out that the man Ebby saw you push to his death was a guy called Hill, Oliver Hill.'

'After all this time.' Bowler pulled heavily on the cigarette.

'So you know what we are talking about?'

'I didn't say that.'

'As good as.' Webster peered into the haze of shadows and tobacco smoke.

'Not as good as, it meant nothing and I know my rights. There's no solicitor here.' Bowler paused. 'But yes, I knew Halverson and yes, we did a few jobs, a little bit of enforcing, a little debt collecting but I won't admit to anything in the form of a statement.

I tell you now, if you do interview under caution it will be "no comment" to every question but I will tell you that Halverson is a very bad lot. Don't mess with him unless you're mob-handed.'

'We'll bear that in mind but we'll be talking to others in your old crew. The first one to cough will be doing himself a favour.'

'You won't,' Bowler sneered, 'I ... we ... we're more afraid of Halverson than the police. No one will cough. Anyone coughs they get their throat slit.'

'You think?'

'I know.'

'We'll be calling on them anyway. We can offer protection.'

'Protection?'

'We can offer it,' Webster replied. 'So think about it.'

'Second point,' Yellich pressed, 'is that someone like Halverson will have enemies.'

'Yes?'

'So who'd want to do the dirty on Halverson?'

'Why? Has someone shafted him?'

'Probably.'

'By doing what?'

'Topping his son.'

Bowler whistled. 'There'll be blood in the Vale now. Halverson won't take that lying down; he'll be out for revenge.'

'So who would want to harm Halverson?'

'Purves. Try him.'

'Purves?'

'Daniel Purves. You'll know him. Same age as Halverson, same age as me, late forties. Those two, they've been enemies for years and Purves is just sick enough to kill Halverson's son to get at Halverson. How was his son murdered?'

'Shot .22 calibre. Close range. Double tap.'

Bowler nodded. 'That's Purves, his prints are all over that. It's just his style.'

'What's Halverson's game?'

'Anything that makes money. Twenty years ago it was heroin and cocaine, now it's likely to be people-smuggling. Big money in people-smuggling and light sentences.'

'Purves, Daniel.' Webster wrote in his notebook.

'Do think about what we said,' Yellich advised. 'There's a deal in it for the first one to tell us about the murder of Oliver Hill. I mean information that will lead to a conviction.'

Bowler shook his head. 'I tell you, no one will talk about that, not from my gang, but off the record I can tell you that Oliver Hill was working for Halverson, he was a desk jockey and Halverson thought he was skimming, so I seem to remember.'

'So Halverson hired you and your gang to murder him, for stealing from him?'

'No comment.'

* * *

Carmen Pharoah found the casually dressed Emily Shaddick to be a spirited if slightly annoying woman, middle-aged, slight, wiry, close-cropped hair. She drove the small Japanese-made van in which she and Carmen Pharoah sat in what Pharoah thought to be an irresponsibly dangerous manner: talking incessantly, looking sideways at Carmen Pharoah, only occasionally glancing at the road ahead and resting one foot on the accelerator and the other on the clutch. Very early on in the journey Carmen Pharoah had decided that whatever the outcome of the visit she would take the return trip with Ventnor who followed in an unmarked car at a discreet distance. Bloodshot, bleary-eyed he might be after another night of excessive drinking but he at least watched where he was going.

'I needed a name when I decided to do this and I used to live in Hull. Funny place is Hull, do you know it?'

'Not really.' Carmen Pharoah gripped the door handle tightly as Emily Shaddick took a bend at what Carmen Pharoah considered excessive speed.

'Well my boyfriend at the time was living with his mate in Leeds and I used to go over and see him and they'd say, "It's 'er from 'ull, what comes and does." I mean, as though I'd clean up after them ... I mean, as if, but then I got laid off from the bread factory and I was too young to retire and I've never been on the dole. So I used my redundancy pay to set up as a house cleaner, I also iron shirts. It's a real growth market, a lot of elderly people that can't dust and vacuum anymore, gardening is the same for the same reason, both good lines to be in with the UK's ageing population.' She paused as she overtook a slower moving vehicle. 'So I have bought this van and some equipment. Then I had the van liveried. There is a big firm called "Maids" and a small two-woman team called "Mrs Mop", so I called myself 'er that comes and does'. It's on the side of the van, big red letters on a white background.'

'I noticed.' Carmen Pharoah's knuckles were white.

'So there's only three of us in York, Maids, Mrs Mop and little me and yes, you are right, this guy wants contract cleaners, so one of us had to be the one. Is that why you phoned?'

'First on the list, alphabetically.' Carmen Pharoah closed her eyes as she thought Emily Shaddick was going to ram a parked car and opened them again when, as if by some miracle, the expected collision did not occur.

'Lucky to get me just as I was on my way out and not just on my way out but on my

246

way out to clean his home ... coincidence, otherwise you would have to wait another week. Only clean once a week you see.'

'Yes.' Carmen Pharoah gasped as the van hurtled round a blind corner.

'He's a sour old goat he is. If he finds out you're a cop he'll cancel my contract and then make things difficult for me.'

'Are you worried?'

'Naw, the Maids have already told me they'll subcontract work to me and I've got plenty of other customers. I'm not bothered about losing Halverson, pays well though, big house to clean. I've got no roots in York; I can always go back to Hull and start up there. Or Leeds or Sheffield. I have three daughters all up and away now, married or at university, so sod Halverson.'

Carmen Pharoah managed a smile but still clung on to the door handle, desperately so, still with whitened knuckles.

Emily Shaddick stopped the van with a vicious jab of the brakes outside Halverson's house and hopped nimbly out of the vehicle and walked up to the gate and pressed the bell. Carmen Pharoah followed on shaking legs and glanced back up the road as she did so to see Thompson Ventnor parking his car some two hundred yards away but in full view. He was guarding her, as a good colleague should.

There was no answer to the bell so Emily

Shaddick pressed it again and then produced a key. 'If he's not at home I can let myself in–' she smiled as she unlocked the gate – 'dare say that's useful for you but he's got nothing to hide. I have never seen anything that looks criminal, if I did I would have reported it, just a very neat house owned by a man who lives alone.' She walked through the opening gate with Carmen Pharoah in her wake, feeling conspicuous in the white tracksuit that was evidently the uniform of "'er that comes and does' and handed to her by Emily Shaddick from the supply she kept, 'to clothe,' she explained, 'the casuals I take on now and again'. Emily Shaddick opened the front door of the house with a flourish of keys and then called out, 'It's only me, Emily, the cleaner.' There was no response and Emily Shaddick, for some reason, switched on the house lights and then set to work cleaning. Carmen Pharoah looked at the interior of the house and out of the window at the rear garden, neat lawns, sundial, the roof of the gazebo, and then decided to go to the kitchen where, as she expected, she found a pile of unwashed plates and pans and cutlery lying on the side of the sink. She took a self-sealing cellophane sachet from the pocket of the tracksuit and placed an unwashed knife inside it. She left the house while Emily Shaddick was vigorously vacuum-cleaning the hall carpet and walked to where Ventnor waited.

'Success?' Ventnor smiled.

'Maybe ... got this–' she showed him the knife – 'it's been used as you see and the guy lives alone, it's a fair bet his prints are on it.'

'OK.'

'So let's do it.'

'Here?'

'Why not?' Ventnor got out of the car and walked to the rear of the vehicle and opened the boot. He took the knife from the cellophane bag, holding it gingerly by the tip, and sprinkled iron filings along both sides of the handle and let the excess filings fall off, leaving sufficient filings clinging to the lines of the fingerprints. He placed adhesive tape over the handle of the knife, again on both sides, and peeled the tape off thus lifting the fingerprints in the time-tested manner. He then mounted the tape on a card and placed the card in a manila envelope.

'You can see the prints with the naked eye,' Carmen Pharoah commented as she took the knife from Ventnor.

'Better give that a thorough wash,' Ventnor said, 'and I mean thorough. He'll know the significance of iron filings if he sees them.'

'I'll see to it. Wait for me, I'm returning with you.'

'You are?'

'Oh yes, I'll tell you why later.' Carmen

Pharoah turned and went back to Roger Halverson's house walking with a lightness, yet muscularity of step. In the house she thoroughly cleaned the knife and then out of a sense of obligation to Emily Shaddick, attacked and demolished the washing up, doing it for her, not Halverson. She left the house waving a cheery farewell to Emily Shaddick who was singing a merry song over the noise of the vacuum cleaner.

George Hennessey had found himself enjoying that day up until the instant that he saw the young man riding the motorbike. Hennessey had spent the earlier part of that morning at his desk after reviewing the progress of the case or cases with his team and determining tasks to be done and allocating the work to individual team members. After his team had dispersed he read the files and familiarized himself with the Hill and Halverson murder investigations; also upon the spate of car thefts, on DC Pharoah's caseload; the alarming rise in sneak-in burglaries being addressed by DC Ventnor; the purchase of a prestige vehicle by a forged bank draft being investigated by DC Webster; and DS Yellich's progress in the case of an elderly man that might, it was believed, be linked to a serious assault of a physically disabled youth. The attacks were similar and both victims very vulnerable and unable to defend themselves. As he read the files he found once again that he was growing more and more comfortable with his increasingly sedentary role and had to admit, somewhat grudgingly, that Commander Sharkey might, after all, be correct: he was getting too old for the field and it was indeed time to settle in behind his desk, to keep the overview but allow the youth to do the legwork. At eleven a.m., after the meeting with the Commander, he returned to his office and put on his brown fedora and white summer raincoat and glanced out of his office window at the walls of the city. He walked slowly down the CID corridor and 'signed out' at the enquiry desk and stepped into Nunnery Lane just across the road from Micklegate Bar. The weather that day, he noted, remained that strange and perplexing mix of comfortable warmth with dark overcast clouds at nine-tenths in RAF speak, and a very low overcast at that. It was also completely still, not a breeze, no wind, nor even the occasional zephyr, just still ... still ... still. It was just as the newsagent had growled to him early that day, 'This dammed weather just doesn't know what it wants to do.' Hennessey stood on the pavement for a moment and pondered which route to take and decided to indulge himself in a walk along the walls from Micklegate Bar to Baile Hill. It was, of the three sections of the wall, Hennessey found, the least popular and yet also the most pleasing. To his right, as he walked to the wall, without the wall were the less desirable properties along Nunnery Lane and to his left, within the walls, an elevated lawn terrace and the more prestigious terraced houses of Lower Priory Street, Newton Terrace and Fairfax and Hampden Streets. The houses on either side of the wall were separated by only a few hundred feet but were massively different in value. Hennessey continued to walk, to stroll perhaps because he was in no hurry, he was in good time for his rendezvous and entered the small copse at Baile Hill which always seemed to him to have a mystical quality and which marked the end of that section of wall. He descended the narrow stone staircase and crossed Skeldergate Bridge. He saw that the rain and constant threat of same had not deterred the tourists and the Ouse was busy with traffic. Small, two-seater petrol-engined launches competed for space on the river with large, double-decker ferries and intermingled with them were oars, both multi- and single sculls. Turning his attention to the road traffic, he crossed Tower Street with some agility, the volume of motor vehicles being both rapid and heavy. He continued on to Castle Mills Bridge, over the small and sluggish River Foss which he had always seen as one of the gateways between tourist York and native York because, once over the bridge, he was amid an area of dense terrace housing but with sparsely populated streets and which could be anywhere in the United Kingdom. It was in fact, he thought, very similar to Greenwich, at the bottom end of Trafalgar Road and it was then, by coincidence, also thinking of Greenwich, southeast London, that he saw the young man on the motorbike. The motorcyclist was doing everything correctly, he was well attired in helmet and leathers, he seemed to Hennessey to be in total control of his machine, he was comfortably within the speed limit, working with the traffic as it approached Castle Mills Bridge, a motorcycle enthusiast, not a reckless 'biker', but it was often like that for him, just an unexpected sight of a motorcycle and rider and his mind would turn. It always triggered the memory; it always triggered the haunting and the emptiness, the sight of a figure all in black upon a silver machine.

He was eight years old, living in Colomb Street in Greenwich, with loving parents and an older brother, Graham, who had a motorbike, a beloved Triumph which he polished and cleaned each Sunday helped by George. If the weather was good, he would take George for a ride, sometimes just round Blackheath Common, but more often, the real treat, up through Deptford and into

Bermondsey, then across Tower Bridge, then into the West End and back across the river via Westminster Bridge. Happy days. Then it all fell apart, so suddenly. He was lying in bed, listening to Graham start his machine, kicking it into life, and then driving away down Trafalgar Road towards the Maritime Museum and the Naval Hospital, climbing steadily through the gears until the sound of his bike was lost in the night. Later that night, but not very much later, there was the classic police officer's knock upon the door, tap, tap, tap (a knock that Hennessey would learn to use). It was followed by hurried voices, then his mother's wailing, then his father came to his room to tell him that Graham had ridden his bike to heaven 'to save a place for us'. No one was to blame for the accident he would come to learn, no other vehicle was involved, rather it seemed that Graham had skidded on a patch of oil upon the road surface. Like George Hennessey's wife, some sixteen years later, Graham had died in the summer, and for the first time he saw the incongruity of a summer funeral, the coffin being lowered amid birdsong and rich foliage and the distant jollity of the bells of an ice-cream van, unseen but clearly heard. His father had died in the winter months and his grave had to be dug in rock-hard ground. His coffin was carried there after a very well attended service in still and utterly silent weather conditions and as the priest intoned 'dust to dust', his cassock was lifted by a slight breeze which brought with it a snow flurry, all adding such poignancy. Just as summer gives to a wedding, so, observed George Hennessey, winter gives to a funeral.

He often wondered what manner of man his brother would have become. He thought of how he had lost his life after alarming his parents by announcing that he was going to give up his safe job at the bank to go to Art College to study photography with the aim of becoming a photojournalist. That would have been Graham, not the tacky world of fashion photography but the hard hitting world of photojournalism, braving war zones and disaster areas, to capture a photograph that would change public opinion. That really would have been Graham Hennessey; a good father to some lucky children and a good uncle to Charles Hennessey. Instead there was the gap, the emptiness that George Hennessey had felt all his life, a hole which should be occupied by an older brother. The memory as so often was again triggered by the unexpected glimpse of a motorcyclist riding his bike.

Hennessey turned into Piccadilly and then right into the area of housing that he thought could be anywhere in the UK. He emerged into narrow Walmgate where he turned right and then left into Navigation Road and then right again into Speculation Street and walked towards a sign which protruded from the line of buildings and which read, 'Ye Olde Speculation Inn'. He walked to the pub and entered it through the narrow and low doorway and turned left into the snug. Shored-Up, sitting alone in a corner seat, nursing a whisky, smiled warmly at Hennessey as he entered the room.

'Shored-Up,' Hennessey nodded at the slightly built, smartly dressed man. 'Usual, I assume?'

'A double please, Mr H.' Shored-Up raised his glass. Hennessey walked across the floor to the serving hatch which served as the bar in the snug of the Speculation and rang the small brass bell that stood on the counter, and which was pleasingly, he thought, not chained to the wall. The brass bell had been part of the Speculation for the twenty years George Hennessey had used the pub, and probably for a long time before that. The bell was such an inviting item to steal and it said much of the local residents' affection for the pub that no one had clearly done so. He bought the drinks from a friendly barmaid in her twenties, a whisky for Shored-Up and a lime and soda for himself. 'Single,' he said as he put the whisky in front of Shored-Up.

'Oh, Mr Hennessey,' Shored-Up groaned but picked up the glass, eagerly so. He poured a little water into the whisky. 'Must not drown it,' he said lovingly, 'there's a skill in drinking whisky.'

'Which in your case is getting other people to buy it for you.'

'Oh, Mr Hennessey, have I not earned the small amount you have bought me from time to time over the years?'

'Yes, you have, that I concede but I was really thinking about the other folk that buy whisky, the elderly widows who drip with pearls and hang on your every word, so lonely, so unfulfilled after the passing of their husbands and a charming gentleman, retired Lieutenant Colonel no less arrives into their lives like a ray of sunlight.'

'So poetic, Mr Hennessey.' He sipped his drink. 'Have you perchance been able to speak to my probation officer yet?'

'Regrettably...'

'Oh, Mr Hennessey, I received a letter this a.m., threatening me with breach proceedings. This could very well mean prison. All those rough boys and a short spell inside will mean a shared cell and you know how delicate I am, sensitive as well, and the plumbing facilities in a shared cell—'

'Delicate! You are an ex-serviceman – you have to play the part.'

'A tool of the trade, Mr Hennessey, and not a widow in sight at the moment, dripping with pearls or not. Pickings are slim,

257

like I told you. Have to widen my search area.'

'Rather you listened to your PO and get a job.'

'A job!' Shored-Up reacted to the suggestion with genuine indignation. 'I did that once and it definitely did not agree with yours truly, not one little bit. It only took me a few weeks to work out that there must be easier ways of making a living. Haven't looked back really ... well, a few phases as guest of the Crown, but all in all, better than having to get up in the mornings in order to make another man rich. So, how can I help you, Mr Hennessey?'

'Halverson?'

'It is a name I know but I have been busy trying to find out about "Two Tone" Bowler, like you asked me to.'

'Forget about him now.'

'Forget him?'

'Yes, we found him, didn't get anywhere and the walking stick you mentioned, well that's now become two aluminium crutches.'

'Well, well. So age has wearied him?'

'Seems so, but Halverson?'

'That name rings distant bells.'

'Really?'

'Would he be aka Shaw?'

'He would. He has an enemy, one Daniel Purves.'

Shored-Up leaned towards Hennessey.

'Take care,' he hissed, 'take care, Mr Hennessey.'

'You know the names, clearly.'

'Know of them.'

'Tell me.'

'Nothing concrete, Mr Hennessey.'

'Alright, what do you know?'

'Rumours that fly in the night. You know your reporter does not always move amongst the genteel elderly with a little cash to spare.'

'A lot of cash and none of it to spare, but carry on.'

'Well, some circles your reporter moves in are ... well, I do so loathe the word, Mr Hennessey, but I dare say I have to accept the fact that I am a criminal.'

'Good for you, Shored-Up, good for you. That is the first step towards redemption. Your probation officer will be pleased.'

'Oh, Mr Hennessey, yours truly redeemed? Never ... won't happen, I know no other life.'

'Carry on. You were saying...'

'The point is that I also have to keep in with the crew.'

'The crew?'

'My name for the criminal brotherhood, the boys who would not like me talking to you but fortunately for me they do not seem to know that this lovely old pub exists tucked away down the end of this little street in York YO1. Long may it remain that way. So I do have to tread carefully, but the majority of my brothers in crime sleep late, even as late as this hour. They tend to be nighthawks.'

'I know.'

'That's when the jobs are done. A lot avoid the daylight to keep their eyes adjusted to the dark.'

'I know that as well. I'm close to retiring and I have been a copper since I stepped off a destroyer at the end of my National Service, so I know, but carry on.'

'It means I can drink here at lunchtime and chat to you, sir ... Mr Hennessey, keeps me in with you and my PO maybe.'

'Maybe,' Hennessey growled.

'Keeping my options open. So I have to drink when and where they drink, can't just show up when I need some information to feed you to help me get my PO off my back, so I hear things.'

'Halverson?'

'And Shaw ... and Purves.'

'We know little of them, a few petty offences but it seems they are bigger fish than that. Nothing known of Halverson/Shaw or Purves for ten – fifteen years. At the moment my officers are obtaining Halverson/Shaw's prints by means that are less than ethical but we'll know if he is who we think he is.'

'Mr Hennessey–' Shored-Up beamed – 'you push the edge. I am impressed. Good for you.'

'So tell me about them.'

'Big names in the Vale, Mr Hennessey. Big in the underworld that is. Real villains. Never do the dirty themselves, but they're behind a lot of jobs. They have separate empires but don't want a turf war. They are a bit like India and Pakistan.'

'What do you mean?'

'They keep their guns pointed at each other and apart from a few spats they have lived in a sort of uneasy peace but just waiting for the other one to start something and then blood will flow like the Ouse in flood.'

'Didn't know you were so well versed in current affairs, Shored-Up. I am impressed.'

'It's part of my stock-in-trade, Mr Hennessey. I can't persuade elderly widows to invest in my tin-mining operation in Bolivia if I reveal ignorance of the world in which we live now can I? I have to look and sound the part.' Shored-Up drained his glass.

'I see ... I see ... dare say you could use another drink, another wee goldie as my Scots friend would say?'

'Oh, so kind, I really don't mind if I do, Mr Hennessey.' Shored-Up reclined in a self-satisfied manner and smiled as Hennessey stood. 'I don't mind if I do.'

Once again seated, he with a soda and lime, Shored-Up with another whisky, Hennessey pressed for more information about Halverson/Shaw and Purves.

'Halverson and Purves – rivals all the way

up from their youth and petty crimes committed therein, Mr Hennessey. The Vale can't be easily divided, not like London or Glasgow, one side of the river or the other, one gang on one side, one gang on the other, but they seem to have made a reasonable stab at dividing it.'

'What's their business?'

Shored-Up shrugged and sipped the whisky and then added a little more water. 'You name it ... but never front line, bank-rolling robberies, extortion, people-smuggling lately. It was hard drugs but they have moved into people-smuggling, big money, lenient sentences if you get collared, as I said once or twice before. I never get a glance at either of them; they're never seen in the thieves' dens. They are approached through their lieutenants and who they be I do not know.'

'I see.' Hennessey glanced out of the stained-glass window past the 'Sanders and Penn's Fine Ales' sign and noted raindrops beginning to fall on the pane, lightly and infrequently but rain was definitely falling again. 'So you have no contact with them?'

Shored-Up held up his hands in a defensive gesture. 'Well out of my league, Mr Hennessey, I don't want to be known by them. People disappear you know, if they get known by them ... so it is said.'

'Really?'

'Well, as I say, so it is said. People are not taught a lesson, nor are they made an example of, they just vanish without a trace, even the slightest infraction, even a suspicion and the person disappears from the planet. His or her body is just never found, neater that way, no body, no murder enquiry. The Ouse is a deep river.'

'Is that where they're put?'

'Or directly into the Humber. So I must be careful.'

Hennessey smiled. 'There's too much of the survivor about you, Shored-Up. Your feet will always be dry, as dry as a bone.'

'I do hope so. It's rumoured they go in alive with a weight round their ankles.'

'Really?'

'Really. Heavy boys, Mr H. and well pro-tected.'

'So what do you know about Roger Hal-verson's son, also Roger?'

'Roger junior? I have heard he is being inducted into the Halverson Empire ... like father, like son. As cold as his old man they say. It is the talk of the den that Roger junior has been iced.'

'Yes. No secret has been made of it.'

'I can say, don't look at Purves.'

'No?'

'No–' Shored-Up sipped his whisky – 'whenever Halverson and Purves have lock-ed horns it's always been tit for tat and

Purves has children, two sons and a daughter and a grandson by the daughter. Purves respects Halverson, hates him but respects him, a bit like the Nazis and the Soviets hated each other, but they commanded each other's respect as soldiers, that sort of respect.'

'Understood.'

'So Purves will know that if he iced Halverson's son, then Halverson will ice one of his children. In fact the rumour is that Purves has already contacted Halverson, offered his condolences and assured Halverson that his hands aren't dirty over the murder of Roger junior. Not only that but it is also the rumour that Purves has offered Halverson his resources to nail the culprit. And that I can believe, that is how Daniel Purves would respond, it is exactly how he would respond. He values his own kin. Neither is he keen for a war.'

'So it's in-house, you'd say?'

'More than likely. More than likely in Roger junior's little house, than Roger senior's big house. I heard the body was found in someone's house?'

'Yes, it was.'

'Found by a burglar?'

'Yes, though that has not been made public.'

'No, the boy is talking, telling folk what he found. So it has reached the den. It didn't come from a loose-mouthed copper.'

'That's a relief.'

'But zap zap zap, three lightning strikes to that couple's house; flooded, then burgled, then used as a mortuary ... blimey, those citizens just ran out of luck big time and I mean big time.'

'If you could make some enquiries? Even if you hear something by the by?'

'I'll contact you, Mr Hennessey but I need a wedge for this and a promise of a word to my probation officer, Miss Pratt. Pratt by name but not prat by nature. She doesn't suffer fools, nor can she be charmed or manipulated or intimidated. I know, I've tried every angle and breach proceedings is approaching me like an express train.'

'Well, I need hard information if I am going to be able to help you.'

'Appreciate that, Mr Hennessey. Hard information–' Shored-Up sipped his drink – 'and we can't meet in York.'

'So long as it's not Rotherham again, of all the godforsaken, depressed and depressing ... populated with malcontents ... but if the information is good, I dare say I'll meet you anywhere.'

'I'll phone you, Mr Hennessey. I have a reason to come up with the goods, if not I'll be inside for Christmas. Young Miss Pratt has picked up my scent; she is running me to ground. Christmas inside ... oh.'

Hennessey stood. 'So you're motivated, that could help us both.'

At the close of the working day Somerled Yellich drove home to his new-build house at Huntingdon, north of York. As he drew to a halt outside his home the front door swung open and Jeremy ran out smiling, arms wide to greet his father. Yellich braced himself for the impact of an affectionate twelve year old. Then, greetings exchanged, father and son walked into the house and Yellich was in turn greeted by his wife.

'He's been very good.' Sara Yellich uncoiled the powdery arm which she had lovingly curled round her husband's neck. 'He's helped me with the baking since he came home.'

'Good, good boy.' Yellich smiled at his son who beamed with pride. 'Well, let me get changed and we'll go for a walk shall we?' Jeremy Yellich nodded vigorously.

Somerled Yellich took his son to the meadows where the stream was swollen with recent rain but not flooded and where they looked for minnows and frogs and identified wild flowers. Further to their left upon the meadow that lay beyond All Saints Church, a group of boys played cricket and the 'thwack' of the cork ball against the bat echoed loudly across the green sward, against a backdrop of trees in full foliage, under a blue and at that particular point, an unusually cloud-free sky. Yellich and his wife had known the disappointment that all parents know when told that their child will not be 'normal'. In their son's case the defect was that of 'Down's syndrome' but in the event Jeremy had brought delight, as a new world had opened up to them as they met other parents of similar children in the York area, and from the support group real and lasting friendships had developed. Jeremy had remained childlike, never to go through the testing, troubled, demanding teenage years and the Yellichs had been told, with love, stimulation, education, he might, by the age of twenty years, achieve the functioning level of a twelve year old and be able to live a semi-independent life within a supervised hostel.

Later that night Sara and Somerled Yellich sat side by side on the settee, sipping wine and listening to a concert of eighteenth-century music on Radio Three. It was all they needed, to sit with each other, in silence, at the end of the day.

In the house Norman Budde remained conscious just long enough to feel his fear lead on to terror.

It was Thursday, 23.42 hours.

Seven

Friday, 1st July,
10.00 hours – 12.22 hours

*In which Yellich and Ventnor pay a house call and
Pharoah and Webster visit a 'beaver'.*

Halverson received Yellich and Ventnor in his
sitting room, which Yellich found to be
exactly as Pharoah and Ventnor had described: neat to the point of obsessive perfection.
The house, he thought, of a so-called 'control freak'. Yellich found Halverson to be a
stern-faced individual, no warmth or humour being in evidence, just cold, piercing
eyes, a tight-lipped mouth and a very muscular build beneath the blue tee shirt and
white summer slacks.

'Why do you call yourself Shaw?' Yellich
asked after the preliminaries of introduction
and condolences for the loss of Roger Halverson junior had been completed.

The question clearly stung Halverson who
seemed to flinch at the realization that the
police knew that he was an 'also known as',

or aka in police speak. He stared at Yellich.

'Cross-referenced in our computer,' Yellich explained. 'Your son, your late son's prints are on file, he is aka Shaw, probably means that you are aka Shaw, seems reasonable since he is following you into your business empire, or so we learn.'

'Learn from who?'

Yellich replied with a smile.

'No reason,' Halverson said. 'Shaw is just a business name I use. I like to keep my private life separate from my business dealings. I am not using it to mislead anyone or escape creditors ... if anything.' Halverson's voice trailed off but Yellich felt it safe to assume he was going to say, 'if anything they owe me'. Had he said that it would have opened up a useful line of inquiry, a minefield for Halverson, a goldmine for the police.

'So what is your line of business?'

'Stocks and shares.' The reply came quickly, a little too quickly to be genuine in Yellich and Ventnor's view, a little too prepared, a little rehearsed, too polished and practised. 'Made some good investments, paying well now or sold when they were worth substantially more than I paid for them. Got out at the right time.'

A bluebottle found its way into the room and buzzed loudly and angrily on the windowpane. Halverson eyed the insect with distaste and undisguised anger. He was a man, thought Yellich, with a short fuse who knew not the meaning of tolerance.

'I see.' Yellich didn't want to press the question. He glanced out towards the neatly tended back garden, seeing, as Pharoah had done, the lawns, the sundial, the roof of the gazebo. He knew it was futile. Yellich was at Halverson's home at DCI Hennessey's request to take the measure of the man in the light of information supplied by Hennessey's confidential informant, whose identity George Hennessey kept a well-guarded secret but of whom he said had 'proved useful in the past'. 'So, your son, sorry your late son, also Roger Halverson—'

'Yes.' There was a note of anger in Halverson's voice, a note which seemed to Yellich to say, 'Someone will pay for this.'

'Have you had a chance to rethink your answer as to who you believe might have wanted to murder your son? He was clearly targeted. He wasn't just in the wrong place at the wrong time. Someone wanted him dead.'

'Still the same, no one I know would want to harm Roger,' he said coldly, defensively, as if between the lines he was really saying, 'I am making my own inquiries.'

'Not Daniel Purves?'

Halverson's eyes narrowed.

'We know about Purves.' Yellich smiled gently. 'We understand he deals in stocks

270

and shares as well.'

'Not saying anything, but it wasn't Daniel Purves. We know each other, and yes, he's in stocks and shares, same as me and yes, we don't like each other but this is not his doing and he knows I would ... well, let's say he has more to lose than me.' Halverson smiled menacingly.

'I see, so that's what you mean by stocks and shares, is it? We know about Daniel Purves' stocks and shares you see.'

'No comment, but he stays on his side of the street and I stay on mine.'

'I am interested in the world of stocks and shares.' Yellich relaxed in the deep armchair in which he had been invited to sit but sensed that Halverson was far from relaxed. 'What did Oliver Hill do for you ... twenty years ago now?'

Halverson remained silent. He stared intently at Yellich.

'Who owned the green van, the van that carried Oliver Hill to his death, over the bridge into the icy flood waters? Can't keep a secret like that forever, folk are beginning to talk.'

'Who's talking?'

'Folk,' said Yellich, smiling, 'just folk. So you do know, or you do remember Oliver Hill?'

'I do?'

'Yes, you do, the name means something

271

to you.'

'I want you both out of my house.'

'Not yet.'

'You have a warrant?'

'No, we don't.'

'Then go.'

'We do, however, have a police car waiting outside which could take you to the police station, so we can talk here or at the police station.'

'I have nothing to hide.'

'So we'll carry on.'

Halverson continued to eye Yellich coldly but he was defensive and he glanced angrily at the bluebottle, which buzzed up and down the windowpane. It was evident to both Yellich and Ventnor that the wretched insect would have little time to live once Yellich and Ventnor had departed the house. Halverson needed a victim, even if it was only a Musca domestica.

'So, tell me about Oliver Hill.'

'I don't know that name.'

'Others say that you do.'

'Which others?'

'Well, people who were not involved in his murder.'

Halverson remained silent.

'But folk talk to folk who talk to folk who talk to folk and the rumour is that you had Oliver Hill murdered because he was skimming money, taking a little for himself.'

Halverson remained stony-faced but his eyes burned into Yellich. So Hennessey had asked Yellich and Ventnor to take the measure of the man and the measure they had taken was a man who likes control and order, a man used to getting his own way, a man who had to work hard to control his violence and a man who knew very well who Oliver Hill was and a man hungry for revenge over the murder of his son. It was remarkable, Yellich pondered, that this man had remained virtually unknown to the police and for so long.

'Which others?' Halverson pressed.

'Can't tell you.' Yellich smiled. 'Confidential sources. Like you and Daniel Purves, we keep to our own side of the street. So we are here chatting.'

'Chatting!'

'So who did you have murder Oliver Hill and why?'

'No comment.'

'Careful!' John Penn stood as he shouted the warning as his son stepped out of the shrubs. 'Stay still! Don't move!' Penn walked slowly but purposefully from the place by the lake where he and his wife sat, enjoying the lull in the rain, enjoying each other's, and their children's, company and their children's joy, indulging in quality time. It was the sort of time that Penn felt he had missed out on when he was Sergeant Penn in the Yorkshire Regiment. Penn approached his son and carefully removed the gun from his son's hand and put the safety catch on. He removed the ammunition clip and breathed deeply. He turned to his wife and, raising his voice so that it carried over the grass to where she sat said, 'This damn thing is loaded and the safety was off', and his wife, with shoulder length auburn hair, a trifle overweight she might think herself, paled and removed the mobile phone from her handbag.

'Little Andy' Barnes revealed himself to be a man true to his name, a man of slight build and short stature whose frail appearance was exacerbated by the large-size prison-issue shirt and jeans he wore. He seemed to Ventnor to peek out of his clothes, akin, he thought, to a young girl he once saw in her parents' house, lying on the sofa wrapped in a duvet with just her eyes showing as she soaked up daytime television. Barnes had an unexpected and very distinct effeminate manner which probably, thought Ventnor, made him very popular and very much in demand over the years. He grabbed the cigarette that Ventnor offered. 'They say you can't smoke in pubs, not no more.' He held the cigarette to the flame of Ventnor's lighter and inhaled gratifyingly.

'They say right.' Carmen Pharoah also thought Barnes cut a strange figure, a hybrid, she thought, both comic and pathetic.

'How much is a pint now?'

'Two pounds.' Ventnor put the cigarette lighter back in his jacket pocket.

'Blimey.' Barnes took another deep inhalation. 'I don't get enough smoke, so this is heaven. I get offered a lot of tobacco, the other cons pay me to keep them happy because I sometimes remind them of their girlfriend or wife, but I also need protection. I am not a very big boy and so it comes in one hand and out of the other. Seems I am just a funnel for tobacco to go through. I handle a lot but use very little and I have another five to serve, minimum. Dare say it will be four pounds a pint by then, and no smoking in pubs ... can't imagine a pub without smoke ... strange. What am I to do?'

'The smokers sit outside and have a fag,' Carmen Pharoah said. 'Other pubs have smoking areas outside, like a large conservatory. One pub in Ireland bought an old double-decker bus and put it in the corner of the pub car park.'

'Well, I knew the old world would be changed when I got out, but really expensive beer and no-smoking pubs? It will be a strange homecoming for me.'

'It will probably–' Carmen Pharoah took

out her notebook in readiness – 'but at least it will be a homecoming, you are getting a bit old to be in here.'

'Yes, well, I didn't think of that at the time, just picked up the knife and ran him through, so ... life ... done ten. I haven't been a model prisoner otherwise I might have been out by now paying two quid a pint and smoking in a double-decker bus in a pub car park. You can upset the system, even shorties like me, if you know how. I learned eventually, calmed down now but I've blown any chance of early parole, so I reckon another five years, but two quid...'

'You'll get pre-release training so it won't come as a shock,' Ventnor offered. 'Possibly.'

'Yeah–' Barnes took another deep drag on the nail – 'is that just as daft as daft can be? Spend fifteen years institutionalizing you and then six months undoing all the damage.'

'Well we might be able to help you there,' Carmen Pharoah suggested.

'Oh?'

'Yes.' She looked Barnes in the eye. 'The old story, you help us, we'll help you. Five years is a long time, it's a big chunk out of anyone's life. We could reduce it; bring on another parole hearing with a good word put in for you.'

Barnes nodded. 'At my age life just doesn't stretch before me like it used to do. It used to be that life was like a railway line that stretched all the way to the horizon with no end in sight.'

'And now?'

'Now, now I can see the buffers at the end of the line. No smoking in pubs, that I really want to see.'

'Tell us about Roger Halverson, aka Shaw.'

Barnes glanced to his left and exhaled through his nose. 'Don't want much do you? Tell you this, he's a dangerous man, he's one heavy old geezer but that's not a name I have heard for a while.'

'Could be you're safe from him.'

'Safe! From Halverson? Not a chance. No way … nowhere … uh-huh.' He shook his head. 'He's got guys in here. I'm over the hill now, whatever Halverson is up to I am not part of it so no one will suspect me of talking to you about him, I hope. I'm just an old soldier, pensioned off but doing bird for manslaughter – got it kicked down to man-slaughter.'

'We know–' Carmen Pharoah spoke coldly – 'you were lucky. He had his life ahead of him.'

'He was making too much noise. I wanted to sleep.'

'Still closer to premeditated murder than manslaughter.'

'Shaky witnesses. I pled guilty in return for a reduction in the charge, makes no difference, same amount of time served.' He glanced up at the thick slab of opaque glass set high in the wall of the agent's room. 'Natural light,' he sighed, 'don't get a lot of natural light in prison but you get even less in the grave ... and Roger Halverson doesn't take prisoners.'

'Is that why he had Oliver Hill rubbed out?'

Barnes' jaw sagged. 'Ollie Hill?'

'Yes. He was pushed to his death into a swollen river by Walpole Moulton and "Two Tone" Bowler and a few others, possibly including you.'

'How—?'

'Ebenezer Moulton told us.'

'Ebby? Ebby grassed on his old man?'

'No, Walpole Moulton is deceased.'

'Wally,' Barnes groaned.

'Yes. As soon as Wally was under the turf Ebenezer reported the murder he saw when he was seven years old. He walked straight from the cemetery to the police station. That was just at the beginning of this week.'

'Oh, Walpole's lad, he was a footballer wasn't he? He was going places.'

'He was until he got worked over one night, now he walks on sticks.'

'Halverson will be behind that.'

'You think?'

'I know.' Barnes shook his head. 'They don't call him the "Field Marshall" for nothing.'

'So Halverson was behind the Oliver Hill murder?'

'Maybe, I won't give evidence or sign a statement but an early parole...'

'Well, let's see where we get to,' Ventnor probed. 'Who owned the green van?'

'Green van? Geezer called Hamlyn, with a "y".'

'Hamlyn? We don't know that name.'

'He wasn't in Two Tone's crew but you'll know him, he has track but he owned the van and he drove it out to the bridge with the boys in the back sitting on Oliver Hill. Halverson believed Hill had stolen from him. Hill pleaded innocence all the way to a mighty blow to the stomach which put a stop to any more from him.'

'Who punched him?'

'Walpole Moulton, so I heard.'

'We must caution you.'

Barnes held up his hand. 'No caution is necessary, I didn't say anything, nothing is going on paper but I still want a good word put in.'

'We'll see what we can do. What is Hamlyn's first name?'

'Gregor, he's about the same age as me, mid to late forties.'

'So you heard?' Carmen Pharoah asked.

'Yes, I wasn't part of the murder of Oliver Hall. Cast-iron alibi, I was doing a month for receiving stolen goods but the boys were all

279

talking about it when I came out.'

'I see.'

'Told me they sent Oliver Hill for a swim on the orders of the Big Man because Hill had been skimming.'

'The Big Man being Halverson?' Carmen Pharoah clarified.

'The one and the same.'

Ventnor offered Barnes another cigarette which was readily accepted. 'Just tell us what you know.'

'Alright, write down as much as you want but I won't be signing anything. I have to live, even if it's in here, I still have to live.' He paused. 'Well, Gregor Hamlyn, he was just seventeen or eighteen at the time, he wanted in the team and he had a little green van, a fifteen hundredweight, and he used it to earn a little pocket money by carrying folks' goods for them. You know, the man-with-a-van sketch but he was off the estate at Driffield, same as me and Two Tone and Big Andy and the rest, and he knew what was going down around him and, like I said, he wanted in. So when they needed a van to shift Ollie Hill to the bridge for his final dive, he was asked if he wanted to earn a wedge and he leapt at the chance. I was doing bird at the time so this is just hearsay but it's good hearsay.'

'Understood.'

'No good as evidence though but I still

expect a favour.'

'We'll see what we can do. Carry on.' Pharoah was stony-faced.

'So anyway, he bundled the accountant into the van. He was tall but lanky, no strength, he was no street fighter. They said it was no worse than carrying a big rag doll for all the resistance he put up. Three of the boys sat on him in the van and Walpole and the other guy followed in Two Tone's car with Walpole's little lad in the back seat. Stupid to take the little lad along but that's what they did. Got to the bridge they say, all went according to plan, dragged the guy out so his head banged on the road, half knocked him out that did, planted him a couple in the old bread basket to knock the wind out of him and over he went. Only a little splash was made so they say. Half expected his old body to get washed up somewhere and be taken for a drowning victim, I mean an accident, not deliberate like, but it never did wash up, stayed below to feed the fishes I reckon, so he disappeared, which is what tends to happen to folk who cross Halverson.'

'Who was involved?'

'So far as I hear, the entire crew plus Gregor Hamlyn on his first job but that's the entire crew except yours truly being as I was in Wakefield nick at the time, twenty-eight days for receiving.'

'So where will we find Hamlyn now? Do you know?'

'He's known to you, quite well in fact. He's inside now.'

'Really? Which nick?'

Barnes smiled and pointed to the floor. 'This one, "B" wing.' He continued to smile. 'I tell you something else; he's not a very happy beaver. He's been different to me. He's worked towards his parole or move to a category B prison from day one. He's not a popular boy and hasn't a lot of protection. He'll deal, especially now Halverson's son has been cooled.'

Ventnor and Pharoah looked questioningly at Barnes.

'We hear things,' Barnes said. 'In here we hear a lot, often before you do. With Halverson's son gone, there's no one to take over Halverson's empire. Halverson's vulnerable. Hamlyn knows that. He will deal.'

'You think so?'

'See for yourself. Just don't tell him it was me that fingered him.'

Gregor Hamlyn, when he had been escorted to the agent's room in which Ventnor and Pharoah waited, after Barnes had been removed amid the sound of jangling keys, revealed himself to be quite the opposite of 'Little Andy' Barnes. Hamlyn seemed to burst out of his prison clothing like a moth escaping a chrysalis, so thought Carmen

Pharoah. Ventnor in turn was reminded of the women he often met at the night club who insisted on wearing a size twelve dress when their figure screamed for a fourteen. Hamlyn had heavy tattoos on his forearms and an old but deep scar on his cheek; he was missing a few teeth from his upper set. He eyed Ventnor and Pharoah with cold grey eyes and did not conceal his dislike for the police. He had clearly come a very long way from being a seventeen year old with a little green van who wanted to be part of 'Two Tone' Bowler's gang. Ventnor and Pharoah had the clear impression that he had long ago eclipsed 'Two Tone' Bowler and could possibly step into Halverson's shoes once the 'Big Man' had been pushed aside. Little wonder, they thought, that he might be ready to deal.

'We're acting on information received.' Ventnor leaned back in his chair after introducing himself and Carmen Pharoah.

'From Jellyfish?'

'Who?'

'Barnes.'

'Can't tell you.'

'I'll find out. This is East Ashby, the cons run this ship. I saw Jellyfish being taken from the exercise yard, he comes back and then the screws collect me. You don't need too much upstairs to work out who fingered me.'

'We understand that you once owned a

green van?'

'Once ... in the early days ... useful things. So it was Jellyfish, he was around when I had that van. My first motor. You always remember your first motor. Jellyfish is a dead man.'

'Well, if anything happens to Barnes we'll be coming for you and you can forget early parole or a move to a Cat B or Cat C.'

Hamlyn's eyes narrowed. He glared at Carmen Pharoah.

'So think about it.' Carmen Pharoah held the stare. 'A lot of men are in here because they didn't think before they acted. So think before you act. Learn from their mistakes.'

'We can help you.' Ventnor sensed the atmosphere needed easing if some good was to come of the interview.

'How?'

'We need information about Roger Halverson.'

'Powerful man, though not so powerful now he hasn't a successor to his "stocks and shares" as he calls his empire.'

'So we believe. So you drove the van that carried Oliver Hill to his death. What was he like? Pleading for his life all the way?'

'No–' Hamlyn shook his head – 'he was quiet. All the way. He knew struggling was useless. Actually that makes it worse to live with. He was a brave man. If he had been a whimpering nothing it would be easier to live with.'

'You are admitting conspiracy?'

Hamlyn smiled. 'I am admitting nothing, no tape recorder in here, you haven't cautioned me and I won't sign a statement.'

'Difficult to see how we can help you if you won't provide information.'

Hamlyn laughed. 'Hey, you wanted to see me, pulled me out of a game of five-a-side. I didn't ask to see you.'

'Fair point.' Ventnor nodded. 'But you did seem to listen when we said we could help.'

'I'm in for murder. It was a fight. I still feel it was self-defence. I collected life but I have been working to help myself. Never been a problem in here, attended all the courses, joined the Christian Union, enrolled for a degree from the Open University, a real eager beaver. I won't give information about the death of Oliver Hill though, that will work against me. I am not a dumb beaver. Nobody will say anything to you – not officially – about Ollie Hill's murder. But ... this old beaver can give you something that will nail Halverson for something else and with no need of witnesses...'

Walking away from HM Prison, East Ashby, Ventnor and Pharoah disturbed an elderly rook drinking from a rain puddle that had formed in the car park. The bird laboured slowly and sluggishly with disarrayed wing feathers into the air at their approach.

It was Friday, 12.22 hours.

Eight

Friday, 1st July,
13.20 hours – 19.35 hours

In which arrests are made.

'The third rock from the sun, Harold Ford.'
Hennessey, seated at his desk, smiled. 'He
trifles with us. Methinks the felon doth
trifle.'

'Well, he's given us something to go on,
sir.' Carmen Pharoah looked at the computer printout. 'He's playing a game alright,
not wanting to be too cooperative with the
police. That's his private agenda, his attitude, but he wants parole or a reclassifica-
tion as a Cat B or Cat C prisoner and so he
has to give us something and he has done.
So, Harold Ford, murdered–' she glanced at
the printout – 'six months ago. I remember
it, no leads at all. Thirty-two years old when
he died, a known criminal, found in a field,
multiple stab wounds but little blood at the
scene. So murdered and insanguinated elsewhere and then the corpse dumped where it

286

was found by a farm worker. Ford was a known associate of Halverson aka Shaw. Only one given relative ... his wife, whose last known address was in Holgate not far from here.'

'So what on earth did he mean by "third rock from the sun"?'

'Just as you said, sir.' Yellich sat back in his chair. 'The Earth. *"My-Very-Easy-Method-Just-Speeds-Up-Naming-People"* – Mercury, Venus, Earth, Mars, Jupiter, Saturn, Uranus, Neptune, Pluto. It's a memory aid that I once learned, except that Pluto has now been downgraded, but the first four planets are terrestrial, the rest are balls of gas, until you get to Pluto which is also terrestrial, also a rock.'

'That's very interesting and I will tell my grandchildren that memory aid but where does it get us? So far we have a cold case and a riddle and while I have the patience for one, I do not have the patience for the other. Riddle me not, jester, I don't get paid enough.'

'He's giving us Halverson,' Carmen Pharoah said, 'he told us we won't be able to prosecute him for the murder of Oliver Hill, but he's giving us evidence linking him to another murder. No one will talk to us about the Hill murder and I doubt anyone will talk to us about the Harold Ford murder but ... perhaps nobody has to...' Carmen Pharoah's

287

voice trailed off.

'You have realized something DC Pharoah?'

'I don't know but when I was at the house, that is Halverson's home, I glanced out of the back window at the back garden as I said goodbye to the contract cleaner.'

'The sundial!' Yellich gasped, pointing to Carmen Pharoah.

'Yes.' Carmen Pharoah turned to Yellich. 'There is a sundial in the garden and the garden is neatly landscaped so, not the sun, but the sundial and not a planet but a rock, literally a rock. Possibly, possibly Hamlyn left something, or knew of something that is under the third rock from the sundial in Halverson's garden and which will incriminate Halverson in the murder of Harold Ford. Possibly, possibly, possibly.'

'More than a possibility I'd say. We are looking at a probability. So, you and Thompson Ventnor, you pursue that, obtain a warrant and search Halverson's home and garden, make sure the warrant covers every base, it has to be in Halverson's name, aka Shaw.'

'Yes, sir.'

'And for the entire property of whatever is Halverson's address, house outbuildings, garage and grounds.' Hennessey paused. 'Yes, ensure you use the word "grounds" because that's all inclusive. "Gardens" is exclusive. He might have an area of waste at the bottom of his garden as I have at mine which a clever brief might argue is not part of the garden.'

'Understood, sir.' Carmen Pharoah smiled with a set jaw. 'Grounds it will be.'

'Good. Take plenty of uniforms with you.'

'Yes, sir.'

'Now I have something to report, that is that the gun that was used to murder Roger Halverson junior has been found.'

'Really?' Webster gasped. The other officers beamed with pleasure at the news.

'Yes, really, but it could so easily have been a tragedy. A young boy found it in a stand of shrubs. He was picnicking with his parents, brave of them in this weather, but they saw a gap in the rain clouds, there was the yellow thing and so they packed lunch and went out to eat ... boy went exploring. Anyway, fortunately for us the father was a recently time-expired army sergeant and made the thing safe. The boy had picked up a loaded weapon which had the safety catch in the "off" position.'

'Oh,' Ventnor groaned.

'Yes–' Hennessey again noticed the blood-shot eyes and heavily minted breath of Thompson Ventnor – 'it could have been nasty. Anyway, it had plenty of latents. Many belonging to a felon named Downes, Freddie Downes, who is but twenty-two years and has previous for minor offences. So, it's a big step up for him to murder the only son of the Vale's most feared and formidable. Wetherby came back very quickly. It is definitely the murder weapon. So that's another warrant, for the arrest of Frederick Downes. I want you and Webster on that, Sergeant.'

'Very good, sir,' Yellich snapped.

'For my part, I have received a phone call from my informant wishing to meet me outside York. He wants to see me outside York when he is frightened and when he has good information to trade. He's a little fearful of his probation officer – too many missed appointments.' Hennessey smiled. 'So, we'll have good stuff. So we all know what we are doing?'

'Yes, sir.'

'Yes, sir.'

'Yes, sir.'

'Yes, sir.'

'Good. Every journey has a turning point, the point when the traveller is nearer the end than the beginning. So does every investigation. I feel we have reached the turning point in this investigation. I feel it is beginning to conclude.'

George Hennessey could never seem to take to the city of Kingston-upon-Hull, or Hull as it is more commonly known. It may be the home town of William Wilberforce, the antislavery campaigner, the town where HMS *Bounty* of mutiny fame is believed to have been built and the town from which Alexander Selkirk, Defoe's inspiration for Robinson Crusoe, sailed, and also has many other claims to fame but it was still not a city that Hennessey ever felt comfortable in when he had occasion to visit. It was not caused by anything he could identify, anything he could put his finger on but the unease he felt when visiting Hull was palpable. It certainly has a reputation for being a 'brown envelope' town, where contracts can be secured with the help of the contents of a brown envelope but in fairness, that sort of malpractice goes on in all cities. Nor was it the case that for George Hennessey Hull had been the setting of a personal tragedy or unpleasant associations, it was simply that each time he approached Hull by train or motor vehicle, the moment that he passed under the awesome grandeur of the Humber Bridge he felt the sensation of going down into something and when leaving, once the bridge was behind him, he felt the sensation of rising up into something.

It's life, Jim, but not as we know it.

That Saturday, disliking motor transport for the highly personal reasons of which the gracious reader is now aware, George Hennessey chose to travel by train to the city. He had always found the York to Hull Trans-

Pennine Service exceedingly speedy and efficient but once again, he had that sensation of descending as the train slowed upon the approach to Hull Station which, in places, still bears the original name of Hull Paragon.

Hennessey left the station by the exit to his right beyond the ticket barrier, the original entrance now being the plush foyer of a prestigious hotel. He strolled into the Old Town and to a pub accessed down an alley on Silver Street. Within was stained panelling, low ceilings, deep red carpet, a warmth and a gentle hum of hushed conversation. Ye Olde White Hart was a most pleasing hostelry, Hennessey found, a little gem of a pub in a strange city. Shored-up sat in the corner of the left-hand bar in front of a glass of whisky.

'Interesting pub.' Hennessey sat opposite him and settled into the chair.

'It is where the Civil War was begun,' Shored-Up advised.

'The Civil War? I believe we have had five such conflicts in our right little tight little island.'

'The big one ... the bloody one, Cromwell versus Prince Rupert, that one. This pub was already over a hundred years old when that war was fought and it started here ... upstairs.'

'Upstairs?' Hennessey glanced around. He

could well believe that the building was over five hundred years old and still a functioning pub.

'The plotting parlour is upstairs.'

'The plotting parlour?'

'A small room now renovated. The beams in the ceiling are original; little else is, apart from the dimensions of the room,' Shored-Up explained. 'But it was in that room that the decision to keep King Charles out of the city was taken and remember, they were saying "no you can't come into Hull", to someone who believed, and this was believed by monarchists, that he ruled England by Divine Right. Big challenge.' Shored-Up pushed his glass towards Hennessey. Anyway, that led to the war which led to the overthrow of the King and the introduction of Parliamentary Democracy. It all started in this pub.'

'Didn't know that you were such a historian, Shored-Up.'

'An interest of mine and like the importance of keeping up with current affairs, it helps my ... my way of life. It adds to the aura.'

'So, if you are not Lieutenant Colonel Smythe retired, you can be Professor Smythe?'

Shored-Up turned his palm upwards. 'What can I say, Mr H.? What can I say? Have you had a chance to talk to Miss Pratt yet? I am most desirous not to return to the custody of HM Prison. It would be so inconvenient.'

'Inconvenient?' Hennessey raised a suspicious eyebrow. 'Why? Are you in the middle of another "job" for want of a better expression? A scam? A sting? What term would you use?'

'A negotiation, Mr Hennessey, but alas no, I am resting at present.'

'A negotiation?' Hennessey sighed. 'Housebreakers talk of "missions" and you talk of "negotiations" anything to bring a little respectability in your eyes into it.'

'Perhaps but prison would be inconvenient because I could not afford to pay the rent on my flat and would be homeless upon my release, a slight irritation that I would wish to avoid if at all possible.' Shored-Up nudged his glass.

'So why am I here?' Hennessey asked after he had returned from the bar with drinks, lime and soda for himself, a whisky for Shored-Up.

'Mower.' Shored-Up reached lovingly for his drink

'Mower?'

'As in lawnmower.'

'Yes, I gathered and only one possible spelling of that name, so tell me.'

'Goes under the nickname of Motor.'

'Motor?'

'Yes, "Motor" Mower, you see.'

'Alright. So why have I journeyed to not my favourite place in the world to hear about someone called "Motor" Mower?'

'He shot Roger Halverson, junior,' Shored-Up grinned. 'Was that worth the journey? And more importantly, is that worth you picking up the phone on my behalf?'

'Possibly and probably in that order.' Hennessey stared intently at Shored-Up.

'And a meal here—' he raised a finger – 'the food upstairs is ... past pleasing.'

'Perhaps. Is this reliable intelligence?'

'Very. I fear gaol. It is very reliable, most reliable.'

'So tell me about "Motor" Mower.'

'A budding criminal who is running before he can walk.'

'You know this?'

'Yes, he is now most shaken by his deed and most unwisely talking about it, although he believes his victim was called Shaw. He was talking in "the den" ... not sensible. Roger Halverson senior will have heard by now and he'll make the connection easily and quickly. It's a question of who gets him first. I tend to think that he would rather it be the police.'

'I can imagine. Does he know the danger he is in, this "Motor" Mower?'

'I think not, not fully. He was told to stop talking but by then his fate was sealed.'

'Age?'

'Early to mid twenties.'

'Blimey—' Hennessey shook his head — 'they get younger and younger. Used to be you were not a gunsmith until your thirties, it'll be teenagers next.'

'Already is, Mr H.' Shored-Up savoured the aroma of his whisky. 'Already is.'

'So, Mr Mower. First name?'

'Alexander, known as "Sandy", sometimes "Alex" but most often "Sandy".'

'Any previous?'

'I do believe he has, Mr Hennessey, I do believe he has.'

Hennessey plunged his hand into his pocket and extracted his mobile phone. 'Let's hope we are in time,' he said, jabbing Yellich's number.

'Adams', 'Bell', 'Budde', 'Davis'. The names had been called out each school day morning and when Budde heard 'Davis' called he switched off until 'Young' was called which triggered attentiveness again. So, he had picked one of the names and had given his name as Norman Bell. But the constable wasn't new. The constable saw fear in the boy's eyes and looked again at the right arm, heavily bandaged, ending in a stump just below the elbow. 'Is that your real name?'

Budde nodded.

'Well, they'll keep you here for a day or two

in case you go into shock, which could be fatal,' the constable explained. 'That'll give you time to think about things. If you want us to find the people who did this–' the constable pointed to Norman Budde's arm – 'then we need help from you.' He stood and caught the eye of a young nurse who glided swiftly along the ward about some pressing purpose and who smiled at him approvingly. 'And you know, giving your real name would be a help.'

Freddie Downes revealed himself to be a drawn, fearful, emaciated, pale-skinned youth and had, thought Yellich, a criminal's face. It had a pinched appearance, piercing eyes, a weak chin, a pointed nose, a receding forehead. He wore his hair greased and flattened upon his skull. He wore faded and inexpensive denim, so inexpensive that Yellich thought it didn't even look like denim. Downes retreated back into the terraced house as Yellich and Webster entered, uninvited. The officers saw that the interior of the house was basically, very basically, furnished and decorated. So basic that it was little more than a bare shell – a cushion on the floorboards for a chair, an old portable television rested on a cardboard box ... basic, basic, basic.

'Thought you'd come.' Downes' voice was weak, trembling, high pitch, whiney. His body shook with fear. 'You're the law, yes?'

'Yes,' Yellich replied sharply. 'So you're expecting us?'

'Yes. I know that woman saw me.'

'Oh?'

'Yes, and I knew she recognized me, if not by name but she knew where I lived. She walks past sometimes and looks in the house if I am sitting on the step with the door open and each time she looks into my drum she sniffs and walks on. Well, it's not much but I was homeless and this is where they put me. I'm drawing the dole and waiting for a loan to come through to buy furnishings and so I live like this, and that woman, that woman looks down her nose at me, so I knew you'd come but I don't get any money for a while. I want a chair and a table to eat food from and so I knocked her over and stole her bag but I didn't hit her hard and there was only twenty quid in the bag and then I looked up and there was the woman who walks past my house and sniffs when she does so ... looking at me. She saw me rob the old chick. I mean, that's why you're here isn't it?'

'No.' Yellich shook his head. 'Interesting as it is, it is something else we have called about.'

'Something else entirely.' Webster strode forward and placed his hand on Downes' shoulder. 'You're under arrest on suspicion of murder, you do not have to say anything but it may harm your defence if you do not mention, when questioned, something which you later rely on in court.'

'Murder!' Downes gasped. 'I have not murdered anyone. I didn't kill her, I just knocked her over.'

'Save it for the police station. We'll be searching your home. Will we find anything of interest?'

'Just a bit of blow under the old mattress I sleep on but that's for my use, you know, just enough for me. I'm not a dealer.'

'I see. Anything else?'

Downes shook his head.

At the charge bar at Micklegate Bar Police Station, Downes, Frederick, twenty-two years, was formerly charged with the murder of Roger Halverson junior. His belt was confiscated as was £250 in used five- and ten-pound notes.

'So where did you get the dosh from?' Yellich asked in the interview room after the preliminaries of introductions had been completed and as the twin spools of the cassette recorder slowly spun.

'A job I did for someone.' Downes looked down at the table top. 'It was nothing to do with the old dame, it wasn't her cash she just had twenty pounds on her.'

'Yes, we'll be charging you with that but right now we're interested in the murder.'

'Like I said, I didn't kill anyone ... no one

at all.'

'Well, we think different–' Yellich leaned forward – 'and we can prove different.'

'Hey, if I didn't do it, you can't prove I did it, it stands to reason...'

'Yesterday,' Yellich spoke slowly, 'yesterday, a little boy came out of some bushes he was exploring, he was about ten years old, he was picnicking with his parents and he walked out of the bushes holding a .22 automatic pistol. It proved to be loaded with live ammunition and the safety catch was off. Supposing he had run up to his little sister and pretended to shoot her with the toy gun he had just found? Fortunately his father had just been discharged from HM Services and the gun, once in our safe hands, had proved to have your dabs all over it and the gun with your fingerprints all over it was used to murder a young man called Halverson a few days ago. So myself, and my colleague, Mr Webster here, do believe that you have a little explaining to do.' Yellich did not think that Downes could turn any more pale, but he was proved wrong.

'What can I do?' Downes appealed to the solicitor who sat beside him, a portly man in a pinstripe suit who had introduced himself as 'Baguley, esquire, of Ellis, Burden, Woodland and Lake & Co.'

'I would advise you to cooperate, young man–' Baguley smelled of expensive after-shave – 'with this weight of evidence you are ill-advised to try to wriggle out of it. I might be able to negotiate a lesser charge for you.' Baguley turned to Yellich. 'I wish to negotiate the most favourable outcome for my client. He hasn't signed anything yet and despite the fact that this interview is being taped, the tape is only a guarantee of freedom of coercion, it's not acceptable as evidence in itself.'

'We know that–' Yellich pursed his lips – 'but we can only help your client if he helps himself.' Yellich paused. 'I have been a copper for a fair few years now and I have met many murderers and frankly, your client here does not strike me as being of that ilk. So I am inclined to believe him in myself, and only in myself, when he says that he has not murdered anyone; but his prints on a murder weapon, the Crown Prosecution Service will run with that.' Yellich turned to Downes. 'I don't think you realize the mess you are in Freddie, you're in very big trouble.'

'Trouble?' Downes looked questioningly at Yellich.

'Classically between a rock and a hard place.'

'I am?'

'Yes, you are in trouble with the police ... that's the rock, and the hard place, well, that's the father of the boy you killed, he is a

301

very dangerous man, not a clever move to get on the wrong side of him. People tend to disappear if he takes a dislike to them.'

'That could be seen as coercion, Detective Sergeant,' Baguley growled.

'Well, if it's coercion, it's still in your client's interest to know that it is also true. I know whereof I speak. That boy's father is indeed a dangerous man and people who cross him do tend to disappear. The man will be looking for your client's blood. Once he finds out that your client is in the frame for the murder of his son, your client is in need of protection, even our witness protection scheme is not one hundred per cent safe.'

'I was told to throw it in the river—' Downes spoke slowly – 'but when I got there, there were folk everywhere so I hid it in some bushes. I was planning to go back later one night and pick it up and toss it in the river then, but that's how I got my prints over it. I was paid £250 to throw it away. I didn't know it had been used to murder someone, but £250 ... I could furnish my drum without needing a loan.'

'Crucial point.' Baguley held up a gold-plated ballpoint pen. 'My client was ignorant of the fact that the weapon in question had been used in a murder. If he is telling the truth—'

'I am,' Downes pleaded, 'that's what happened. £250 quid to throw a gun in the

302

river, that was a good deal.'

'You see he is not even guilty of accessory after the fact. We are looking at reduced charges already.'

'Perhaps.' Yellich reclined in his chair. 'The police don't frame the charges, the CPS does and even if your client did act in ignorance of the details of the offence, it is reasonable to expect him to assume that the gun had been used in the commission of a crime and your client has previous convictions. I think a charge of accessory after the fact will stick, it depends on your client's further cooperation.' Yellich turned to Downes. 'So who was it, Freddie? Who gave you the two hundred and fifty smackers for your trouble?'

'That question–' Baguley glanced sideways at Downes – 'that question I advise you to answer.'

'He'll kill me.'

'Well if he doesn't, Halverson will. Custody is the only safe option for you now, Freddie.'

'Halverson, is he the guy you mentioned?'

'He is. Why have you heard of him?'

Downes nodded. 'He has people rubbed out.'

'We know. We just can't prove it ... yet. So who gave you the gun?'

'Mower, Alex Mower, he gave me the gun and the money.'

Just then Yellich's mobile phone vibrated in his pocket.

By virtue of a convenient train, George Hennessey sat talking to Somerled Yellich ninety minutes after taking his leave of Shored-Up in Hull. 'So, Downes is charged with accessory after the fact, that's good, keeps him safe. The CPS might choose to prefer reduced charges but that is for them to decide.' Yellich smiled. 'He's not in a hurry to leave the station, sir, he knows of Halverson by reputation. He is a very worried young man at the moment.'

'Halverson will be out for blood, even if it is only the blood of the felon who threw the murder weapon away, but the interesting thing is that both he and my informant mention Alexander Mower–' Hennessey patted the file on his desk – 'and we do know Alex Mower, we do indeed know him.'

'Small time villain,' Yellich offered, 'young enough and stupid enough to try to climb the criminal ladder by offering his services as a hit man. Last known address in Tang Hall. Shall we go and pick him up, skipper?'

'Yes.' Hennessey nodded. 'Yes, I think so, even if it's only to take him into protective custody before Halverson's tentacles wrap lovingly around him.'

Yellich stood. 'On my way, boss.'

'Good. I have just found an interesting pub in Hull.'

'Really, sir?'

'Yes, do excellent food. I'll tell you about it sometime, a good place to take Sara and Jeremy. Who are you taking with you?'

'Webster, sir.'

'Good. Just you two?'

'I think so, sir. It's all that is needed. I think Mower will be grateful for the protection, he'll know that Halverson's looking for him now.'

The 'sun' was, as Yellich suggested, the sundial in Roger Halverson's rear garden, which stood to the right-hand side when the garden was viewed from the house. Beyond the sundial was a row of large pieces of sandstone that marked the boundary between the closely cut lawn and the neatly tended, fully weeded herbaceous border, each rock being placed at equal intervals. Beneath the third rock from the sundial was found a butcher's knife, very carefully and conveniently wrapped in a black plastic bag. Ventnor extracted the knife from the bag and held it gingerly between thumb and forefinger and examined it briefly. Dried blood was discernible along the blade. He placed the knife back inside the plastic bag and placed it, in turn, in a large production bag. Carmen Pharoah, who had been standing next to Ventnor, turned and walked back into the house where Halverson sat in a still, catatonic-like state as if frozen in a cold rage, staring fixedly into space. Reassuringly for Carmen Pharoah two very large constables stood on either side of him, wearing crisp white, short-sleeved shirts, serge trousers and highly polished shoes. Carmen Pharoah said, 'Roger Halverson, I am arresting you in connection with the murder of Harold Ford.' She then recited the caution, after which she said to the constables, 'Put him in the van, please.'

The woman smiled at Yellich and Webster. 'Alex is not here, not at home.' She beamed. She was short, clad in an apron and slacks. She held a duster in one hand. The flat smelled of furniture polish and air freshener. 'He's with his young lady.'

'And where does she live?'

'In York, in Heslington, Hall Place, number ninety-three. If you take—'

'It's alright, Mrs Mower,' Yellich said, smiling, 'we know exactly where that is.'

'Shall I phone him to let him know you're on your way?'

'No—' Yellich turned to go – 'please don't bother.'

'But you must want him for something?' A note of alarm crept into her voice. 'Is it trouble again? Are you the police?'

'We sell double-glazing,' Webster explained, 'just responding to a form he filled in and sent to our company.'

'Ah–' the woman beamed again – 'I thought ... no matter, but he'll be with his young lady ... Hall Place.'

'Many thanks.' Yellich turned away.

'Yes, thank you.' Webster smiled warmly and followed Yellich.

Janet Nash flung the door open annoyed, furious. 'What!' she demanded. She was dressed in a man's shirt and little else.

'Police.' Yellich showed her his ID. 'We were told that Alex Mower would be here.'

Janet Nash paled. 'You're the double-glazing salesmen. His mum phoned us, right when we didn't need a phone call. She phoned us when you'd gone because she said you didn't look like double-glazing sales-men. She said you were not warm and friendly enough. We should have known.'

'Yes, a little untruth,' Yellich explained, 'we didn't want to alarm the lady.'

At that moment Alex Mower walked up behind Janet Nash. He was muscular, short, neatly cut black hair. He wore a pair of jeans.

'Put the rest of your kit on, Mr Mower. You too, Miss Nash.'

'Why?' Janet Nash demanded.

'Because we said so,' Yellich growled. 'We want to chat to you about the murder of Roger Halverson.'

'How...' Janet Nash appealed.

'Quiet!' Mower snapped. 'Quiet! Quiet!'

'Just pull some clothes on,' Yellich repeated. 'Please.'

Freddie Downes sat hunched up on the floor in the corner of the cell, trembling it seemed to Hennessey, trembling with fear.

'We need more,' Hennessey explained. 'If you want us to help you, we need more.'

'More?' Downes whined.

'More. Alex Mower could not have managed to move the body by himself. He needed a boat, a rubber dinghy or something and he needed help to get Roger Halverson's body up the stairs of those folk's house and into their bed. So who was it?'

'Padget. Nicky Padget. He was standing with Alex Mower when Alex gave me the shooter to get rid of. He's known to you, try Padget. This will help me?'

'Yes.' Hennessey walked out of the cell. 'It will help you.'

'We've got six hours to charge or release you–' Hennessey spoke sternly to Mower who stood motionless in his cell, as if trying to wake up from some unpleasant dream – 'and believe me we won't be releasing you. We're bringing Paget in now.' Hennessey paused. 'Oh yes, we know about him. The first one of you to talk will be doing himself a huge favour.'

Mower remained silent.

'I'll come back once Paget's in another cell. Give him an equal opportunity to talk before you. Do some clever thinking.' He paused. 'If it helps to clarify your thinking and if you have been otherwise informed, the dead man was also called Halverson. Does that name mean anything to you?'

Mower paled. 'She said his name was Shaw.'

'I'll tell you what I know. I'll tell you everything.' Janet Nash sat on the bed in her cell wringing her hands.

'Good for you,' Hennessey said. 'I'll be back in a moment with a woman police officer to take you to the interview room. You're entitled to a lawyer.'

'Don't need one. My dad always told me if I ever got caught bang to rights, the only thing to do is come clean, hope for leniency of sentence and start working towards your parole. Don't suppose I'll be walking down Lavender Hill now but at least it won't be the Bangkok Hilton.'

'Well not for a while anyway. I'll get a lawyer to sit in on your interview. We'd prefer it that way.'

'I'll need protection.' Janet Nash looked at Hennessey with a childlike expression. 'You don't know what Halverson can do.'

'Yes we do,' Hennessey said smiling, 'but don't worry about him. He's got troubles of his own. He's in the next cell and won't be going anywhere for a very long time.'

Hennessey saw what Shored-Up meant. Having Miss Pratt for a probation officer would indeed be like being hunted by a raptor especially when compared to his previous PO who was happy to talk about fly fishing and wasn't too concerned by the odd missed appointment. The woman eyed Hennessey coldly though unashamedly large spectacles – the sort which transmitted the message – 'I am a woman and I wear glasses and I am proud of both facts.' Her black hair was worn tied back. Her suit was dark grey pinstripe. She was not, he thought, a day over twenty-four years old and he doubted if she had ever learned how to smile. She was, he further thought, insufficiently equipped with life experience or warmth of personality to make a good probation officer.

'It is highly irregular,' she said coldly. 'This offender has missed three appointments already. I am framing breach proceedings.'

'He has been very useful to us, Miss Pratt.'

'He will be useful to you again, when he comes out of prison.'

'He gave information which probably saved a young man's life.'

'He did?' Miss Pratt paused.

'Yes. He did.' Hennessey noted her office

to be neat and clean and Spartan. 'And helped solve a serious crime.'

'Very well. I will offer him another appointment. But he has to keep it otherwise I will breach him. And he must not mistake my kindness for weakness.'

Hennessey stood. 'Thank you. I will ensure he keeps it.'

'No,' Miss Pratt spoke firmly, 'don't ensure anything. It is up to him and him alone to keep the appointment.'

'I understand. But thank you anyway.'

'And I will make it an 8.30 a.m. appointment. If he is not over the threshold of this building by 8.35 on the day in question, I will initiate breach proceedings. I will spell that out clearly in the letter I send him.'

Hennessey was to see Shored-Up in the street a few weeks later and noted the man looked downcast and preoccupied, but at least he was at liberty. He had clearly kept his last chance appointment with the ferocious Miss Pratt.

Thompson Ventnor sat in the armchair in the living room of his house and poured the first glass of cheap red wine from the large bottle he had bought. He intended to demolish the contents that evening. He hoped to make himself very ill. Very ill indeed. He hoped for a mother and father of a hangover.

He felt he needed that to stop him drinking.

It was Friday, 19.35 hours.

The following January an observer would
have seen a middle-aged couple strolling
calmly, arm in arm, along the esplanade of
the North Bay at Scarborough.

The man glanced to his left to the sea
which was calm and still, with only small
waves lapping on the shore but yet, he felt it
had a menacing quality about it, with its hue
of battleship grey. Above the sea was a low
cloud cover, also still, also grey, so much so
that the man had difficulty discerning the
horizon. At seven miles distant, the sea and
the sky seemed to merge. He turned to his
right and looked up at grassy banks criss-
crossed with pathways which in June, July
and August would be thronged with joyful
tourists, but which were now deserted.
Above the bank was the terrace of hotels
which formed the skyline, all white, and all,
like the pathways, empty. The man had
always felt there to be a certain poignancy
about seaside resorts in the winter months
but refrained from comment. He had made
that observation many times and he knew
that his lady companion knew what he was
thinking. Instead, he said, 'Strange case, that
one in the summer I mean.'

'The corpse in the bed? That one?' The

woman turned to him.

'Yes, that one all wrapped up in five days, starting with a man on sticks hobbling from his father's funeral direct to the police station. Had a satisfying and an unsatisfying feel about it, both at the same time.'

'How do you mean?'

'Well ... satisfying in that we were able to convict Halverson senior for murder and also seize his house and the large amount of cash we found in his loft. He could give no account of how he obtained the home or for his possession of the money and so they were adjudged proceeds of crime. His lawyers are appealing so said assets will be frozen and will remain so for a long time. He won't be able to have access to them. He collected life anyway so he'll be inside for a good few years and yet we'll never know the extent of what he did. He probably was responsible for the deaths of many people, people who are still listed as missing persons, but he left his prints on a knife which was covered in the blood of one of his victims.'

'How did you find the knife?'

'A tip-off from a con doing himself a favour. He never explained how he knew the knife was where he said it would be. I largely think that was because he was part of the murder. He saw Halverson's prints on the knife and the victim's blood also on it and was probably told to get rid of it but instead,

313

secreted it. A sort of investment, something he could use to bargain with or use to protect himself from Halverson, but again, we'll never know.' The man paused as he watched a herring gull glide over the ice-cold surf. 'And the murder of Oliver Hill, we know what happened now and the prematurely ageing Mrs Hill can have some closure. We were able to tell her that her husband was murdered and did not abandon her for a younger model but any conviction will rest on the eyewitness accounts of a seven-year-old boy and some twenty years previously. The CPS decided not to pursue it.'

'So the gang got away with murder?'

'Yes. They cut pathetic figures now by all accounts, but yes, they got away with murder. So that's a bit unsatisfying but that's often the way of it.'

'Win some, lose some.'

'Yes, can't win 'em all. That's a valuable lesson to take on board.'

'So who did murder the corpse in the bed?'

'Oh, that was his girlfriend, Janet Nash and her new lover, bloke called Mower.'

'Mower?' The woman smiled. 'Like lawnmower?'

'Yes. They were lovers and wanted Halverson junior out of the way so they could become an item. Got some help to dispose of the body. So they collected life and the helpers collected ten years each for being accessories after the fact. They all made a clean breast of it and won't serve a damaging length of time. Nash and Mower might be out in five years and their helpers in two or three.'

'As little as that?'

'Yes. They all went "G", as my son would say, and demonstrated remorse. That sort of thing impresses the parole board. But they'll be looking over their shoulders all their lives because when Halverson senior gets out, he'll be burning up with the need to avenge his son's murder.'

'Will he be out soon?'

'Doubt it. You might have read in the papers, he went "NG" as Charles would also say. Pleaded not guilty despite compelling evidence and showed no remorse. That will not impress the parole board. His attitude will give some time for Nash and Mower and their helpers to cover their tracks. But he knows their names. The story hasn't ended.'

'Again, unsatisfying. I see what you mean.'

'It's a never-ending story really.' The man sighed.

'The chaos theory ... everything connects with everything else.'

'Yes, you could say that. So what shall we do for lunch?'

'What do you suggest?' She smiled at him.

'Well, how about a drive up the coast to Whitby?' Hennessey suggested. 'There is a fish restaurant there whose seafood casserole is excellent.'

'Sounds ideal.' Louise D'Acre squeezed his arm. 'Sounds perfect.'